SCARLET NIGHTFALL

Gothic Poetry

Marisa Loretta

Table of Contents

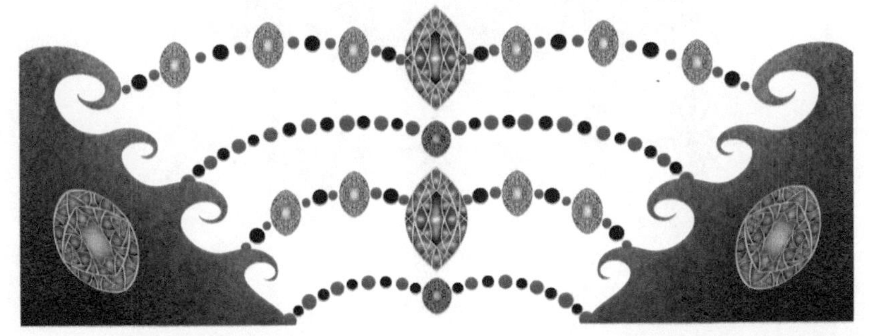

Supernatural Fantasy

PROCEED
WITH GRIM
CAUTION

VIOLETVALE
MANOR

BEWARE
WHAT LIES
WITHIN

Violetvale Manor

Upon an eve so late, even ravening wolves cannot fight exhaustion's call
Submit, *they must*, to their fatigue, slumbering until mockingbirds sing
But the Violetvale Manor, near a Neptune-tinted ocean, never does rest
Erected from demonic carcasses as ivory wood and tacky blood as grout
Exuding an unspeakable aura of madness, inviting innocent prey within
Step into my skeleton, the door begs, *let me seal your fate in sorrow, forever*

Beyond the corpselike entryway of the manor, grave torment takes over
Floors seem to slither beneath your feet while ceilings rattle from wrath
At your own risk, face the unnerving, unnatural perils swarming inside
Encounter the winding staircase carved from corroded planks of timber
Climb the decayed steps before entering an incessant cycle of confusion
For the end is nowhere near—it does not exist upon this elaborate path
Decomposing walls distend with angst and undulate from despondency
As clawing contours of crushed appendages demand to be emancipated
Silhouettes of skulls and outlines of mouths press up against the plaster
Hoping their scratching hymns will reverberate and a savior will appear
But within the Violetvale Manor, the dawn of salvation will never shine
Amble past haunting passages ornamented with bronze-framed mirrors
Though, as your tear-stained eyes fall upon the glass, distortion follows
Regard the dire illusion where your reflection screeches like a shrill siren
Unsteady lips bare your swollen pharynx, bellowing from writhing pain
Echo of your existence—whose features contort from undiluted danger
Twist away, lest the deception cons your mind and the images turn true
Dozens of chambers line the halls—harboring ineffable horrors aplenty
Cross over the threshold, become accosted by hot-tempered behemoths
Plunge through agape portals, a one-way-ticket to the pits of purgatory
Sink into unsavory seas where Krakens glorify the bitter perfume of fear

Teeming with induced terror, the manor's foundation deteriorates daily
Sconce light bulbs explode, paint peels away, and russet bricks dislodge
Fright infects the air you inhale to survive, polluting your lungs instead
Even still, quivering from vexing unease, your exploration does not halt
Entering rooms you shouldn't, *yet your hand is already turning the handle*
Once you enter the Violetvale Mansion—escape becomes unachievable
And though the sanity of your soul abates, your body never does depart

Pearlescent Oracle

Ivory irises—as bleached as bone—drowning in divine visions foretold
Slotted within the preternatural sockets of she whose stare stretches far
Whose spirit softly beckons to regard the validity of her potent dreams
Beneath the volume of imminent intuitions, her figure begins to thrive
Until pallid flesh glows with a gilded shimmer, the sign of a true oracle
Telling trances immerse her senses before spouting from her critical lips
Within the ocular realm of prophecies, pale eyes emulate oceanic pearls
Purer in hue than ever before, for pigment flees when insights transpire
Godlike gaze, wielding the cherished skill to transcend this fixed terrain
Enraptured within an imminent portrait of the future, her skin tremors
Impending tempests twine around her capillaries with visceral warning
While these revelations impatiently glide across the grooves of her skull
Swallow them all down, she must—until they reside behind her ribcage
Before lapsing lower, dwelling within her soul, sentient of their veracity
Humming, her head drones that fate is final, and all she may do, is wait

Evil—apathetic and arctic, akin to an ice shard slicing against her heart
Artfully crawls around her consciousness—keeping to the unseen edges
Waiting for an unexpected opportunity to surface like a burrowing vole
As tangible as a scalpel, ready to smother her omniscience with its blade
Evil awaits its escape—though it rages at the notion of anyone knowing
Of anyone hindering the malice latently living below, beside the beetles
Soon, this odious entity will rise from polluted sludge with vile stamina
Zealous to activate the lawless reign this prophetic individual is privy to
And so, the beast haunting her divinations hungers to halt her heroism
Aspiring to fillet her tongue into fleshy ribbons with a corroded cleaver
And amputate her all-seeing eyes from their essential holes with finality
Nevertheless, the damage is done—for the instant her foresight finishes
Stark irises convert—now stained ebony from the approaching iniquity
As if the optical, opaline pearls she once bore sprang from their abodes
Only to be replaced with dual orbs of onyx—blackened, limitless voids
Evil is nigh, as told by brisk breezes gossiping of how it wakes and wails
This is how it starts, with a flash of something deviant ready to rupture
Something soulless and starving—who converses intimately with death
Evil arrives with mercenary strategies as the crestfallen psychic collapses
For destiny is sculpted by the stars, and the cosmos never dares to falter

Gashes and Gems

Observe her regency ballgown, the lavish fabric strewn with petite gems
Jewels press into her bones, pining to leave distinguishing marks behind
Draped upon her sensual frame, gauzy pleats of fabric pool at her ankles
Luxurious in its elegant design, extending all the way up to her jawbone
Twirling over her neck until the second she turns and the material shifts
Silently sliding down to her collarbones, though she does not yet notice
You, however, have been regarding her with longing amid all the revelry
And as the first hint of her nude skin is exposed, a sting of shock ensues
For what should have been a beatific view of an immaculate complexion
Is riddled with bite marks and viscid tar, tricking out like gruesome rain
Spellbound with blunt unease, you cross the distance between you both
In doing so, an impulsive draft awakens—prancing over her naked flesh
Alerting this enigmatic individual that her mottled grazes are detectable
With disinterest, she lifts the fallen textile and fastens it back into place
Doing so without concern for the bites or the blood or the implications
When you finally reach her side, you ask, *no, you beg*, for an explanation
Unhurriedly, she meets your stare without any worry lining her features
Murmuring that you must be mistaken—for she is not in peril nor pain
As she speaks, baffled tears accumulate—welling in your overcome eyes
For your gaze may be water-logged, but the mutilated portrait was clear
Abnormally touched by your devastating concern, she soothingly insists
With an ephemeral expression of empathy, that she is more than alright
Pacified—you watch as she gracefully sashays across the congested floor
Readying to depart until a supernatural gentleman suddenly dashes out
Capturing her palm, he raises it to his mouth before turning, *just slightly*
Placing a kiss upon her wrist—thinly cloaking the veins lying just below
Note the look of hunger deepening his stare with primal need, with lust
Though, perhaps the gaze he gifts her is simply a trick of the moonlight
But, it is no such illusion, for carmine proof begins to engulf his tongue
Bellow at the blood so clearly glinting upon his carnal lips, she does not
She only trails one manicured nail in the fluid upon his achromatic skin
Before dragging her finger through her own lips—sucking and savoring
Beaming with erotic famine over her wanton display, he waits no longer
Swiftly, he hooks an arm around her midriff—hustling them both away
And while some defenseless souls dread the dark, waiting to be rescued
This woman, covered in gashes and gems, requires no such saving at all

Seven Deadly Sins

Seven Deadly Sins skated upon a grim wind, allied as one immoral unit
Certain to obey their dissolute vows, the oaths amid their unruly minds
Say their names—Pride, Lust, Sloth, Greed, Envy, Wrath, and Gluttony
Scavenging the eccentric junctions of these lands for mortals to demean
Conquering, cutting, crushing the individuals they fixate upon stalking
Stay silent, lest the sins hear the echoes of your exhalations, and pounce

Pride, whose stifling narcissism spawned the cells of this proud creature
Arrogance overflowed within their organs—an unending well of vanity
Boastful being who cringed at the inane notion of welcoming humility
With an escalating ego, Pride believed themself to be greater than gods
But still, they required visible verification of their superior prominence
And so, Pride set about degrading every drop of dew and glob of grease
Until surging waterfalls froze in place, as rebuked lilies and lilacs wilted
Only when swollen with smug accomplishment did Pride elect to cease
Leaving the world lifeless—never again able to be reinstated or renewed
Lust, who writhed with an abysmal ache, a boundless burning for desire
Believed bodies were designed to be worshipped—flushed with wanting
Carnal creature—utterly consumed by unashamed fantasies of yearning
Communing only by slotting their mouth against the lips of their lovers
Vaccinated with arousing serums, mortals misjudged desire for devotion
But Lust did not enlighten them, for their endless worship was exultant
Ultimately, the truth came forth as sore hearts cracked along the center
Agonized by the Lust's rejection, for mortals merely wished to be loved
And this brazen sin could only ever offer a fleeting, yet heavenly, touch

Sloth, who sluggishly shuffled through life at a dragging, practiced pace
A drowsy being who never desired or pined or dreamt of anything at all
With indifference, the sin harbored no interest in gardening or growing
Ignoring all duties—until crops failed to sprout and branches grew bare
Mortals starved, yet Sloth never did fake a single modicum of sympathy
Sunken stomachs howled, and underfed forms sidled down to the grass
Laying upon their backs—too weakened from hunger to ever rise again
Sloth looked upon the fields occupied with motionless, moaning bodies
Openly marveling, for the kingdom had begun to live just as the sin did
And he did not even have to raise a finger or speak a word to make it so

Greed, with an egotistical existence addicted to chanting *more and more*
Covetous sin who wailed and whined, never grasping sincere fulfillment
Not until they gulped the sum of the ether, asphyxiating earthly tenants
Mortals strained to heave any lingering gulps of oxygen into their lungs
But no particles persisted, and their crucial presence would never return
And when Greed inevitably developed an appetite for something *unique*
Wheezing mortals were hurled down the gullet of the sin's needy throat
Horrifically swallowed, bones and all, never to feel daylight's heat again
Envy, queasy from jealousy, howled from the hollows of their jade heart
Green-eyed soul who blinded the fair irises of their countless courtesans
Warranting that their lovers would never perch their gazes upon another
Preys of Envy's possessiveness became jailbirds, captive to strict darkness
Gutted of their sight, these stunned, unseeing mortals were fated to fall
To tumble off the edge of the Earth and descend down a gulf of vacancy
When destiny called, this sin was not incarcerated in a cell of mourning
No—Envy only felt relief, for the late mortals would never love another

Wrath, lone progeny of ire, delivered from the razor-sharp ribs of devils
Enraged bundle of fevered energy who convulsed with unrelenting fury
Eager to infect the innocent—to tower above all in the midst of carnage
And so, a war cry ascended from Wrath's throat, and rage was exorcised
Neon troops lined forest floors, and tornados engulfed vagabond clouds
Victorian castles collapsed, reigning kingdoms fell *until nothing survived*
Ecstatic, Wrath extinguished the infernos and smothered the monsoons
Disposed to take their satanic body to the next realm—already doomed
Gluttony, obsessed with discovering the limit of their voracious hungers
Even though their bloated body was nourished, ravening they remained
Insatiable individual harboring a palate for attention, approval, affection
Thirsting for anything to quench their engorged soul, if only for a while
As years passed, Gluttony could tolerate no more of their unfulfilled life
Fraught with famine, the sin urgently nibbled upon this spacious world
Gnawing until nothing remained but the celestial sun and cosmic moon
And so, like Angroboda's wolves—Gluttony heartily devoured those too

All too soon, the universe became vacuous, save for the famed seven sins
Forever hexed to live in mayhem—though for them, it was no hex at all

Thorned Beauty

As mesmerizing as a flower blooming in the pastel throes of springtime
Indecently dulcet, not unlike the covetous syrup of candy-coated agave
With a botanical moniker—constructed from dashes of sugar and spice
The Rose, they breathed, though not to illustrate her picturesque façade
Underneath her sparkling body, a decadent husk, devious and deluding
Lived something corrosive, demanding to slash epidermic layers of skin
And burst through the vitalizing surface—like jagged surprises of harm
The Rose concealed penetrating thorns within her emboldened skeleton
Vital to her existence, lining her veins like spiked rows of emerald gems
Relentlessly—*The Rose* was connected to her codependent thorns in life
And would be mirthlessly fused even in the freezing clutches of demise

Born a hypnotic being who grew terribly troubled when the barbs arose
For the prick of her pristine skin ripping open—spilling carmine beads
Was almost as intolerable as innately knowing what would happen next
After her thorns were laid bare—a floret of a foreign species she became
No longer perceived as a diamond in the breathing garden of humanity
Exhilarating charisma overlooked, for the thorns could never be unseen
Barks of revulsion, of real trepidation, replaced former sighs of worship
One graze and your own flesh would be mangled—split open with ease
While goosebumps of horror ornament your limbs, you would gaze up
Finding her magnetic irises shining, glassy with the warning of weeping
Succinctly, you would experience a pang of pity germinate in your heart
For she did not ask for this fate—no more than you asked for your own
Banish any lingering empathy and grasp how suitable her name truly is
For *The Rose* attracts with her beauty before wounding with her bristles
Leaving you both bleeding and broken, but still, you cannot look away
For whether it be splendor or shock, a remarkable rose she still remains
And you hate her for that, as she hates herself—and the cycle carries on
Eventually, the thorns tunnel back beneath, and the carnage rinses away
Leading you to dreamily marvel once more, for she really is so beautiful
What harm is there in moving a little closer only to inhale her fragrance
Just for one second, for roses are always everyone's favorite—so popular
Right up until the moment you decide to cradle one within your palms
For her thorns will find flesh—*as always*—leaving you tearfully contrite
While *The Rose* drowns in her own tsunami of sobs, long after you leave

Briar's Decision

Sprouted from the earth as both a pious cherub and impertinent demon
Awash with the pearly glow of paradise and the misty abyss of perdition
Half of Briar's soul was dipped in the iridescence of romantic innocence
While the rest was doused in the delectable depravity of Lucifer himself
Delicately virtuous, with indexes of ethics cycling throughout her mind
Cruelly impish, with files of torturous techniques drilled into her bones
A living, languishing contradiction—dubious of how to feel, who to be
As ever-changing in her demands and disposition as a fickle chameleon

When magnolias thrive in the month of May, Briar becomes breathless
Just as rhythmic crashes from the ocean in midsummer pacify her spirit
Simultaneously—Briar comes alive with glee at the prospect of disarray
Celebrating the portrait of chaos painted by a hazardous thunderstorm
While sinking her filed teeth into her arm, idolizing the biting imprint
Whether it be benign pecks upon her throat from floating flower petals
Or hemorrhaging lacerations maiming her jugular like vampiric gashes
Briar appreciates the sensations—inoffensive or injurious—all the same
What an existence to experience gingerbread proclivities of saccharinity
Alongside virulent penchants of sin, equally swarming with fire and ice
Though as time ticks by, Brian struggles with her forthcoming decision
For a set of jeweled tiaras await her in the realms of those who bore her
And yet, only one may lastingly rest upon her luxuriant, licorice tresses
Deciding her authentic nature and destined vocation—once and for all
Champagne circlet of angels, stippled with gold leaf, covered in charms
Exhibited in a beatific kingdom where seraphs soar, and purity prevails
Denigrated wreath of demons, magnificently barbed, gloriously beaded
Displayed in a crooked domain where spite feels as heady as springtime

Briar looks within—trailing the yarn roving down her cylindrical throat
Gawking as it wraps around her heart of garnet and blood of brimstone
Dragging her down deeper still—into the charred caverns of corruption
Imitating the perpetual hellfire wildly raging amid Briar's rightful home
For any residues of holiness have now ebbed away into smoke and ashes
No longer distressed by her divided soul, Briar claims her cutting crown
Basking in the satanic glory of darkness, just as she was always meant to

Lupine Transformation

As the lofty globe of opalescence diverges, entering the next lunar phase
Radiance of totality ensues until the argent satellite appears whole *at last*
Under a full moon, the pending sensation of change lands in the clouds
As the clatter of ropes and restraints, welded with silver, clangs outwards
For the *allegedly mortal man* knew his transformation was crucially close
And so, he prudently immobilizes himself, impeding any threats of ruin
Once the modification initiates—any restraint over recklessness will flee
Abating into the nightfall sky like roving smolders from a dwindling fire
When moonlight strokes his erratic skin, mortal traits are stripped away
Starbursts of pain paralyze his senses as if the devil doled out this abuse
Inept to halt this kaleidoscope of cruelty—for thus was his lupine curse
With a crack, his anatomy accommodates the feral animal breaking free
For this sequestered creature resides beneath his humanoid complexion
Even amid the nights when the comic orb above does not reveal its face
Only now is the caged animal granted enchanted permission to surface
Mirroring the events of the previous month—muscles bulge under flesh
Inflating until the configuration of his cells becomes wolven once again
Taupe membranes turn into pewter fleece—as insulating as a wool quilt
Fanged canines, arctic irises, and saw-toothed claws emerge—all at once
As his rabid heart triumphs—coursing with the adrenaline of a *werewolf*

Yet when dawn breaks after an altering eve, the sins of shifting are bared
For the vexing glower of a solstice sun exposes the secrets of yesternight
Breaking his fitful slumber, the dazed man, once again mortal, awakens
Bidding to piece together what uproar befell based on the debris nearby
Disoriented, he assesses his battered physical state with mounting panic
Throat sore from snarling, chest inflamed, knuckles slashed from unrest
Swollen wrists, mulberries-hued, throbbing from prying at his manacles
Silvered cuffs meant to hold him captive, yet the sight of broken chains
Mortifies his shamed soul, for clearly, a riotous getaway had been made
Though, what transpired when his mind was lost to his werewolf needs
Only the melody of a new morning, afloat with floral dew, will divulge
As the ether shudders from wretched screams, his dreads are confirmed
For those shrieks are laced with devastation—and he is likely the culprit
Ideas of ingesting wolfsbane fill his mind as viscous gore sullies his flesh
For though his mortal and lupine lives would end, so too would his disgrace

Odessa's
Inferno

Odessa's Inferno

Blistering angel of arson— forged in untamed fires and eruptive embers
Illuminating the witching hours as soon as the moon supersedes the sun
Odessa, whose organs lurch with violent abandon, as hyper as Maenads
Goddess of seething sparks, kindling combustible logs of control within
Living lighter, inferno ignitor, erecting wildfires with a flick of her wrist
Even torrid flashes of daylight recoil at the temperatures Odessa invents
Stoking firestorms and provoking furnaces with her heedless ambitions
For Odessa does not merely control the flames; no, *she is a flame herself*

Oven-like anatomy—with a bloodstream replaced by pitchers of butane
Whose veins are set alight with a never-depleting supply of lighter fluid
Odessa's skeleton resembles a Russian nesting doll, exquisite yet riveting
With every layer you lift, more incinerating warmth rises with intensity
Simmering with power, magma spills from the goddess's molten mouth
Drizzling outward on a downward incline, lapping at her explosive skin
Lawless locks of heat braid themselves into Odessa's mane of vermillion
Even the goddess's pupils are as bloodred as matching pomegranate orbs
Making it difficult to discern where her blazes end and where she begins

Douse Odessa's smoldering figure in a tempest of rain—drown her in it
Watch her sultry combustions continue to sway to the tune of torching
Fire yields only to this breathing matchstick, never to wither on its own
Odessa longs for this flammable land to adorn the ambiance of ignition
Writhing with the need to create an apocalyptic pyre from lush terrains
To turn what was once earth into unthinkable piles of cinders and coals
And though Armageddon will ascend, her threatening flares will live on
For she is Odessa, idol of pyromania, and her fires will never extinguish

Graveyard Schemes

Circling crows pinching carrion between their beaks—a moody sight
Lurching in-between headstones garnished with disintegrating violets
Destructive ropes of rain displace heaps of rubble atop ignored graves
Overhanging branches jut out at unnerving angles like ruptured arms
Eternal necropolis—far less empty than your vision could distinguish
Populated by trapped spirits secreting chronic vapors of despondency
Souls are separated from their corpses and extracted from dour crypts
Arising as ghouls wandering the graveyard they cannot abscond from
For whenever the troposphere turns icy, the climate is never to blame
Phantoms harbor such heartache—despite their merciless reputations
Languishing in nonexistence, sulking over their lost lives—now adrift
Hounding for the heady feeling of being alive, of being *acknowledged*
Merely mist they may be—though ghouls beg to yank their lips apart
And release a sonorous scream, souring the bloodstreams of passersby
But alas, ghouls remain alone in their existence—mournfully unheard

Disheartened spirits hunt for carnal skeletons of warmth to slink into
For their own bodies are exiled below—hidden under sludge and soil
Drowning in the cologne of dirt and surrounded by swarms of larvae
In their pursuits to be pardoned from their fates as spectral prisoners
Ghouls bother those who visit the graveyard—bearing beating hearts
Rabid from their inner hopes to pillage the skin off of a mortal's back
Foaming with the hunger to possess these tangible individuals, always
Sick with the need to save their sanity by feeling *anything besides mud*
By sensing something besides maggots settling atop their waxen flesh
Yet, when ghouls venture to acquire breathing bodies for themselves
To sense the winds of humanity, swirling with the verve of mortality
Ghouls fall straight past their corporeal targets—foiling any schemes
Leaving graveyard guests untouched as ghouls wallow in their failure
Longsuffering spirits may never again reenter their own putrid forms
Compelling ghouls to turn to the carcasses they are laid to rest beside
Before licking the rotting features of others, amenable to *any* remedy
Eager to reach past the decay and uncover any lasting vestiges of life
But, dolefully, their plots are futile, denying the ghouls their renewal
Now empty of hope—ghouls reminisce upon their mortal existences
For those memories are the closest they will ever come to *living* again

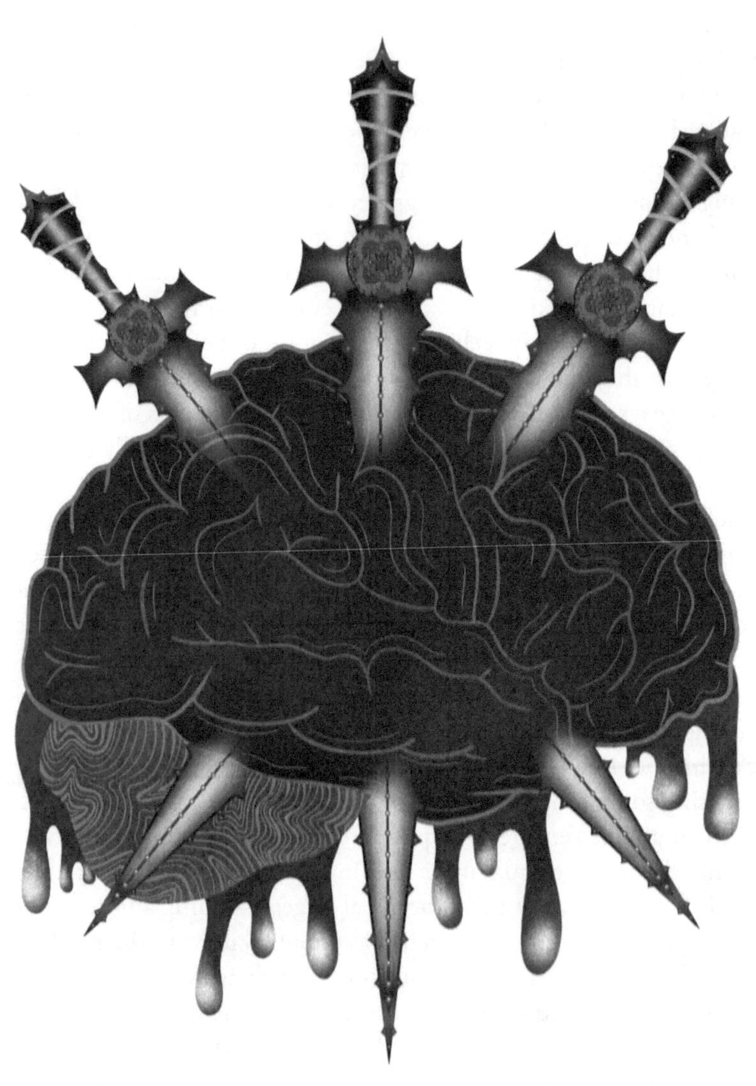

Empress of Nightmares

What manic madness inundates a skull drowning in the seas of slumber
As the lunar disk glimmering within the universe croons a cosmic track
Eclipsed depths of a drowsy mind fall victim to haunting hallucinations
Spine-chilling, flesh-jolting, blood-curdling, lips-shivering, pulse-racing
Soundless screams haunt the ghostlike lair of dreams enveloped in smog
Caught in an epidemic of decline coined by the Empress of Nightmares

Veiled within the vapor of shadows, saplings of torture flock to her side
As expected as the tip of a longsword finding itself caked in ruddy gore
Detested empress, admiring the misery bleeding from a comatose mind
Yet, she never does demand to dirty her own unsullied, porcelain palms
For the monarch cannot permit the roars of screeching to stain her soul
Thus, heathens of her own design, sculpted from pure sin, are spawned

Generated from the empress's will—demons germinate without protest
For there are no angels who dare to cry out, imploring to impede them
Led by brutish instructions, the demons infiltrate impressionable brains
Molding minds as pliant as clay, a punitive method of indelible pottery
Foul pincers hold dozing bodies captive within their villainous custody
Until the skies turn away, sweet dreams blacken, and nightmares attack

Disembodied fears slip into material shapes—able to murder and maim
Hurling victims into vortexes where unlikely trepidations turn tangible
Skulls nearly explode from the encumbrance of inescapable persecution
As the Empress of Nightmares glories over the essence of maltreatment
Ricocheting off the comatose brains damaged by her deathly daughters
All while hedonism blooms in her chest, where her ruby heart *should* lie

As the brightening horizon beckons the termination of unruly nightfall
Nightmares never follow in the footsteps of the evening's extermination
For the maelstroms brutalizing convulsing minds during moonlit hours
Seep into the cartilage and delve beneath the collagen of pitiable bones
Until unconscious visions of fright thrive, even as amber sunlight glows
Vowing that no matter the time, the empress will keenly remain nearby
And her nightmares, enduringly embedded within, will never conclude

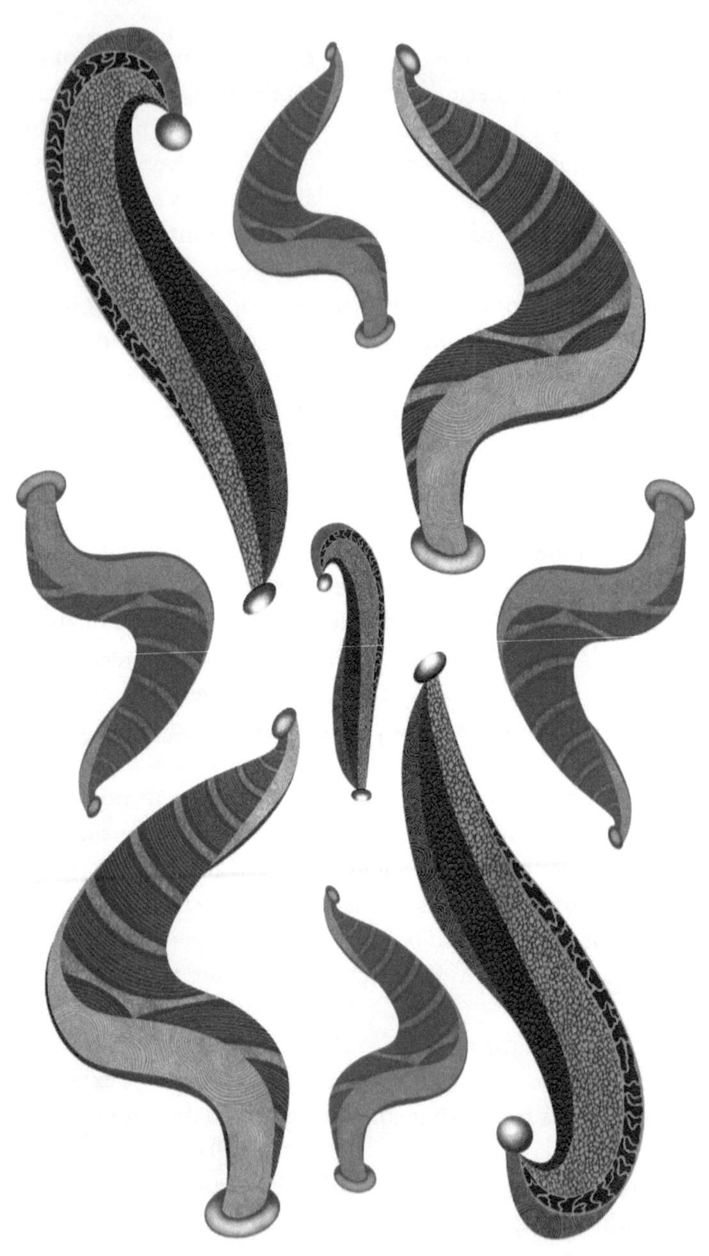

Leech of the Lagoon

If only his skeleton stayed static, never changing at the strike of twilight
Plasma would not be pilfered, wounds would not stimulate termination
And lives would remain living—never victim to the leech of the lagoon

Within the moonless galaxy, not a trace of starlight loiters and listens in
For all planetary creatures and stellar clusters have cowered from dismay
Far too horrorstruck by the detestable felonies transpiring below to stay
Condemning this land to an evening of absolute obscurity and oblivion
And yet, the figure strolling along the shoreline requires no illumination
In order to unveil his transformation, beginning and ending with blood
Pints of plasma rearrange, elongated appendages shrivel, flesh fluctuates
Until, *at last*, a scrounging pest, nothing but a writhing, wretched worm
Occupies the space where seconds ago, an ordinary body of bones stood
Detrimental tendencies flood the cranium of this person turned parasite
Craving nothing but the copper tang which only palatable plasma offers
Upon the bank of the ultramarine lagoon, death lies in enthusiastic wait
As the invertebrate leech shadows their quarry, like a predatory detective
Gluing themself atop coursing veins—the creature slices before sucking
Guzzling and groaning—caught up in a hedonistic, carnivorous fantasy
Hemoglobin-ridden gore smears their lips as a macabre form of makeup

To be slaughtered by a vampiric leech is a slow-moving, suffering ordeal
Becoming frigid with anemia, one has time to realize what is happening
Forced to experience their prolonged death with unbearable expectancy
One must never try to peel a parasite off, for it will only tighten its hold
Panicked at the thought of separating from their newfound blood bank
And so the victim is left to indolently expire in stop-motion increments
After gulping down far more than their body weight in slurps of scarlet
Sickening refrains of swallowing dwindle as the leech withdraws, at last
Leaving their host to faint, for even though they were not fully drained
Their bite won't mend, their blood won't clot, and their evacuation endures
Hemorrhaging alongside the lagoon until they are as hollow as a casket

Molting their gummy flesh, the leech shifts until only a human remains
Overfed with the stolen, internal vermouth of life, slackening their pace
As their lack of remorse makes room for the buzz of feeling fully gorged

Spider Silk Temptress

Macerate your mind until the secrets in your skull trickle out in droves
From reminders of appalling deeds to liabilities with libidinous sinners
Expose these intimate memories from the private crypt of brain matter
As the well-informed Spider Silk Temptress hangs onto every last word
With a bronzed body—like burnished metal melted down until molten
Varnishing her flesh as an ethereal enamel—incomparable in luminosity
Curtaining seductive features lie silken cobwebs like a diaphanous mask
Lily-white filaments seem effervescent upon her opaline garment of lace
An arachnoid aura adheres to her sultry form, like a noxious nightingale
Urging you to feel feral over her pheromones and savage over her aroma
Wishing for you to grow torturously tempted—*a goal long ago achieved*
Discreet spiders sinisterly suspend from the shoulders of their temptress
As alabaster yarns of their own weaving permanently hold them in place
But, the arachnids could never conceive of straying from their sovereign
Too loyal and too unversed with an existence upon the earth to ever flee
Gangly beings note the hypnotic declarations you divulge to the cosmos
Padlocking priceless confessions away, guarding them all like gemstones
Only after their temptress samples the ambrosial admissions, just a taste
Enough to whet her appetite, as stolen words always salivate her tongue
And agony will linger in the air until her lips finally close around a *secret*

Vulnerable you become—for your mind's sealed vault has been pillaged
Uncovering your now naked spirit, deprived of your mysterious essence
As if an explanatory marquee spelling out *prey* balances above your head
Reeling from the magnetic trance of the temptress's seduction—look up
Notice the clouds amending their course, shifting the night's astral light
Before meeting the troublesome glower of the temptress and her spiders
Shiver, for her dreamlike figure of fantasies swiftly feels all too ominous
At once, find yourself imprisoned within a gauzy web, like a silky snare
Constructed by her servile spiders, promising your permanent captivity
Scandalized sensations arise as the temptress walks into her actual form
Bloated ink-like body, legs upon legs upon legs, upsetting and unsightly
Crawling closer, nothing within her features feels inviting, not anymore
Brace yourself as she devours your skeleton—just as she did your words
Spider Silk Temptress—she will not bring your confessions to her grave
No, the only cemetery that this sham femme fatale will tour is *your own*

Nikolai's Dungeon of Bloodlust

Hostage: the disenchanted moniker that currently depicts my existence
Destined to remain within this isolated dungeon, drenched in suffering
All because of Nikolai: my cryptic captor, both gentleman and monster
Depending on the hour, for under the forgiving moonlight of nightfall
Beauty immerses his sculpted face, like a vampiric Adonis of attraction
But when twines of starlight arise, vestiges of guilt fill his contrite irises
And as the despair of dusk gives way to the warmth of a budding dawn
Any remorse is substituted with ravening feelings of salivating *bloodlust*

Congested with the burgundy glucose robbed from my dwindling veins
Nikolai wishes to lick the fretful perspiration off my nape as an aperitif
To assuage his dehydration—as yearning as scalding sands of the Sahara
With a thirst pleading to be remedied, a pair of whetted fangs protrude
Swiftly plunging into the unprotected breadth of flesh upon my jugular
Indulging in indecent gulps of *my* own blood, Nikolai sinfully swallows
Swaying in euphoria, yet this nocturnal being longs for enough patience
To fill a goblet with this delectable juice, to savor it like a vile sommelier
But alas, he cannot waste even a moment to prepare such a heady drink
Content in his ruby trance to consume straight from the wincing source
And only when his features bloom with drunken bliss does he pull back

Unstable I become, for my body cannot bear much more embezzlement
On the verge of termination, my head swings wearily with hopelessness
As Nikolai, now shockingly altruistic, heals the perforations *he* inflicted
Coasting his firm hands over my frayed throat as if caressing a lost lover
Delirious, my eyes creak open, only to be met with the sight of his own
Swimming with creeks of sympathy and currents of shame all over again
As if the fulfillment of his famine has reinstated an iota of his humanity
And that portrait mends me more than any of Nikolai's healing touches
Despite the lethal fog revolving within my mind, fooled I would not be
For my puncture marks may be missing, but death still prowls in the air
My concerns are confirmed when Nikolai's savagery hungrily resurfaces
Although there cannot possibly be much life left within me to consume
Helplessly, I yank upon the iron bindings pushing into my bruised skin
Imploring for a miracle when Nikolai stalks toward me for the last time

But my chances of fleeing are crushed as his eyes glint with viciousness
For the only thing which has escaped is the mercy within his grim gaze
Repentant gentleman no longer, for the inhuman monster has returned
And this time, his appetite will not be assuaged *until it is utterly too late*

With a brooding sense of déjà vu, Nikolai soaks his lips in my lifeblood
As a dutiful creature of the night, he gulps until his tongue grows numb
It is only when he endeavors to resume devouring and comes up empty
That he learns he has sapped me dry, rendering me an unfilled skeleton
With this abject revelation, the gritty hourglass of time hastens its pace
Triggering the light streaming into the dim dungeon to shift once more
Appearing again as a worldly man, Nikolai's supernatural appetite ebbs
Any echoes of starvation vanish into a chasm—replaced by raw anguish
While my heart abates, growing as static as his own unresponsive organ
Until the reaper, *always lurking nearby*, arrives to collect my limp figure

With a mandible still drowning in the wetness of my withdrawn essence
My undead abductor folds my unresponsive body into his taut embrace
Before brushing his lips against mine, willing my blood to return to me
To sink into my skin, to cartwheel down my gullet, to fall into my veins
Nikolai longs to hack at his chest if only his palms would stop shivering
Not hesitant of the troubling pain which would ensue from his cleaving
But feeling stifled by pressure, discerning the urgency he must act with
For he knows he is full of the blood I need—the blood belonging to *me*
But, regrettably, even if Nikolai submerged my corpse in the scarlet sap
As a fruitless attempt at resurrection, miraculously awaken, I would not

Eternal ether—ridden with tinges of plasma—keens over my departure
Even Beelzebub grapples with despondency over my heartrending finale
As for me, the final melody which dashes into my ears amid my passing
Happen to be the rattling of my chains—torn off my inert hands at last
Paired with the reverbs of Nikolai's shouts, devolving into sobs of regret

Still swarming with my blood, I remain Nikolai's captive, even in death
But I will always be with him, *in* him, and with that thought, he beams

Twilight Stroll of Stone

Gothic gargoyles, hewn from granite, axed from marble, reliably gazing
Observant eyelids never waver—not even when aerial clouds dismantle
Or vials of sunlight shatter, coating the realm in cascades of luminosity
Lest they miss one significant moment of all they were crafted to guard
For their sense of duty is resolute, embossed into their mineral makeup
Yet, their bones yearn for twilight to flower, for daylight to disintegrate
Giving way to moonbeam brooks, steeping the empire in evening glory
Only once darkness develops may gargoyles mercifully meander in awe
As sterling stars gradually uncover themselves within Oxford-blue skies
Gargoyles embark upon their awaited decline, like a hike of excitement
Inclining until their heels meet the infamous ground, which they resent
For unburdened mortals tread upon the territory as often as they please
While gargoyles linger overhead, wanting and wishing for that freedom
Presently, with the canopy of midnight as a veil, liberation is discovered
Stretching sedentary limbs, gargoyles set out on a hushed nightfall stroll
Drifting with no destination in mind and no commitments to complete
Only looking to nourish their souls— starved from living stagnant lives
And so, they roam until their boulder soles throb from unversed fatigue
Still, these aches are welcomed, for they were triggered by idyllic strides
Gargoyles emphatically gasp, honoring the view of their heaving chests
Gawking at the overjoyed ability to move—to exist just like the mortals
Even the commonly unfeeling elements delight in the gargoyles outings
Winds blithely cavort over their wideset forms, like willowy tour guides
Urging them forward—propelling their strides with the powers of ether
Granted such scant hours upon soil, gargoyles do not halt their footfalls
Not until glimpses of daybreak peek past the fog of a blossoming dawn
Only then, with weighty sighs, will gargoyles pause their traveling paces
Solemnly making their way back to the dreary apexes of their buildings
For they have no alternative but to resume their roles as stone sentinels

Back in position, stained glass windows recoil off of their stalwart backs
Reflecting the calico tones of sunrise upon their dismal, sculpted bodies
It is only when the shades of the skies shift again, beckoning the sunset
When afternoon hours wither, surrendering to a stint of cathartic night
That the gargoyle's immobilizing spell is temporarily, thrillingly broken
And their pipedreams of promenades become active realities once again

Fairy-Dusted Destruction

Radiating ethereal verve, dreamlike wings rival the refinement of a swan
Glowing extensions of all fairies' hearts, entirely insubstantial in weight
Extremely psychedelic in appearance, like a crystalized rainbow of color
Welded onto flesh with a symphonic aura relaxing their possessor's soul
To sadistically sever the most requisite feature from these beatific beings
Is a sin even Lucifer, harbinger of limitless cruelty, would never approve
Even so, uncaring of the resulting penalties from barbarous kings below
An ax, whetted with wickedness, cut across the air in a furious upswing
Only to descend upon the dainty wings of the fairy with atrocious ease
Maiming vertebrae, marring cartilage and ligaments, massacring nerves
Disconnecting the fairy-dusted gossamers preserving the wings in place
Darling drips of blood sullied with the scent of woe sifted out in spades
Though, this mutilator never did waver nor weaken in his brutalization
Until the fairy's favorite limbs, slashed with dour finality, fell to the soil

Once, her wings flourished against her spine, an illustration of splendor
Decorated in the hues of pears and peonies—flecked with golden flakes
While frolicking across prairie fields and floral pastures, her wings shone
For they were as glossy as liquified daylight, dripping with honied luster
But now, her willowy wings lay buried under the proof of this butchery
As the fairy dissolves into luminous tears in an intense spell of sobbing
Harrowing devastation arises from the amputation, obscuring her spirit
Sharply screaming, nothing earthly or ethereal could overpower the din
Defiled with matching scabs upon her back—which she forbids to heal
Desiring a bodily memento, tainted with gore, of what she experienced
To keep her woe alive, stoking its sparks until the day it turns into rage

Over time, a fresh set of wings begin to blossom—an agonizing process
But the fairy does not weep, for her tear ducts are now bolted with steel
Mutely, she only grinds her teeth—for she has experienced much worse
Newfangled wings, bereft of brightness, eventually breach through skin
As jet-black as the Cephalopod ink gushing from a squid within the sea
Evil warnings circle the bitter fairy's scarred spine like cautionary clouds
Daring someone to wave an ax in her presence, to wander by her wings
For if they try to steal from her, this time, it will not be *she* who bleeds

Masquerade at the Cherry Lake Chateau

Herrin lies your invitation to the Supernatural Masquerade,

Amid an auspicious eve, one fortnight away, an exclusive ball will begin
Respectfully requesting the presence of creatures with paranormal cores
Rallying leechlike souls with still hearts and monochrome complexions
Beckoning fabled spirits void of flesh, from golems to kelpies to ghouls
Arise from sarcophagi, emerge from austere alleyways, ascend from seas
Leave your lairs and release all inhibitions and insecurities, *just this once*
Embark on the expedition to the raptly regarded Cherry Lake Chateau
Whose archaic exterior betrays nothing of the opulence revealed within
Gothic chandeliers studded with medieval gems swing from the ceilings
Waiting to shower eclectic guests in the warm glow of their amber light
Upon mahogany walls, beside windows featuring intricate stained glass
Prolific artwork painstakingly produced by artistic hands hangs proudly
From delicate, reminiscent watercolors to haunting, cathartic charcoals
Arrive in jeweled masks of papier-mâché—projecting enigmatic privacy
Enter the haven of the esteemed estate and divulge your genuine forms
Shapeshift with glee—shed artificial skin, giving way to authentic scales
Muggy forms of fabrication are not needed upon this sympathetic night
As all in attendance understand the inhuman plight of living insincerely
Within these halls, none will criticize, just as none will slander or shriek
Untie your masks and exist exposed, just as mortals are able to *every day*
Zip your skeletal figures into hand-sewn gowns—let your bones jut out
Adorn your piercing claws with rings, embellish your horns with hoops
Wrap your unearthly bodies in fabrics catering to your innermost wants
On this promising eve, swig crisp vermouth and citrus-flavored punches
Allowing even incorporeal beings to indulge, able to savor the sweetness
Freed from spectral burdens forcing any liquids to pass straight through
For the powers of this night are endless inside these accepting corridors
Elysian symphonies flow from stringed instruments and seraphic voices
Letting invitees frolic and foxtrot the evening away—at least until dawn
Only sunlight signals the conclusion, leaving guests to lament in earnest
Always begging to stay for the rest of their lives—infinite as that may be

Beyond the crimson gates of the Cherry Lake Chateau, live freely—at last

Midnight Annihilation
Written by:
Narcissa Nightshade

Prolific Playwright

Veins peeled open like the skin of a plum, ejecting bloodred sustenance
Streaking the undying palms, youthful as ever, of the prolific playwright
Nowhere closer to a mortal demise than she appeared to be decades ago
Inhaling acutely, she drags her elongated quill along her tarnished flesh
Before exhaling in wild mirth—now equipped to pen her tale of torture
Rifling through her intellect for the ideal words to stamp onto papyrus
Though—the playwright never needs to look too distantly or arduously
For her inspiration crops up like a truthful daisy, never a fictitious weed
With dexterous hands inscribing like waves—solid and steady and sure
The playwright spins a saga of a woman seeking shelter amid a tempest
Scurrying toward a medieval manor—one not as vacant as she assumed
For the owner could not bear to leave, even after all these solitary years
Tethered by memories of hosting revelries in the brisk equinox months
And star-gazing upon his balcony when the spring air pleaded to be felt
Yet, this venue matters little, for the audience only cares who will enter
And more pointedly, who will be lucky enough, *living* enough, to leave
Still, the owner ushers her inside, like a saint, away from the rough rain
Not knowing, for it happens that you never do know until it is too late
That as he closes the doors behind them—he is not locking danger out
But rather welcoming peril within, with trustful arms and a naïve mind
Squandering no time—the woman depletes all life from the proprietor
For it may have initially been the inauspicious storm that pulled her in
But it is the hushed promise of mayhem that hastens her ministrations
Nicking her dagger across his neck, notching her blade astride his chest
As her victim wheezes for reviving air—while writhing in wretchedness
Until his lungs collapse and his life depletes, with haunting permanence
Soon, the gaping wounds marring his corpse finally cease their bleeding
As the manor watches with horror—mourning their trustworthy owner
Not in any state to note the fleeing woman—now thankful for the rain
Washing away the brutal evidence dripping from her dependable dagger
Allowing her identity to remain covert, though her story will be known
Finished—the playwright cracks her sore knuckles like bursts of gunfire
Admiring her plentiful words—flecked with the gloss of thieved vitality
Yet her quill is now bare, and the morbid gore upon her skin is now dry
And so, she must wait under her hands are once again filthy with blood
To begin anew, restarting this grisly cycle for the rest of her eternal days

Thunder of Dragons

Featherlike clouds shift, exposing the epic view of a thunder of dragons
Hatched from bronzed eggs of life, wrongly delivered upon earthly soil
Birthed with a deafening rumble before departing into the freeing ether
As it was always envisioned for these grandiose beings to soar into space
Flying as a unit with daunting exteriors through never with deadly aims
Magnificently gothic beings—coasting in a perfect, practiced formation
Leading dragon at the fore—flanked by the others in devoted deference
Astoundingly thrashing their thorned tails, fluttering their veined wings
Idolizing the buoyant utopia of the universe as notable dragons of thrill

Behold the fabled thunder, named after their guttural refrains of roaring
Cherry-picked fivesome comprised of diverse species with distinct skills
Each more revered in reputation than the last, with unparalleled talents
Bracketing their frontrunner, a frozen duet of arctic dragons materialize
Imitating polar icebergs with stainless-steel scales upon their abdomens
Known by their frostbitten flesh, icicle horns, and shivering respirations
For their sighs yield midwinter snowfalls, like blizzards of hypothermia
Beside the subzero beasts, a blurred twosome of vapor dragons drift by
With charcoal bodies disguised in fog and hazy wings shaped from mist
Breathing out blankets of smoke, serenely coating the skies they inhabit

Piloting their path as principal ruler, the energy dragon directs his pack
Enveloped in radioactive scales—the ultraviolet hue of neon mandarins
With exhalations releasing beams of electricity with superlative voltages
Infusing a galvanizing sense of excitement straight into the stratosphere
Aloft dragons orbit their fruitful kingdom, bounding with raw pleasure
As mystical a display as a colony of macabre bats sailing over the moon
Coasting with aerial powers reinforcing their scales, fueling their wings
Worshipping the frenzy of flight, leaving land-living mortals speechless

Czarina
Of
Cemetaries
Sovereign
Of
Crypts
Sovereign
Of
Crypts

Czarina of Cemeteries

Sovereign of Crypts—sternly governing the subzero kingdom of Russia
As austere as a harvester of casualty, as solemn as an investor of tragedy
Settled upon the spine of an owl, an unfortunate insignia of expiration
Monarch of Mausoleums hurdled from unsympathetic skies to the dirt
Drenched in the morose aura of midnight, she materialized from smog
As an immortal figure, draped in ebony tulle and lavish lengths of satin
With rich ringlets so luminous, they embodied a smattering of starlight
A never-ending carcass coated in flesh, lounging upon a skeletal throne
Amassed from a mixture of broken ribs, bruised clavicles, brittle femurs
Both sinister and striking—an unsettling seat for an unnatural empress

Queen of Tombstones—governing the putrefying corpses of the lifeless
Manipulating spirits with the puppeteering cords of her calloused heart
An organ unfilled with commiserating sentiments or concerned queries
Remember that she is no reaper, for her hands employ no severe scythe
Only death pilfers concluding breaths from the failing lungs of mortals
Before shoving slain souls into a decrepit realm, empty of light and life
Within that tainted land of termination, a menacing destiny is foretold
While a reprehensible verdict of suffering and subservience warbles out
Chiming from the unhinged lips of the ruler like an entombment dirge
For she does not murder, but she does relish in deciding phantom fates
Aflame with the despotic desire to reign over the spirits *she* condemned

Czarina of Cemeteries—shackles her dreary subjects with steel bracelets
Until the souls mutely weep—though their haggard cheeks remain dry
For when their lives were drained of verve, so too were their briny tears
As the queen's voice rumbles, rows of rotting bodies rise for their queen
Like an undead army— trained to obey bloodstained orders of anarchy
Annihilating grating intruders who long to hunt and harness the spirits
Until any mortals who wish to control the departed befall an ironic fate
Becoming as extinct as the deceased spirits they hankered to command
For the cadavers of this cemetery are forever chained to one lone leader
And the only being who may brandish those bindings is the sinister Czarina

Headless Horseman

Headless horseman, a chilling moniker imparted upon an innocent soul
Eclipsed figure of enigmatic fear whose title ignites furnaces of loathing
A disheartening fact—tarnishing his spirit with blemishes of self-hatred
Racing upon an unyielding steed with an equestrian coat emulating coal
Careening through graveled paths, traveling beneath the stars with grief
Enigmatic horseman—whose contours of his complexion appear intact
Thanks to the privacy night offers and the mirage his raised collar crafts
Hiding the reality that a gorge of oblivion lies where his head should be
A lifetime ago—the previously head-bearing horseman was decapitated
Mercilessly severed from his spinal cord with ensuing splatters of blood
When his dear head fell upon the terrain as a new home for earthworms
So, too, did his saddle and stirrups tighten—hexed to resume his riding
Banning the horseman from ever again feeling the dirt beneath his feet
For dismounting was decreed to be hopeless—sealing his galloping fate
Now, the divided body of the headless horseman spasms with mourning
While his heart aches—musing upon the moment his head was thieved
Remembering that he could not even drop to the floor to cradle his loss
Trapped upon his steed, forced to leave his head behind in tragic defeat
Discarding any optimistic dreams—*that is*, until this promising evening

Jezebel enters the scene with cinnamon flesh and titillating rosebud lips
Hurrying along an out-of-the-way route in a threadbare gown of tatters
Aware that the trinkets once sewn into the refined taffeta are long gone
Undetected beneath fallen leaves and tawny acorns from aged oak trees
It all began as Jezebel left the Valentine gala within the Calla Lily Castle
Ready to return to her cottage and drift into a dream-inducing slumber
When she took notice of a silhouette upon a stallion headed toward her
Jezebel snatched a lantern lingering upon the granite stairs of the castle
Before skittering away with the haste of a hyena—as the figure followed
Thus commencing the tumultuous journey of Jezebel's nighttime chase
Now, uneven cobblestones slice into her feet—though she cannot falter
Conscious that while this remote road is bathed in outlines of obscurity
Far more than just the curious shadows are watching her fortune unfold
Trailing her stanch and swift steps, regarding the tension in her features
When all too fast, her stolen lantern flickers like a firefly ready to perish
Leaving Jezebel in unmitigated darkness, though not in benign isolation

Enfolded in the gloom of dusk—Jezebel heeds the neigh of a lone mare
With an alabaster coat, like a timely lighthouse of luster in the dimness
Jezebel heaves herself up onto the blonde steed, hollow of any hesitation
Needing to escape the rapt horrors focused upon wolfing down her soul
Jezebel's palms flutter atop the reins—while her spirit remains persistent
For the tender edges of her spasming heart—carved from parcels of love
And the timid energy coiling within her irises and etched into her spirit
Changed and calcified the moment Jezebel initiated her fleeing journey
Sentimental behaviors and beliefs now harden with unwavering tenacity
As she senses the festering cinders of vindication stir just below her skin
Pushing Jezebel onward in her ominous odyssey, powered by adrenaline
Craving to emit an aura of hellish aim—worse than that of her pursuer
No longer will Jezebel cower like a cat, not when she has made it so far
It was now, during this enthusing epiphany of defiance for our heroine
That the failed lantern gripped by Jezebel's hands—looking utterly pale
The hue of peaches and cream—drained of all pigment from clenching
Begins to blink back to life as if a distant flame felt the alarm of danger
Bellowing within the nighttime ether, alerting the air of imminent peril
Urging the spark to battle its way through the dark and into the lantern
Portraying an illuminating glimmer of saving grace amid this gothic eve
Finally cast in luxuriant light, Jezebel is now able to regard her predator
And though her mind is more rebellious than it was this brisk morning
Some entities still exist that even the most gallant of beings cannot face
And so, Jezebel's fright suddenly returns with an undeniable vengeance
Until she feels no choice but to lead her mare in the opposing direction
Evading this unnerving sight, she absconds to her calm cottage—at last

Unbeknownst to Jezebel, the horseman harbored no desire to hunt her
It was only that he had detected a glint of jewels and a gaze of empathy
Daring him to conjure sanguine feelings of fraught hope one final time
The decapitated jockey wanted for nothing but Jezebel's relieving hands
To sever his doleful curse and dismount his jinxed figure from his steed
Allowing the headless horseman to sink to his knees and search the soil
Before joyfully reuniting with his lost head, just as he had so wished for
And yet, Jezebel did not help, nor did any of the others he had tracked
Leaving the sullen horseman eternally tearful and everlastingly *headless*

Darkened Anarchy

Astral moon with an elysian anatomy fatigued from her lunar existence
And drowsy irises stinging from the blinding gleam of her metallic aura
Suddenly vanished along with her sisters and daughters within the skies
Never again did the saffron sun awaken the earth with her torrid beams
And no more did the carelessly sparkling stars race across the milky way
No, only a vacuum of vacancy remained within the astronomical galaxy
Everlastingly swathing the cosmos within a varnish of absolute darkness
Lightyears away in a remote empire, humanity was propelled into havoc
For the descent into drawn-out nightfall awakened the true colors of all
Complacent monsters were raiders of the sorcery rocketing across space
Drawing upon the potency of astronomic magic to fortify their powers
But amid the hostile shadows—every beast was defenseless and drained
Bereft of speed and strength and supremacy, mourning their dominion
Becoming as fragile as the endangered mortals they haphazardly stalked
When they were tipsy from tyranny and uncaring of their consequences
As victimized mortals foamed at the mouth from this fateful gift of luck
For the inhuman injustice which hounded this land had been equalized
And for once, astonishingly, mortals seized an advantage over monsters

As a cocktail of rage and reprisal brewed within their browbeaten minds
Bitter outlines of obscurity assisted their livid bodies to move unnoticed
As the mortals trailed and tracked the frightened monsters of this world
Utilizing the same heartless fashion once implemented upon themselves
How the tables had turned as monsters were left unable to pilfer plasma
Or emotive tears or vitalizing energy from the caverns of panicked souls
Incapable of blatantly ransacking supreme sway from the interstellar air
Powerless to burgle anything at all, for their vision was wholly impaired
Without the auspicious flair for sight, they were left subdued and sullen
Still—their tenacity had not fled along with the effulgent constellations
And so, when the fight broke out, the undermined monsters were ready
Ruthless battle, long overdue—waged in shadows, though not in silence
None were able to view the stomach-churning onslaughts of spilled life
Just as none could witness the rewarding spectacle of belated retaliation
Only the cheerless howls ringing out acted as proof of the lawless battle
Steadfast cries and horrorstruck bellows ascended toward ebony clouds
With no sign that their echoes would ever wane from the cloaked ether

Blueprints of Sin
Blueprints of Sin
Blueprints of Sin
Blueprints of Sin
Succubus's
Lair
Of Lust

Succubus's Lair of Lust

Seducing, sensual succubus, with saliva pooling atop her brazen tongue
From the delectable dustings of souls wafting in this land of ample lives
Hellish minx, immeasurably immodest, hatched to entice and embezzle
Symbolizing a suggestive goddess of temptation, sultrier than perdition
Originating from an unsated empire of *hunger* with a provocative figure
Devised from illicit blueprints of sin—as tantalizing as vinegar is to flies
Though not even the tissues comprising her organs feel rested or relaxed
For exhaustion razes her mind while her energy levels radically dwindle
And only the carnal deeds of touching and tasting will awaken her fully
Coquettish demon in disguise, luring males into her wanton lair of lust
Who skate into the spell of her sultry eyes, like a waking coma of *want*
Before massaging the unholy flesh of her bare midriff with raring hands
Succulent pheromones infiltrate their senses as an aromatic aphrodisiac
While a sexual spell of desire settles into their veins—begging for more
Mesmeric succubus trails her swollen mouth over their writhing bodies
Tangling her expert fingers within their disheveled hair—tugging softly
Lapping at their pulsating throats, savoring the feel of their purring skin
Consuming their erotic energy and feeding off their salacious yearnings
Tapering her teasing—she *finally* lowers her shameless lips to their own
Like a fatal snake bite, for a succubus's kiss is both defusing and deadly
Amid this intimate act, euphoric waterworks trickle from her tear ducts
As she becomes unabashed with a thirst only rabid beasts can recognize
For her powers of persuasion blossom each time her tongue meets theirs
In a carnal dance of dominance, one the succubus leads with conviction

But soon—this flirtatious, yet tender kiss, does not feel ample anymore
Deepening her ministrations, the succubus, with inhuman lungs of steel
Ingests their soul and imbibes their spirit, draining with fiendish elation
Letting their earthly essence soar down her gullet like masculine nectar
While floating in a conscious dream of the unaffected joys of hedonism
As she lethargically slays these aroused mortals, her touch never departs
For she continues to leisurely graze her nails across their heaving chests
Yet the moaning males do not entertain objecting for one scarce second
For the intense pleasure of her devouring mouth is perfect in every way
Well—that is until they are left with only a drained body, a dazed brain
And a gaping corner within their skeletons where their souls once lived

Dichotomy of Demetria

Peer into an abyss of ambiguity, where two halves do not make a whole
For Demetria's beauty is binary, depending upon the direction she faces
Twisting toward the sunlight, she appears as a prima ballerina of beauty
With blushing irises of burnished butterscotch and a sumptuous mouth
Whose immaculate skin, flawless and fetching, is often mistaken for silk
As ravishing as a star, with layered tresses in the hue of heated chestnuts
And a physique that deities gossip over in the ivory palaces of Olympus
Demetria's features are no fallacy, though never may they be duplicated
Much to the devastation of painters and sculptors alike who have failed
Whose cloth canvases and clumps of clay are splattered with their wails
For nothing may ever truly replicate the exquisite nature of her exterior

But then, shifting toward beams of blackness, her attraction evaporates
For this half of Demetria's complexion is merely an emaciated skeleton
Repugnant fragments of flesh flaking away from her once enviable face
Revealing corroded bones freckled with filaments of nauseating mildew
Gaunt and decaying, grey and dismaying, Demetria is far from faultless
And no great lengths will be taken to imitate her appearance any longer

None know better than Demetria how attraction is analytically regarded
When speaking from her superficially lovely lips, her words matter little
For people become too enamored by her splendor to hear her thoughts
But when speaking from her rotting lips, her words mean nothing at all
For her views are entirely discounted, as society only favors the striking

Even Demetria herself cannot recollect when her dual exterior emerged
Or which side—the blissful or the brutal—showcases her original form
Although now, she can no longer bring herself to feign care or concern
For she furtively reveres the dichotomy she has been destined to live as
As her spirit is not composed of only one shade, of only one sentiment
What a gift it is—that her face and figure have the chance to echo that

Unassailable Monster

Though the slope of the blade is sharp, it is not absolute in its strength
Hoist the dense hatchet high—drive it down in an allegedly final blow
Thrust a bronze broadsword through robust muscles and renal kidneys
Ladle a bushel of belladonna down the ravine of this infinite individual
Wrench his femurs and fibulas from their positions with dreadful force
Strip the flesh from his immortal chest, fileting piece by piece by piece
Buckle to the unforgiving earth in defeat when he continues to live on

Many have insolently endeavored to massacre this unassailable monster
But none ever prevail, not in granting true termination or lifelong scars
Even the sulfur-scented reaper will *never* harvest this recuperating being
For his name has foiled death himself, to the point of incensed madness
And it is a rule older than the hands of time—that all anonymous souls
Will dodge the sour traps of demise, so long as they remain unidentified
Released from the always-looming stopwatch ticking down to departure
Only to be assigned to the permanent purgatory known as immortality

Brutalized being incapable of expiring, yet agony finds him all the same
For every assassination attempt ends with abysmal lagoons of his blood
Marring the soil below him as he swims through his own plasma to flee
Lacerations line his sternum as bones lay splintered at nauseating slants
Forced to feel the caustic burn of every slash, of every gouge, every day
Patching himself together in solitude—*more excruciating than execution*
Suturing limbs, spooning life into depleting veins, cauterizing incisions
Waiting, in horrible haste, for the last of his extensive wounds to repair
Reattached, restitched, resurrected, like an everlasting, crimson phoenix

Though instead of sailing from the threshold of death on intrepid wings
This monster—brought to life from fabled pages of mythological beasts
Thought to be fictional, yet his tangible waterworks tell a different story
Only wallows in abject torment, waiting for his next mutilator to arrive
For what good stems from an eternal life—if it only produces such pain
Immortality, the cruelest of curses—breathing in air while living in hell
Invincible monster, *needing* the next slayer to succeed so he may depart
For the lethal gift of lasting death would finally free him from his woes

Aerial Odyssey

Gaze through the looking glass, seize the hand of the hare, and descend
Become unmoored from the gravitational grasp of the embrace of Earth
Tumble through untrodden realms, veiled within this immense universe
Experience what lies in the in-between as a pioneer of unforeseen paths

Start amid the lackluster kingdom of the living, congested with mortals
Before slipping into a surreal chasm, forced to follow the winding track
Careening with bewilderment, weightlessly lapsing like a listless feather
Tripping past atomic breezes whistling by while ogling the foreign void
Unwittingly embarking upon an aerial odyssey—dissimilar to any other

Jump into the sphere of all spirits where the atmosphere is melancholic
Submerged within haunted hues of dismal greys and phantasmal silvers
Infinitely clamorous in ambiance from the grumbling protests of ghouls
Nostalgically mewling over the torn cords of their embezzled existences
Yet—their mourning dirges constantly cascade into the skies unnoticed
For mortal souls with earthly ears had never been granted ghostly entry
Within this unnatural world while parading flesh flushed with liveliness
But now, every apparition stands agape, blatantly gawking with interest
Witnessing your diving form gracefully lurching with swelling swiftness
At once, the spirits swarm to you, thinking you have come to save them
And yet, despite their gauzy expressions of hope—nothing can be done
For you are just as helpless against your falling fate as they are to theirs

Heed their grief-stricken snivels while you exit the domain of phantoms
Only to enter next a realm starring unceasing consequences of foul sins
Arrive at the wayward territories of Hades, the concentric circles of hell
Where smoky constellations consist of flaring skulls infinitely blistering
And gushing rainfalls are nothing but surges of gore from severed veins

Begin by passing through the original circle, limbo, a state of ambiguity
Engulfed in solitude, leaving lasting scabs of loneliness upon your heart
Then, accelerate through the arena of lust, windswept yet never wanton
And the frigid dome of gluttony, where even the ether tends to tremble
Pass by strenuous greed, where caches of gold no longer appear desirable
Encounter the circle of wrath, echoing with infuriating wartime bellows
Face the land where heresy reigns, broiling with punitive fires of reprisal
Only to fly past detailed rings of rioting violence and falsehearted fraud

Cagily reach the terrain of treachery—the illicit, red-hot abode of Satan
With opaque skies—like the universe's complexion in the dead of night
Brimming with traitorous spies, bristling within a polar zone of penalty
By this point, your brain is irrevocably scarred by all you have regarded
And so, with bleeding eyes weeping berry-tinted tears, you continue on
Relieved at your freedom—thrilled to have your vision wrenched away
From the night-terror-inducing representation of the underworld *at last*

Soar once more, stumbling into a heavenly realm—not unlike your own
Yet this province seems far more picturesque—like a paradise of serenity
Survey the merry garden of utopia you have been charitably placed into
Bursting with benevolent wildlife and blooming with eternal hollyhocks
Breathe in botanical dewdrops, a covetous aroma you so yearn to bottle

Ultimately, realize the floral pollen in the atmosphere is actually poison
Just as the petunia petals are hornets and shifting daisy stems are cobras
As you feel blades of grass, revealed to be lawns of thorns, stab your feet
Grasp the notion that your journey has finished, plummeting no longer
Deserted on solid, yet spiked, soil—trapped upon this portentous realm
With only a fractured looking glass, a misplaced hare, and no way home

Legend of the Labyrinth

Below graveled ground, beside petite snails, lies a disorienting labyrinth
Forged in parallel time with the sculpting of the continental Earth itself
Stupefying maze featuring elevated partitions and monumental barriers
Every complicated turn is twisting, and each complex path is perplexing
Impossible to detect how entrenched within the labyrinth one becomes
Uncertain of the distance to the door, unsure how much time passes by
Tread the troubling corridors of the labyrinth, travel in unending circles
Become furthermore ensnared with each perilous tread you dare to take
Although, the mystifying passageways should not be your greatest worry
For the most pressing concern lurks within the walls, hidden from sight
Dwelling under the terrain—covertly molding themselves into the maze
Reside inhospitable behemoths with mortal cravings, salivating to strike
Thrown into the labyrinth by malignant gods as a type of divine theatre
Deities watch on in sinful delight whenever the creatures turn ravenous
Knowing their only prey, their only potential nutrition, are frail mortals
If you hear the beings with sharklike teeth and slicing talons start to stir
You must flee, and swiftly so, to an exit you are no longer certain exists

Departing toward your escape or your end, stagger over heaps of bones
Splinters of skulls and fragments of clavicles—lapped completely clean
For cannibalistic appetites are as endless as the curves within this maze
Resulting in skeletal remnants of those who will never again see the sun
For the labyrinth will now and always remain their eternal resting place
Shove jawbones to clear your path, kicking up what seems to be debris
But in a heartrending epiphany, learn that dust specks are actually *ashes*
Of those who somehow fled the ravenous wrath of the labyrinth's beasts
Only to never find their way out, fated to amble until their tardy deaths
Becoming stacks of lost lives—serving as reminders of your own destiny
Hold your breath and heave your way through—ghastly step after step
Notice something crimson tarnishing the walls in long, tortured slashes
Proof of those who had attempted to claw their way out in desperation
Fearful that each trail led them deeper into the maze, far from freedom
Freedom, which must be a trick—a sweet mirage that will never be true
For the horrors of the labyrinth pluck away any probabilities of leaving
Like picking berries from a bush, one by one, until the branch is barren
Leaving all who enter doomed from the start, like the Minotaur himself

Dahlia's Murderous Aftermath

Dahlia, damsel she was not, for her skin was stippled with scarlet chaos
Painted in the matching anatomical pigment of her botanical namesake
Tinted with bloodied freckles and tarnished with evidence of expiration
Finally—the calamitous splinter of glass lurched from Dahlia's slick grip
For it was murder that she committed in an impetuous, irrevocable way
And so, it was a murderer she had become and would endlessly remain

Before the mess and massacre, a sharp warning of peril called to Dahlia
Injecting her mortal anatomy with the erosive toxins of evil exhilaration
Gushing throughout her capillaries while corroding her breathless lungs
Bathing her flesh with a rosy tint as she found herself before the *monster*
For what else shall you brand one whose soul rains with violent showers
Bearing irises just like Satan's descendants, void of any and all empathy
Flaunting the nails of a jungle predator—signaling his savage character
If the single-minded monster was granted one wish by a mythical genie
It would be the ability to *rip her limbs like a ragdoll* with his snarled lips
While licking her tears—for proof of panic acts as a monsters ambrosia
Although, Dahlia would never break from the dread he craved to incite
And her sobs would remain a baseless reverie within his demonic mind
For her skull never did grasp the importance of deigning to feel rattled

No, Dahlia's enthusiastic ears only ever heard alarm bells of adrenaline
Feeling feverish from impish excitement over what would happen next
For the chess game of carnage, with pawns aplenty, had only just begun
And Dahlia was an all too willing player—acting as obedient as an oath
As she submissively lowered her head, the monster barked his approval
Before curtly prowling forward, supremely pleased with her compliance
Entranced by vicious fantasies of rooting into the ravine of her skeleton
Breaking her bones—exulting in the rapturous tune of the ensuing snap
Blackened blood boiled as his revolting mouth slavered—a foul portrait
As he pursued his seemingly docile target, his hunger clouded his focus
And thus—the monster did not note when Dahlia's eyes tapered in rage
Or when her mouth pulled into a sinister smile—foaming with victory
Before the reaper could apprehend Dahlia *or* what would remain of her
A flare of light reflected off an injuring shard of sea glass upon the floor
A sharpened savior—which would turn the prey into the pitiless hunter

With a crooked appetite for anarchy, the hunting hellion dove forward
Aiming to cleave open the vulnerable expanse where her esophagus lies
But before he got the chance—Dahlia lunged for the makeshift weapon
Sea glass in hand, she thrust herself forward just like a wartime goddess
Forcefully colliding with the rampaging monster with unforgiving force
Finally, close enough to bury the shard into the sheer skin atop his heart

In an instant, he who craved to introduce Dahlia to the dance of death
Gaped as glass tore across flesh—inciting the commencement of defeat
Trounced in one swipe—by she who toed the threadlike line of demise
And while being engulfed by an incarcerating vacuum of infinite expiry
His irises found Dahlia, who hardened her gaze but broadened her grin
Hoping her energetic expression of triumph, now void of any false fear
Would haunt the craters of his head as he faded into nothingness at last
Leaving Dahlia alone, circled only by the blood of the being she slayed
It did not take long before this scene awakened Dahlia's unlimited thirst
A sadistic sort of dehydration, growing and growling within her organs

Before—for her life would now exist in terms of before her kill and after
Dahlia's wispy soul was like a cloud never weighed down by wickedness
After, her blood cells and bone marrow felt outright novel in every way
Dahlia's desires were primal—like the cravings of a lion circling a lizard
Just as her hunger was horrific, like ravens lapping at wretched remains
And though the results of her slaying coated her cheeks like grim jewels
The copper aroma of gore, profusely evident, did not turn her stomach
On the contrary, Dahlia needed more and would do anything to get it

Dahlia, damsel she was still not, though now, human she was not either
Her mortality melted away, her brain shifted, and her anatomy mutated
For she had become the revolting being she had slaughtered in seconds
A punitive penance: for that is the curse the creature had always carried
To unload the ultimate consequence upon any who long to destroy him
Vowing that his murderous legacy would live on *even when he would not*

Now, Dahlia sets out on her own hunt—fraught to gratify her gluttony
Just like the slain creature had been hankering to do when he found her

Basilisk Venom

Beware of the Basilisk, insidious schemer, rattling reptile, virulent being
Serpentine symbol of malice, whose sinister scales are mottled with evil
Cloaked in the unsettling hues of a darkened rainforest, dire and damp
Wily shapeshifter of serpents, calculating architect of innovative snakes
Shedding the eternal flesh of his original form—arising as novel species
Before slinking back into his chilling body, ready to reign over them all

Scaled czar—fated for royalty from labor, carrier of a crown from birth
Born into actuality with the imprint of an imperial circlet atop his skull
Heed the discordant chords of the coldblooded monarch's gruff hissing
Emboldening submissive creatures to materialize from their desert dens
Answering this royal request, they rush to their leader's side with loyalty
Coiling beside this nefarious beast, worshipping his malice-laced words
For the brusque cadence of the Basilisk is supreme, never to be ignored

Bloodcurdling being—veins burning with acerbic cataracts of corrosion
Sense his low exaltations perch upon your skin like mites of destruction
As death waits in the unseen corridors of life—fervently biding his time
For the noxious Basilisk breath reeks of demise, and shortly, so will you
Flinch from his axing teeth and fatal, forked tongue—slimy with toxins
Prepare to perish while his terminal lips sneer—gaping wider and wider
Until homicidal fangs flash in the darkness—before finally finding flesh
Tearing through inconsequential layers of skin, like biting into an apple
Yet, unlike with apathetic fruits, this chaotic feast will only end in *death*

Although—most incurable of all remains to be his stony eyes of venom
For the Basilisk deals certificates of demise without weaponry or words
Only employing his toxic gaze, much like the merciless stare of Medusa
For the gorgon and this reptile are kindred souls, slaughtering in silence
Deserting your motionless body, with empty eyes ajar, the Basilisk flees
Slithering away, leaving only a current of caustic poison trailing behind
Absconding to his imperial throne, shining with an unsympathetic aura
Where the Basilisk's sinuous subjects will be waiting, as they always are
Ready and raring to listen to their king's latest tale of viperous mayhem

GRIMWOOD
PALACE

Phantom of the Grimwood Palace

What suffering to wish for hushed solitude—the docile song of stillness
Only to be accosted by the unremitting thrum of unwelcome company
Relentlessly intruding upon your beleaguered ears—bleeding in distress
Hence is the spectral existence of the Phantom of the Grimwood Palace
Beginning with a bayonet pitilessly impaled into his reddening sternum
Mimicking a pasture of springtime poppies as crimson as a demon's eyes
Finishing with a pair of lifeless lungs—never again to inhale a lick of air
Mortality raided by death, so a spirit he became—chained to this palace
But now, burdened by brazen guests, the phantom lives alone no longer
Condemned to overhear the unsolicited lodgers roaming across his halls
With the assertive gait of those who do not recognize they are imposing
Who have not yet fathomed that anyone is even around to impose upon
Harassed by blinding headaches, the phantom fantasizes about isolation
Dreaming of peace as does each specter tethered to their place of expiry
Innocuously, the phantom wanders the passageways of his stanch palace
Until his presence, alerted by the creaking of rusty floorboards, is heard
Leaving the visitors sure that this nameless spirit must be stalking them
Devising schemes to inflict ghostly methods of horror upon their souls
And yet, the phantom purely wishes to reside within his palace *all alone*

Musing over this injustice, disbelief consumes this entity of the afterlife
For he cannot grasp why *he*, of all people—or, he supposes, of all spirits
Should be the one expected to leave—to be evicted from his own home
In demise, he was stripped of all of his earthly possessions and promises
Why must he also be denied the asylum of shelter, his only lasting asset
For the Grimwood Palace carries not only the memories of his existence
But now, it also holds his soul hostage—clasped in the palms of passing
And so, despite the indignant, shrieking visitors—the phantom remains
Over time, the aura of panic oozing from the guests becomes intolerable
As the phantom frantically tries to find ways to show he means no harm
But his efforts are ineffective, for his pleas are either unheard or ignored
Until the phantom is left with an orb of rage rattling around in his soul
Prompting him to soon *snap*, siphoning all the malicious energy he can
Gathering cargos of grief and resentment from the realm of the undead
Only to unleash it all upon the lodgers in a hailstorm of wicked terrors
For if they are so certain of an evil spirit, then that is what they will get

DEATH'S
DIARY

Banshee of Mourning

In the afterglow of afternoon, darling kisses of harmony graze the realm
Forging an ambiance of stillness and serenity—like a haze of tranquility
Until the jolting tune of warning decimates the calm—as a dreary omen
Keening screams escape lamenting lungs, dispersing like cautionary flies
Blubbering in unmasked bereavement, this banshee's premonition ends
And now—before the reverberations of her somber symphony fully fade
Death will ascend from the underworld—disposed to claim yet another

Inconsolable banshee evermore inundated in a grim gale of foreboding
For she has read the diary of death, now storing his secrets in her veins
And when it is time for the deity of demise to exercise his pitiless blade
Liability presses upon the back of this wailing woman—to enlighten all
Sound waves swarming in her stomach long to be freed, to be followed
Impatient to twist into deafening shrieks as soon as her critical lips part
Until even Mercury and Mars tremor from her thunderous predictions

Yet—a sense of deplorable expectation pesters her fretful consciousness
For the moment when preordained individuals become rotting fatalities
Unfathomable aches of the dying become affixed to this tearful banshee
Cursed to endure the repulsive pangs of removal from this mortal plane
And while their resistant souls are plucked out like pits from a nectarine
An imperative chunk of this banshee's own soul trails the victims down
Into the perturbing realm where worldly existences are finally expunged
Souls bound for solitude garner comfort from the company of her soul
Yet, that relief comes at an appalling price for this troubled being to pay
For the dead may feel soothed, but this banshee with a fragmented soul
Knows nothing but indescribable pain, with no pleasurable end in sight

Though for now, this banshee focuses only on the burning in her blood
Signaling that another mortal will soon perish—as someone always will
For the acquisitive reaper never submits to the hypnotic call of slumber
Powerless to resist—this banshee unhinges her mouth, unlocks her jaw
And emits a bellow spiked with the familiar fragrance of imminent loss

Sun-Kissed Rhiannon

Rhiannon, bewitching pirate queen, seducer of the turbulent seven seas
Born without blood, only a rush of sparkling saltwater in her capillaries
Heart decorated in seaweed, coral reef bones, organs bursting with sand
Tempestuous whitecaps roll in harmony with the orchestra of her pulse
For every natural mineral within every sea she sails over belongs only to her

Effortless glory describes Rhiannon's sun-kissed and freckle-dotted skin
Flesh, face, figure, not a modicum is unpossessed by coastal magnetism
Irises fashioned from baby blue sea glass, amassed from the tides below
Sinuous, coarse curls, daffodil-hued, streaked with contours of daylight
Windswept fringe—brushing over a toasted complexion of awed sienna
Rhiannon securely fastens a laced corset atop her tiered frock of indigo
With an indecent slit torn onto either side, tattered with her own hands
Ensuring her capability to amble across her ship with unrestrained ease
Decorated in jewelries of citrine—from the heavy hoops upon her ears
To the chains and rings and cuffs enhancing the rest of her curved body
Spellbound are all by the aquatic allure of the pirate queen's appearance
And as absolute is her attraction—Rhiannon's magic is just as mesmeric

Rhiannon reigns over the open, obedient seas, steering her noble vessel
Raising her ornamented arms, beckoning and binding water to her will
Creating immense surfs and swells without any overwhelming exertion
Forming tsunamis and tidal wives, as easily as breathing in the briny air
With unstoppable powers as pure and potent as the caress of a jellyfish
Every competing captain and stalwart crew member thinks of her often
Envious of Rhiannon's seafaring magic, of her naturally irresistible aura
Nevertheless—the traitorous essence of mutiny will never mar her ship
For this breathtaking buccaneer will always remain too riveting to hate

Years from now, enthralling as ever, Rhiannon will be woven into myths
Tantalizing tales of a revered pirate queen, transcribed from only truths
Nautical narratives of energizing escapades in search of gilded treasures
Reports of a golden woman, resplendent in blue, peering into a spyglass
Plotting her next destination, certain her loyal waters will take her there

Interstellar Solitude

To exist as a star—what intricate beauty life within the skies must bring
Idling beside radioactive moondust and planets shifting in perfect orbit
Slotted within the milky way with primeval care, luminous and lasting
And yet, their astronomical permanence will soon prove to be unstable
For the quietude of all exquisite things must come to an end eventually
As the fates understand well, bearing this truth with genuine mourning
And when nightfall next descends, the universe must hesitate no longer
With a throbbing feeling of melancholic remorse—gravity finally falters
Stars sewn within the intergalactic cosmos are pulled from their stations
Axed from the ether with an astral bayonet, left only to speedily tumble
Helpless to delay their declining until a fertile floor catches them at last
Having landed upon a foreign realm, the stars search their surroundings
Only to learn their pearly, pointed forms have not survived the journey
For their souls remain unchanged, yet their appearance has been altered
Deprived of their blinding light while gaining corporeal figures of flesh
Displaying long limbs and reddened lips, now glowing in a mortal sense
Fulfilling earthly fantasies they never dared to dream, *the stars finally feel*
Bestowed with the secular abilities of speech, of movement, of sensation
Fervent to experience life like those they had endlessly envied from afar

But—bliss comes with a bill, and so for every star who elects to remain
Contented to dwell beside terrestrial debris and dirt for the rest of time
One unfortunate mortal must leave this realm—unable to deny destiny
Condemned to reside above, within the galaxy, replacing the fallen star
Initially, the victims marvel at the vivid grandeur beautifying the galaxy
However, much time does not drift by before horrific realization sets in
Grasping the magnitude of their situation, forever stranded as starlight
For these mortals may have gained a novel persona of astronomical awe
But so, too, have they been hexed with an existence of endless isolation
Imprisoned in silence—unable to scream, to sob over all they have lost
While distantly, the prior starbursts of scorching light grow remorseful
For the lands they now inhabit are not as notable as they once believed
And humanity proves to be excruciatingly wearying and entirely woeful
But their decisions are fixed, sentencing the stars and mortals to misery
And so, when someone radiant yet regretful passes you by on this realm
Look twice and sense their stellar aura, for not everything is as it seems

Origin of the Original Vampire

Fatefully suspended upon the charcoal wings of an ineffably gothic bat
Foreboding cobwebs of transformation journeyed through sunless skies
Urgently inclining, the overcast mammal extended his jaw and attacked
Inhumane bite, carnage aftertaste, unraveled flesh, hemoglobin rivulets
Altering songs of sewing echoed late into the eve, for change had come
Intergalactic fibers interlaced within the universe added novel filaments
For something mystically murderous was bred below the midnight skies
Astronomical constellations shifted within the cosmos, huddling as one
Nosily bidding to attain an enhanced view of this unprecedented birth
For the stars were regarding the grave conception of *the original vampire*
Once the nocturnal creature of twilight departed, skulking into the dark
Melchior, now immortal, with matching marks upon his jugular—wept
Ensnared within a cyclone of nauseating agony as his blunt teeth shifted
Until filed fangs of destruction tore through his gums, fitting into place
Melchior shivered, for no longer did his bloodstream provide pure heat
No longer did his veins do anything at all, not unlike his inactive heart

Morbidly changed, yet what truly pestered Melchior was his *dehydration*
Aching for copper syrup to glaze his esophagus—like a bloodred donut
A longing as potent as a banshee's urge to release their keening screams
Neither beings brandish a choice, for their desires are entirely inevitable
Melchior dreamt of the metallic scents flooding violent slaughterhouses
And fantasized about vascular ambrosia until he could waver no longer
Tracking soon-to-be sufferers, the vampire then located his ideal victim
Before laying a shameless kiss upon her lips—commencing his carnage
Devouring her mouth, ravishing her tongue, animalistic from bloodlust
Yet, his appetites were not erotic, unlike the wants of his inaugural prey
No, Melchior only longed to lull this mortal into a false feeling of safety
Until her body melted into his—uninhibited from the throes of passion
Allowing Melchior, with an undying spirit and an underfed soul, to *take*
Perturbed stars bemoaned as the vampire cradled the center of her neck
Admiring how her veins remained divinely visible—even in the twilight
Melchior stroked her pulse, careful to heed any changes in vital rhythm
Coerced to do so by the final vestiges of humanity he contained within
But then, restraint ignored, Melchior pricked innocent flesh like a fiend
And euphorically consumed that which he will always crave, at long last

God, Melchior moaned, *never again will bland wines sate my eerie palette*
Now knowing the most potent liquor in this realm is none other than blood
Inciting the most decadent luxury of my existence after merely one mouthful
Frantic from savage need, Melchior—with flesh as frigid as falling snow
Did not dwell upon the aspects of mortal life he would never feel again
Honied desires for angel cakes or humming songs from a beating heart
Hasty confessions or hurried caresses prompted by ephemeral existences
Melchior cared not for any of the dreary, for they did seem so dull now
Facets of an earthly life, vacant of the rapture which only plasma offers
For the eccentric flavor of the garnet liquid lingered upon his tastebuds
As pleas for more harassed his mind, consuming his vampiric thoughts

Unable to look away, the scandalized stars witnessed Melchior pull back
Beads of blood seeped from his prey as her eyes grew glassy from terror
This unrefined spectacle, detailing the devastation the vampire inflicted
Broke the smoke of severe *want* Melchior had found himself trapped in
And though the stars observed from afar in blatant disdain and distress
Gilded spheres of light would never know how from this night onward
Melchior's skull would always be engaged in derisive warfare with itself
Scorning how once tender palms had shifted into sadistically toxic fists
How the scent of coins assaulted his senses as gore tarnished his mouth
And yet, Melchior stayed bidden to his bloodlust, inept to deny its call
Creature of the undead, but even still, he was not yet hopelessly callous
Still abreast of his prey's fading pulse, Melchior knew when to adjourn
For he may thieve blood forever, but never will he venture to slaughter
With a stationary heart, the vampire rebuilt his initial prey's ripped skin
Anxiously attempting to stroke her already sore skin with a calm touch
Watching in appreciative awe as her complexion sutured itself together
Melchior bestowed a lingering kiss, a farewell press of his bloodied lips
Upon her mended throat—then upon her jaw, her cheeks, her temples
Abashed apologies for all he had stolen and for all he would steal again
Melchior departed in hushed silence—pondering his distinctive reality
Battling notions of bloodlust with his already escaping morals from life
And when he reached his wooden abode—intended for daylight hours
Melchior's tongue began to salivate with his scarlet thirst—all too soon

Heralds of Horror

Entombed within an existence of coerced servility, crueler than a coffin
Helpless victims, caught in a gruesome snare, stripped of their own will
Pulse with pain while prostrating at the pulpit of the Heralds of Horror
Within the umbral veins of the triad, undeterred currents of power flow
Extracted from the alarming carols of misfortune still sullying the skies
Immortal unit of the undead, never diseased by plagues nor by poisons
Designed to remain in this territory—quenching their thirst for torture
Until every battered mortal beseeches death to retrieve their souls, *soon*

Original herald, with sturdy fists sculpted from brass, chiseled from ire
Body broiling from the heat hurdling off his uncouth pleas to disfigure
Hands hankering to suffocate lengthy throats and splinter feeble bones
Confiscating ivory spines and sucking upon bloodied vertebrae in bliss
For only the melodic movement of slashing flesh into nauseating strips
Would appease the morbid need for barbarity festering in his vile mind
Subsequent herald, with a wraithlike exterior twisted from fragile vapor
Brainwaves like a marionette's ropes—disturbing victims with delusions
Dropping innocuous psyches into vortexes of dismembering daydreams
As the mirages—*however false*—of murder and mayhem and mutilation
Trigger waterfalls of queasiness to waft from their pores—oozing panic
Until the herald grows heedless with the unhallowed demand for more
Concluding herald, whose vexing voice scampers past their adverse lips
Producing searing words—impaling skulls like sonatas bound in spikes
Slavering to vaccinate prey with the budding spores of explicit disasters
Germinating upon the gruff librettos falling from their heartless tongue
If possible, the herald would attach an amplifier within their esophagus
Heightening their lyrics, only to devour the hurt provoked in all bodies
Absorbing unsavory tears—like a Michelin-starred meal of ruthlessness

In the end, the Heralds of Horror's victims remain traumatically ruined
Nothing but disassembled carcasses, heaps of hemorrhaging extremities
Though, even in parts, these tyrannized corpses will never find freedom
For their skinned flesh and stabbed souls will eternally writhe in misery
As the triad steps over their gutted forms before moving on to the next

Scylla's Aquatic Tragedies

Uncharted sea whose sapphire waters imitated a hoard of molten jewels
Hazardous to all who set sail—as her waves were fickle and unforgiving
Bearer of a beachside aura luring daring pirates into her ensnaring surfs
Tricked into thinking they could traverse the tides as easily as Poseidon
Sailors embarked on a perilous passage, unlikely to ever return to shore
More often than not, seafarers inaudibly disappeared into the unknown
For the riotous crashes of frothy whitecaps muted their screams entirely
Until nothing of their trips remained, save for paltry splinters of lumber
Torn from the felled vessels which carted them to their marine demises
For the sea often deigned to distort, revealing a vulgar beast of atrocity
One with suctioning limbs to steal with and ruthless lips to ravage with
Towing asunder any who piloted slick waves, triggering *aquatic tragedies*

Scylla, female fiend of the sea with a sickening visage and a violent soul
With a dozen grisly tentacles, six ghastly heads, and limitless grim teeth
Inhabiting a yawning den opposite the mythical whirlpool of Charybdis
For peril stalked the seas—regardless of which side you traveled toward
Scylla restrained any who risked drifting near her death-defying domain
Plucking sailors and ships alike from coastlines where air streams freely
Before hauling them all below, where ether they would find nevermore
Scylla tethered victims with her tentacles, imitating makeshift manacles
And when she became flush with too many captives, not enough limbs
Strips of seaweed were knotted around jolting ankles and flailing wrists
Bruising skin with briny shackles, ensuring her prey remained confined
With almighty authority, Scylla would devour their visceral trepidation
Absorbing the aftertaste of desperation, as hopeless as a trout on a hook

Then, vicious as a vulture, Scylla would hold their drowning forms near
Only to place their quaking, puckered flesh between her fanged incisors
And *wrench*, cleaving skin into scraps, an ode to Cerberus, rabid in hell
Shredding until the devils of expiry appear to cheerfully seize their souls
Leaving their frayed remains forever stuck in the canyon of her stomach
And the few who miraculously outlasted the violence within Scylla's lair
Able to gulp lungfuls of salty sea winds once more, will never sail again
For the fates let them flee once—but they will not be so generous twice
Urging the sailors into land-bound lives, left to adore the tide from afar

The Fates

Weaving Sisters of Fate

Omniscient sisters of three, sage oracles weaving upon the loom of life
The Fates, spinning, scheming, shearing—decreeing the destinies of all
Prudent goddesses brandishing crucial skills of the divine from delivery
Draftswomen of transient existences and designers of terrifying endings
Clotho, crocheting critical twines of budding life upon a fateful tapestry
Lachesis, examining the needlework, shaping the size of the embroidery
Atropos, handling essential shears, shredding the filaments with finality
Wise sisters, creators of kismet romances, crafters of intense heartaches
Shielding the crystal balls slotted within their orbital clefts as they speak
Ensuring their all-seeing spheres will never be shoplifted with acrimony
For mortals and gods and mages reproach those carrying shrewd spirits
Acting out with ferocity, outraged when their own insight is in question
Or—choosing to disbelieve their claims, utterly truthful as they may be
As the poor prophet of mythology, Cassandra, will wretchedly attest to
These goddesses, living tarot cards, find significance in ordinary objects
A fruitful cornucopia flaunted atop a banquet board—denoting fertility
A roasting candlestick trickling wax, suggesting radiance and realization
For the Fates endlessly uncover meaning in the most mundane of places
Once, when bored and bursting for entertainment, as deities always are
The trio fashioned a fate so detrimental none would triumph in the end
For once the Fates cement their fortunes into the fabric of the universe
Nothing atmospheric or earthly may invalidate the ill-omened outcome
An aftermath as permanent as Pandora peeking inside her plaguing box
Thus was the oracle the goddesses decreed with calculating amusement
The divination which will emerge from nothing and change everything:

As the stars change their courses, forming sinisterly novel constellations
And the last laurel leaf descends from the lush branch it sprouted upon
Molten mantle below soil will disintegrate, heaving the world into decay
While mortals begin to bear the grave burdens of imminent doomsday
Madness will gush from the ether just as moonlight falls from the skies
Sunshine will char complexions, and fields will spasm until skulls burst
Any souls not yet slain will perish as the terrain cracks down the middle
Wholeheartedly decomposed, the Earth will grow into a realm of rot
For the shocking end will have befallen, just as our knowing lips predicted
And no poems nor proverbs nor prophecies will save anyone, anymore

Rhubarb Jam

Samira's Possession

Invaded gates of Samira's soul creaked wide open with every inhalation
As her diaphragm tensed and her lungs inflated with sweetened oxygen
Samira's tragically agape cherry lips swallowed far more than simply air
While her throat—*unwillingly*—welcomed inside a wraithlike phantom
Who hysterically hoped to rejoice in the rapture which humanity rouses
To detect the essences of honeysuckle and orange blossom in springtide
And to savor homemade rhubarb jam spread upon freshly baked bread
Yet the phantom's ambitions were not exclusively innocent in intention
For his urges also inclined toward the manifestation of palpable horror
In a twist of fate decreed by insolent idols—an opportunity was offered
As Samira, powerless against infiltrations, sensed the phantom creep in
Rummaging beneath her corporal flesh—like a colony of meddling ants
Until, improbably but not impossibly, the phantom felt alive once more
Defying his destiny as he moved with mortal ease, taunting other spirits
As prideful volcanoes of gratification over his conquest ruptured within
Leaving Samira aghast, for her troubled, tear-stained eyes could still see
Though her mind, subdued by the phantom's authority, could not reign
Unable to vanquish he who manipulated her tongue and palms and feet
With each move the spirit made, Samira's autonomy further diminished
For she was but a mortal marionette—directed by a phantom puppeteer

But still, the apparitional control of the phantom was not yet unlimited
And so, Samira felt her hands move—though not of their own volition
Shepherded by a force ten times more tyrannical than her roaring mind
Moving toward her trembling throat, Samira readied herself to strangle
And while her heart faintly hesitated, her confiscated soul did not relent
Leaving Samira with no will or want but to grievously start to suffocate
Only her asphyxiating demise would gift the spirit absolute domination
An opening to shed the final dregs of his phantasmal existence for good
Samira was then assailed by ruin—with blanching lips and bruised flesh
Anatomical blood started to ascend, escaping from her wheezing mouth
Until Samira screamed, emitting mangled shrieks of looming expiration
As newly aerated plasma lined her jaw and vitality left her dilated pupils
Eliciting the phantom to exhale in vile ecstasy, for his new life was nigh
Yet the universe always desires balance, and so as death claimed Samira
The phantom, spectral no longer, took her place, able to truly live again

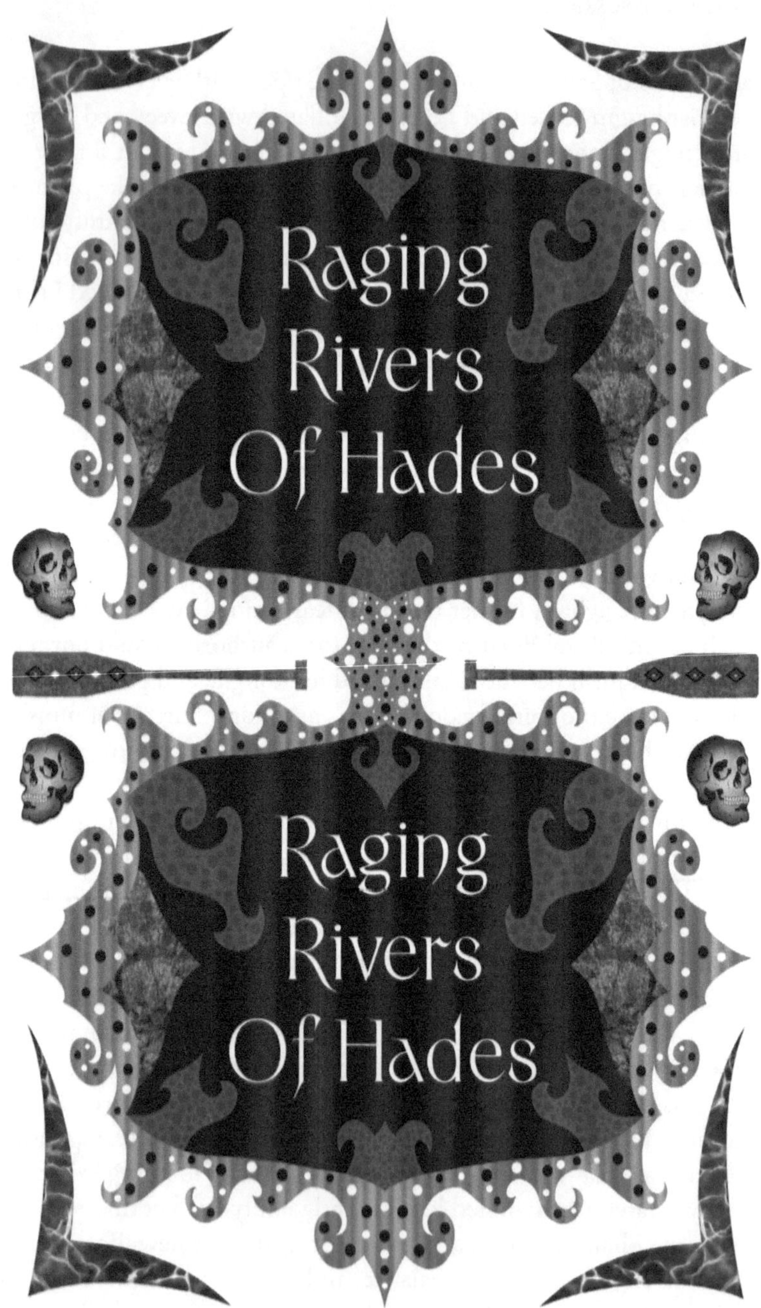Raging
Rivers
Of Hades

Raging Rivers of Hades

Wade within crystalline oceans gushing with briny scallops and salmon
Cherish the notion that the currents do not bellow or burn or brutalize
Unlike the quintet of rivers encircling the reprehensible realm of Hades
Rushing streams promising that dissolute souls will languish in vexation
Upon grisly waves meant for those not dearly departed, only justly slain

Acheron—river of sullen misery guarded by slavering Cerberus himself
Reeling surfs of woeful viridian as harrowing as a heartbroken phantom
Resolute barricade dividing the empire of evil and the land of humanity
Grave river, where undying ferryman, Charon, sailed with the deceased
Demanding burial bribes: silver coins of ceremony from dismal funerals
And if their palms were destitute, frigid ghouls they wretchedly became

Row, *not-so-merrily*, down the Styx—infamous, indigo waters of hatred
Where non-breathing beings journey toward their hostile punishments
Travel further down the flow where the reprimands only become fouler
Within the river of revulsion, illustrious gods vow their infinite pledges
For the molecules wield mighty sway, enough to incite imperviousness
Enough to inject immortality into worldly flesh, like the swift Achilles
Dipped into the freshwater foam by his mother, the sea nymph, Thetis
Yet, Achilles was never fully submerged—much to his tragic detriment

Warily propel down the river of flames, Phlegethon—as searing as lava
Raging penance for souls who engaged in lawless endeavors while alive
Acts that would trigger antipathy in even the most criminal of heathens
Maroon currents of charring blazes appear thick with the arterial verve
Which once heaved throughout the veins of the rivers blistered victims
Yet amid the flaming scourge of suffering and scorching and suffocating
A tender tone of romance floods the foundation of these boiling waters

Styx, goddess and lover of god, Phlegethon, expired due to his infernos
Never did he wish to harm, yet his fires could not resist holding her just once
After her exodus, Hades, newly sentimental thanks only to Persephone
Designed these rivers layouts so the lover's canals could run side by side
Amicably promising that since they could no longer be together in life
At least their eponymous channels could gaze upon each other in death

Lethe, absentminded river of forgetfulness, stimulating obscured senses
Reincarnating souls who succumbed to the reaper—only if they imbibe
Prepare a goblet from the gilded seas of oblivion, swallow with caution
Once ingested, all remembrances of earthly existences will be expunged
Sip the amnesia-provoking broth; heavily guzzle until you hazily drown
Unlatch the hatch found on the floor of your stomach to keep drinking
Feel the bloated curves of intestines fashion rivers of your own making
While everything—past, present, pending—eludes your skull, evermore

Keening river of lamenting, Cocyton, arctic lagoon of ear-piercing cries
Bordered by a lifeless landscape, signaling no expectations for salvation
Ricochets of howling—mournful wails—rebound off the dejected river
Cocyton, portentously assembled as the ninth circle of the underworld
Intended for fraudulent traitors, divvied into a punitive quartet of pain
Caina, Antenora, Ptolomea, Judecca—each round was utterly malicious
Plunging betrayers into subzero waves of torment, like chilling reprisals

Prudently heed the advisory accounts of the hair-raising rivers of Hades
Beware the tides within Acheron, Styx, Phlegethon, Lethe, and Cocyton
Lest you find yourself dourly rolling along these bleak brooks in demise
Perished and paddling—with an everlasting captain at your ship's helm
Drifting with depression toward satanic destinies—entirely unescapable

Melancholic Waterfall

Ethereal meadow, Eden upon Earth, teeming with thriving wildflowers
Floating upon an isle within the Adriatic Sea—a Mediterranean marvel
Where fairies and fawns dwell in harmony within their heavenly home
Just beyond the birch trees, sedative lilts of tropical lullabies chime out
Follow the gushing melody, a serene refrain promising a mystical sight
Do not falter until a draught brushes aside a curtain of vines and moss
Exposing a vista as honied as berries and as inebriating as mulled cider

Opalescent liquid flows from the awed waterfall, as soft as cocoa butter
Saturated in detonations of starlight, soaked in outpourings of sunlight
Utterly angelic, lusciously crafted from the seraphic mouths of cherubs
Petrichor, the pleasing aroma after rain, infuses the island's atmosphere
While the waterfall hypnotizes you like a pendulum of trancing powers
Charmed, wade into the shallow stream and swim beneath the torrents
Until the candid composition of the luminescent waterfall reveals itself

Saccharinity tapers as bawling acoustics shatter the otherwise calm skies
For the lovely cascades were not made by saints—but created by sinners
Amorphous spirits, dipped in despair, mingle with the marine minerals
Who siphon the pitch of their cries, imbuing the ballads into the water
Detained become these deceased souls with their howling lamentations
Until the shimmering falls gleam from the energy of their outraged fear
As unaware mortals only admire the effervescence of the souls' anguish

Ambushed souls confined within this gushing cycle may never get away
For they are spelled to tumble from the loftiest location of the waterfall
Only to be right swept back up and sent to the top, *over and over again*
A diabolical form of perdition—masked in a flattering place of paradise

Mortals—flee from this meadow in haste before you meet the same fate
But even after you depart—even after you cleanse with unsullied water
The impression of spirits swarming your skin, lavishing your bare body
And the ricochets of their tear-jerking shrieks—will never be forgotten

Tahlia's Revenge at the Bayou

Within the backwoods of the bayou, the dewy swamp acted as a refuge
A safe harbor for amphibian creatures treading artichoke-tinted waters
And tunneling mammals lodging beneath the surface of these wetlands
Though, just beyond the murky bog sat a quaint cottage made for two
With shutters the hue of lemons and forget-me-nots in the windowsills
Where a mortal male resided as the only real monster in the marshland
More insolent than any individual upon the hillsides of this lush Earth
More antagonistic than any devil within the netherworld hailing Hades
For this fellow cultivated foul spores in his soul, worsening by the hour
As the sweltering sun of the swamp who sees all would vigorously agree

In her life, Talia was restrained by the careless chains of another's heart
Chrome cuffs of dominance, masquerading as an act of love so stifling
No longer was Talia able to inhale—choked by her coerced submission
Draven, bearing an austere moniker intended only for a satanic mortal
Adored Talia not with tenderness and calm strokes of idolized sincerity
But with rigid fists and lascivious fingers—always grasping and grazing

Talia indulged Draven—for her shackles were silencing yet also familiar
And the notion of prying herself from the domineering ties of his heart
Only to learn what horrors would follow—Talia was not quite ready for
Mindful that the arrow of his moral compass had integrally been askew
Blistering any sense of ethics and empathy—much to Talia's displeasure

Always idling by her side, Draven noted the subtle rejection in her eyes
How her panicked pupils amplified before skating into a state of apathy
So too—did her flesh rebuke his touch with goosebumps of displeasure
Fixated with fury, Draven's rancorous heart gradually deepened in tone
And that scorched dimness trickled into the garish cerulean of his irises
Until Draven gazed at his swamp, at his Talia, with the vision of an imp
Any luster he met, from the daisy-hued ringlets dancing down her spine
To the way the evidence of dawn exquisitely reflected upon her features
Detonated ferocity within his soul, as did all representations of radiance
Blinded by ire, the sadistic shadows of his shifted heart hatched an idea
Harsh enough to pacify the demon developing within his earthly bones

Only when what was recognizable turned revolting did Talia dash away
Escaping across the miry currents within the marsh with petrified haste
Though, she should have known her feet would never bring her too far
For Draven's strides were always swifter than her own, fueled by malice
Upon the clammy shore of their bayou—Draven beckoned Talia closer
And acted upon the sinful pleas haunting the seared scraps of his heart

Demise crawled toward Talia briskly—like a cobra pouncing upon a rat
Yet, in the scant seconds in in-between, no longer living, not quite dead
Talia detected the mirthful snapping of the tethers Draven had inflicted
Allowing her to release one final and full breath of authentic respiration
Liberated at last as the cuffs of Draven's vile love were thankfully severed
And though Talia's body had drowned—suffocated by saltwater torrents
Her soul, huffing with spectral retribution, was not definitively defeated
As her past paramour, the archetype of evil, would soon come to realize

In her afterlife, Talia's damp spirit was not yet ready to leave the swamp
As Draven became bound by the straps of the sins he had implemented
Departed, *though not disposed of*, she manacled herself to Draven's heart
In reprisal for all the times his palms declared ownership over her body
For no inch of Talia had been left unscathed under the guise of passion
And now, Draven was left to befall the same fate he inflicted, evermore
Talia pressed her phantom hands upon the chest of the one she loathed
And while gripping his charred heart, her entombed tears finally flowed
Talia brought Draven to the precipice of demise, only to shift her grasp
Sliding her hands up to his jugular, strangling him just as he did to her
Talia settled her drenched body of vapor over his tangible body of flesh
Tapping his pulse, sensing it sprint from alarm, then falter from fatality
But still, Talia never did allow Draven to feel the relief of lasting expiry
Content to continue her haunting from eternal dusk until endless dawn
Glad her skin was now waiflike—never able to be fondled by him again
As Draven rotted from the plague of her presence, Talia finally felt at peace

Within the backwoods of the bayou, the swamp detected this reckoning
And from then on, the sun above the wetlands shone a little bit brighter

Grecian
Muses
Grecian
Muses

Grecian Muses

Learn of the pantheon of Grecian muses upon their altar of persuasion
Reputed daughters of burly god, Zeus, and memory titan, Mnemosyne
Whose essences were abounding with creative and cultured inspirations
Dwelling in Mount Helicon, offering aids of influence to famed deities
While drizzling originality of the arts upon the derivative mortals below

Calliope, epic poetry muse with a mellifluous voice and renowned quill
Prolific author of the valiant tales of champions and their heroic quests
Emitting a becharming cadence originating from her lilting vocal cords
Promising that her gifted bloodline would yield praiseworthy songsters
And ingenious poets of remarkable chronicles for generations to follow
Euterpe, harmonizing muse of music, originator of aerated instruments
Wielding her woodwind flute—flattering olden ears with her orchestras
Composing rejoicing concertos and pleasing verses—until all were rapt
Erato, softhearted muse of lyrical poetry, as starry-eyed as a turtle dove
Inscribing romantic stanzas with Cupid's love-doused arrow as her pen
And the liquified essence of thrilling admiration as her worshipping ink
Thalia, mischievous muse of comedy—fashioned from comedic energy
Humorously diffusing any solemn situation with flickers of amusement
Melpomene, fraught muse of tragedy laden with harrowing tribulations
Whose glum intonations falter, choked up with sorrow when she sings
Wealthy with splendor and suitors, though real joy still eludes her spirit
Urania, astronomical muse, well-versed with floating stars and satellites
Psychic prodigy, witnessing pending events through galactic divinations
Polyhymnia, muse of sacred hymns and harmony, praising and praying
As meditative as a transcendent soul floating in a pond of introspection
Terpsichore, festive muse of dance and choral songs—as jovial as a lark
Merrily moving like the uninhibited maenads mad from amethyst wine
With as willowy a physique as a winter wind waltzing across the icy sky
Clio, proclaiming muse of history—enthusiast of primordial knowledge
Treasuring historical figures and their fates—venerating their existences
By etching imperative events upon her timeless and fundamental scroll

Instrumental goddesses of nine impassioned those from antiquated eras
While continuing to nurture poets, painters, and playwrights, *even now*
For their imaginative incentives remain as eternal as their immortal lives

Foreboding Fever

Awoken from an uneasy slumber by the fateful cry lodged in his throat
Rescued from infernal dreams, reeled back into reality as a forewarning
Ailing he must be, struck down with a fever of the most untamed strain
For the vexing warmth assaulting his skin drives his skull into psychosis
Escalating the temperature of his festering bones—melting his marrow
Leaving him distraught, desperate to be divested of the fever's fiery aura
Submerging his sweltering body into an arctic bath with subzero waters
Until every limb is immersed in the freezing fluid—like a Siberian lake
Although, before relief can be retrieved, morsels of condensation surface
For any chance of a chill is crushed by the extreme degree of his malaise
Vexingly leaving behind only the torrid existence of the steaming liquid
Leaking tears of frustration, his flushed cheeks begin to string and singe
Translucent firestorms fall from his eyes—scalding flesh as they decline

Hours pass as the aroma of bodily ashes infiltrates the uneasy ambiance
Constellations perch into place, but still, his infection does not improve
Scorching teardrops escalate into charred hands, seared legs, burnt arms
Nothing has ever felt more unbearable, that is, until the coughing starts
Hacking up glossy fires—as if a furnace exploded within his esophagus
In an outrageous occurrence—his body burns alive from the inside out
Blood cells become orbs of ignition, needing to expel themselves *rapidly*
Ashen remnants of his charbroiled organs trickle into his panting pores
And within the midst of this blazing illness, a delirious epiphany occurs
Sending sweat pouring down his spine, expelling any outstanding hopes

Never again will he experience the comforting sensation of frosted relief
Only destined to be incurably hampered by a fever that will never abate
Though, this is no earthly disease, this is nothing made by mortals at all
For this inferno is the insignia of death, warning of his imminent expiry
Encumbering him with a foul taste of the fiendish fate he will soon face
For the diabolic dwelling of his afterlife will be blistering, never blissful
This chronic warmth, bewildering his thermometer, stems from hellfire
Already licking at his marred skin with an aberrant sense of anticipation
Uselessly, he begs, but the gods are inattentive, and the angels are weary
Leaving his cremating mind to muse that if the fires feel this atrocious above
Just how torrid of an arena will he enter when dispatched way down below?

Lamia's Cannibalistic Appetites

Feasting Lamia, flaying garlands of flesh as if spryly skinning crisp pears
Diving barbed incisors into raw tissue and sucking upon skeletal nectar
Chewing upon cleansing livers and crunching upon stripped extremities
Tasting just like bodily bonbons—donated by a carnivorous chocolatier
Pillaging predator, gnawing at her bloodied lips in starving anticipation
With a hunger worse than Cronus, mythical titan who devoured his kin
Although—Lamia's meat-eating appetites were not always utterly savage
Formerly—her features were flushed not from cannibalistic exhilaration
But from the lecherous thirst for lust and the breathless attitude of love

Before catastrophe befell, Lamia reigned as an admired empress of Libya
Loyal to her nation—although nothing bested her devotion to her lover
Lamia's heart was lodged with lovesick needles—dribbling with longing
Deliciously wrapped up in a throbbing affair with none other than Zeus
Wedged in a sultry web of infidelity—basking as his infatuated mistress
Inciting brazenly besotted ice storms twirling with immoral snowflakes
How rich an experience to be illicitly adored by *the mighty god of all gods*
But—the ardent tempest of their tryst receded with heartbreaking haste
When Hera, goddess of marriage, wife of Zeus, learned of their adultery

Swathed in the flames of marital wrath, stoked by coals of unfaithful ire
Hera set out to slay Lamia and Zeus's offspring—navigated by betrayal
Embarking upon the most deplorable act of reprisal she could summon
In the wake of her uproarious children's death cries—Lamia was gutted
Inconceivably infuriated, the former queen's fury turned to famishment
Held within the fog of eternal mourning, Lamia hunted trusting youths
Only to devour them in tearful despair, turning hideous with every bite
All the gore, while pleasing upon her lips, wreaked havoc upon her soul
Until Lamia's unsightly grief infected her previously unblemished figure
Sullying her once-glowing skin with the mutilations of incessant sorrow

At times, whenever Lamia's indignation surpassed her bereaving misery
Whenever her greedy inclinations evolved into something more mature
Lamia would emerge from her lair with the willpower of a past empress
Appearing as pristine as when she was the handler of Zeus's heartstrings
With duplicitous locks spun from fibers of gold and toasted, taut limbs
Behind a stunning façade, Lamia seduced men with her submissive eyes
Kneeling at their feet, tarnishing her gown with soil, bruising her knees
Looking up at them through curled lashes—a vision of sheer innocence

Shameless mortal men hankered for a taste of Lamia's tantalizing purity
Never imagining anything to be astray about the portrait Lamia painted
For beauty is so often misperceived as benevolence—innocently benign
Yet palms need not be tainted scarlet to display the markings of murder
And saccharine appearances disclose nothing of homicidal deliberations
If one were to take a machete to Lamia's chest, cutting along the center
Only to rifle through her catalog of bones and analyze her sea of blood
Nothing but carnal relics of all she slaughtered would be grimly evident
But none cared to gaze beyond her maidenly exterior, blinded by desire

Consequently—because mortals were too hedonistic to sense any alarm
Lamia continued her libidinous routine, coaxing them indecently closer
Beckoning her rage—she slayed with gouging bites and gashing lesions
Dining upon sinewy ligaments, chomping upon slick irises and arteries
Although, even these gruesome massacres did not extinguish her famine
Starved, Lamia pined to close her lips over the sky—*if only she were able*
And so, wiping skin shavings from her jaw, Lamia resumed her chasing
Stalking through leafy forests—gluttonous and hollow from heartbreak
Devouring everything and everyone to satiate the abyss of her suffering
While Zeus, a god unreprimanded, continued to rule with divine power
Feeling more blissful in his rekindled union with Hera than ever before

Fountain of Fantasies

Fish-laden lakes flock toward Daphne—nymph of freshwater fountains
Drenched naiad, feminine icon of wells, bearing watercolor-like beauty
Whose oceanic eyes witnessed the formation of the *Fountain of Fantasies*
Positioned within a scenic cliffside meadow—a geological spring gushes
Cascading swells vault off weathered rocks like striking babbling brooks
Fashioning this spring of splendor, submerged with effervescent waters
Foaming like the blood of Poseidon, tinted jade, like molecules of moss
Bristling with hails of fruitfulness from Gaia, the Earth goddess herself
Raining with melodic couplets from the enthusing mouths of the muses
Awash with trancelike rivers of saliva from Morpheus—deity of dreams
Lured by the cavern's inviting echoes, imbibe from the elusive fountain
Avidly position your slavering lips directly below the descending stream
Sense purring droplets dance atop your tongue as you languidly swallow
Bask in the ballet of power coming to life amid your fatiguing anatomy
Enter a slumbering state while your weary mouth continues to unhinge
Yearning to guzzle as much palatable fluid as your esophagus will allow
For the delectable spring is persuasive, lulling your mortal body to sleep
Sanctioning your hallucinating mind to recreate the sweetest of reveries
Tumble into tailor-made utopias, just like Alice falling into Wonderland
Become mesmerized by performances playing out of the one you desire
Euphoric scenes of romantic whispers and lustful gazes, utterly realistic
Reexperience lost dreams, which long ago, you wished to remain within
If only for a moment longer—before being wrenched away by daybreak
Revisit epic sagas featuring elusive deities, eerie demons, ethereal dryads
Counterfeit as the illusions may be, the results they trigger are authentic
Instigating waterworks from utter elation to roll from dozing tear ducts
As joyful sobs sink into the spring, joining the dream-inducing particles
But—ingest excessively, swallow until waves slosh within your stomach
And dreams will deteriorate—snatching you away from glacé love sagas
Before being propelled into diabolical nightmares—visions of depravity
Wide eyes remain agape, though hauntingly glazed over in abject horror
As your mouth froths with fear, tangled within a mock realm of trauma
Urge your drowsy subconscious to retch, upheaving any ingested liquid
Liberating yourself from the Fountain of Fantasies captivity, at long last
Leave at once, bearing the blistering scars from life-altering nightmares
Deciding that despite the idyllic dreams, this tiring trip will be your last

Death's
Fatal
Kiss

Death's Fatal Kiss

Cower, for I am branded as Death, rousing hysteria with my reputation
Windchimes of annihilation emit their percussive timbre until I awaken
Serrated scythe clenched, my hunt for a novel and naïve victim initiates
Swiftly, my precious prey is procured and paralyzed, unable to abscond
As I murmur a surrendering spell against her nape, nearly affectionately
Articulating in a dialect none can discern—yet she submits all the same
Docilely breaching her lips for me as I brush my mouth against her own
Bestowing my malign kiss of fatality, tender in touch, terminal in effect
Inhaling with sadistic aims and a steady diaphragm, I suck out her soul
Briskly treasuring the sprightly taste—as rich as the stoutest of whiskies
Until her waning essence lands within the bottomless basin of my body
Remaining there with all of the others, like the sailors seduced by sirens
Destined for a damp downfall, sinking to the sea floor, never to surface
My prey turns a stunning shade of grey, which only I would call *glowing*
Delightfully, her concave body becomes barren of all wants and worries
When she collapses, for gravity never has and never will cater to corpses
Promptly, I scoop up my lovely cadaver and wrap her in my arctic hold
For this will endlessly be the most meaningful phase of my provocations
Holding my prey intimately, tucking her into my embrace one last time
Before exiling her soul to the City of Caskets—a skeletal empire of loss
But then, those ominous, discordant chimes cry out for me once again
And as I, Death, prepare for yet another execution, gratitude floods me
For what a wonder it is that this slaughtering sequence will never cease

Listen, for I have faced Death—reeking of his ashen aftershave of sulfur
And nothing concerning my demise nor my destroyer will I ever forget
Possessive arms enveloping me influentially—as if reluctant to let me go
Rumbling, abrasive accent whispering foreign refrains, I wished I knew
Feeling my mind become murky from an overcast mist of subservience
My mouth parting, my jaw hanging—as Death took and took and took
Lapping my soul from my skeleton—as the consummate larceny of life
Heat diminishing from my bones, and hopes expunging from my brain
All at once, my corporeal form converted into a limp shell of inactivity
Now, I am alone, missing the firm embrace Death kept me in as I died
And though Death will hold someone close like that again, never will I
Fated to grasp only air with my *ghostly* arms, never to be touched again

Ethereal Femininity of Mermaids

Evocative vibrations of cyan waters crashing upon surreptitious beaches
Jade lily pads and magenta lotus blossoms floating in divine suspension
Creatures of coastal incandescence swimming within turquoise currents
Never holding their breath below the tide, with no necessity for oxygen
No—the lungs of mermaids demand only fizzing molecules of saltwater
For the cocktail of ether offers little relief compared to the sap of the sea

Adorning an appearance mortals would die for, and trolls would kill for
With almond eyes and ultramarine irises stippled in hues of chlorophyll
Coral-stained cheeks, arched lashes, puckered lips dribbling with saline
Drenched in sea foam and salt, corroding until lustrous skin is revealed
Mesmerically transparent flesh, imbedded with seashells of every shape
Sundials and conches and scallops bejeweling their fabled complexions
Nourished curls patterned with dainty plaits interlaced into their tresses
With highlights of aqua and lowlights of teal, as garish as infrared lights
Never do their locks tangle or frizz like the land-walking females above
Not as the circling sea softens their strands like an unraveling hairbrush
Beyond the coastline, beneath the brine, neon scales adorn mythic tales
While hearts pulse with aquatic passion, glowing under fluttering chests
Dusted with dashes of seafaring magic, utterly unlike any beings before

Rusalka—sparkling mermaids, dark divinities upon shores and streams
Revered as goddesses within the toxic waters that terminated their lives
Vengeful souls, not unlike the spirits of their sea sisters, the choral sirens
Tempting mortal males close, hypnotizing their effortlessly swayed gazes
For their minds tread down a lascivious trail, blind to cautionary alarms
Invited onward until they totter into their own sinking and sodden fates
Drowned in desolation—just like the charismatic rusalka had, long ago
Malicious at times, yet the mermaids are not exclusively engulfed in evil
For these beings emanate an aura of ethereal femininity and gentle grace
Maritime maidens—as serene as a solstice garden when they deign to be
Blossoming alongside the starfish and beckoning behind the sea urchins
Cryptic waves, once the rusalka's death site—now their eternal dwelling
Functioning as their sinister cemetery and restful sanctuary of harmony
Until the doubtful day when the ebbing and flowing tides stop swaying

27
27
27
27
43
43
43
43
27
27
27
27

Grime and Gore

In the skeletal wake of warfare, traces of bedlam laid upon the landscape
Sullied banks laden with grey muck and cranberry blood and briny tears
Sickening reminders of the violence shed from the brutal spine of battle
Morsels of grime and gore ascended, binding together in foreign design
Fashioning an unsightly organism comprised only of repellant remnants
When the unidentified monster arose, the universe flinched—quivering
Initiating blustery winds sailplaning over the realm from the aftershocks
Magnolia trees shivered, coursing sea waves rippled, bee hives collapsed
While miniature woodland animals took cover behind felled tree trunks
Until the universe calmed, recovering from the atypical sight she beheld
Ready to raptly examine the being with a cautious stare and a clear skull

Bred from hemorrhaged blood and topsoil, disjointed bones and sweat
As unattractive as the aura of envy, as unpleasant as the scent of nausea
Beneath the filth, below the grease, no vessels or ventricles dwelt within
Empty of organs and capillaries and glands, void of *essentially everything*
With every tread he took, lingering scraps of discarded grunge levitated
Drawn to him like a paranormal magnet—clinging on with desperation
Flesh upon his figure, if it could even be cataloged as such, grew grainy
Becoming more grotesque with each vulgar veneer of debris he grasped
Daylight fired into his eyes, but the acerbic beams of heat did not blind
Frigid atmospheres sent shudders down his back—but he did not freeze
Appearing allegedly impenetrable as the universe looked on with unease

And yet—the apprehensive soul of the cosmos needed not to fear at all
As the abnormal monster entertained no aspirations for slaughter or sin
Though he was born from wreckage, he needed not to rouse more of it
Purely existing as a sentient entity, harboring the sole emotion of *hunger*
Insatiable to collect all which littered the dirt: ashes and bile and sewage
Like gathering shells upon a seashore or postage stamps at a flea market
Though the mementos he sought were draped in fertilizer, lard, bacteria
For each crumb of waste permitted the unnamed and unlovely monster
To remain in this favorable kingdom with a ticket of permanent tenure
For minds may decline and corpses may decay, *but grime remains forever*

LYSSA

Seraphina's Wyvern

Plights of women are pervasive—even unprecedented Pandora suffered
For it matters little if one is born from earthly ancestry or eerie alchemy
Irate cockroaches of injustice will filter into livid anatomies all the same
Sense the incensement of Seraphina, soaked in undiluted feminine rage
For vitriolic mortals have strained to cleave her tongue, carve her torso
Yet had they succeeded, leaving her body as an ashen bouquet of death
Seraphina still would have fumed, for fury endures, even in the afterlife
Within her womanly marrow, vexing anger becomes tangible over time
Taking on the form of ghostlike shadows, easily eradicated by the wind
Seraphina sinks into the quicksand of deriding acts and debasing words
Until her shadows become solid—with the arcane strength of spider silk
Enriched with the bristles of outrage, molding into unbreakable entities
From the igniting coals of Seraphina's mood—harmless silhouettes shift
Becoming a fully physical figure with the contours of a foreign creature
And thus, conceived from embers of indignation, *the wyvern is delivered*
Trustworthy only to Seraphina, with fuming bile lining her gallbladder
Given the Grecian name, Lyssa, after the simmering goddess of temper
Whose redhot disposition was only ever rivaled by this stormy creature
Lyssa—volatile being with impaling wings jutting from sable shoulders
With thorn-studded horns, the opaque barbs reminiscent of onyx gems
And tapering eyes gleaming in a light show of topaz and tangerine hues
But as time evolves, Seraphina's temper rises, and Lyssa's pupils blacken
As the wyvern exhales gushes of violent verve—acting like cathartic rain
Spitting obsidian saliva infused with unrivaled toxins in raw retribution
There are those who now, more than ever, implore to exploit Seraphina
To secure her wyvern and steal her wrath, now that it may benefit them
Lyssa glories in lapping her calamitous, charring tongue over their flesh
Until reaching their fallible skeletons, right before they erupt into ashes
Seraphina and her corporeal creature butcher those who incite hostility
Delivering them to the gods they desperately, hypocritically preached to
Let them learn if their deities will save them now, with scorched bodies
And blackened souls already cloaked in malice long before their demise
Let them whine when they find the gates of paradise barred and bolted
Seraphina—still swimming in her rage—feels lighter with every reprisal
Riding upon her loyal wyvern, taking back her thieved autonomy at last
While Lyssa's namesake, the rabid idol of madness, looks on with pride

REVA

Reva's Treasure Chest

Only Reva understands the reaper's rapture following a spell of demise
For such extermination delivers a novel soul into death's keen embrace
As the aftershocks of finality gift this nereid something far more prized
Reva, with a mythic reputation and a mortal-like veneer of desirability
As attached to the sea as the fates are bound to their imperative threads
Yet, unlike her openhearted sisters, the stewardesses of maritime sailors
Like saviors amid aquatic perils threatening to harm bodies *or* bounties
Reva refused to speak the same affable vows as her neighboring nereids
Rejecting the oath with her first breath, entirely materialistic from birth
When suffocating victims of drowning or suffering hostages of Krakens
Perish within heaving currents, ineffable Reva does not shriek or snivel
No, she simply awaits their advantageous corpses to descend like bricks
Sinking without their souls all the way to the base of the obscure ocean
Where vivid bioluminescence illuminates the otherwise obsidian waters
Reva, fluttering with anticipation, follows their tumbling, lifeless forms
Stalking as she swims—as eager as a wilted peony in need of hydration
When the corpses may fall no further, settling upon the drenched sand
Reva insatiably thieves from flesh and robs the pockets of the deceased
Pillaging all possessions—*for they will have no use for them in the afterlife*
Gemstones mined from soiled terrains, rarefied tomes, and vital atlases
Daggers with diamonds inlaid within the hilt, witchcraft-infused swords
Reva clutches them all to her purring chest before departing in triumph
Treading ebony streams until she reaches her beloved chest of treasures
A wooden trunk whittled from the drenched lumber of marooned boats
Diligently guarded by a daunting vampire squid beholden *only* to Reva
Suctioning its cephalopods around the chest—like a protective padlock
Within the limitless cavity lies Reva's private hoard of opulent wonders
Curious anchovies swarm the vault, hoping to witness the riches within
Yet, Reva shoos them all away—for these treasures are for her eyes only
Bundles of pearls and glass bottle messages mean nothing to this nereid
For she desires objects which originated from the shore where air surges
Only earthly items will satiate her soul and fortify her saltwater powers
And so, Reva inhabits these ink-colored waters, wishing for shipwrecks
Ensuring the sea monster, *Scylla*, pays captains and crews a ruinous visit
Which will, unsurprisingly, foreshadow their briny terminations of life
And as they anticipate expiry, Reva only anticipates their precious *riches*

Macabre
Musings

Macabre Musings

Ravens arise from cauldrons of weird waters with feathers of morbidity
Only to murmur into the obscured cores of the most macabre of souls
Prattling on about their kindred connection with those drawn to death
Who answer the summons of nightfall, embracing shadows like a lover
Souls who feel more at ease within a crypt versus a countryside chateau
Favoring a crowded cemetery of apparitions over a lavish castle of royals
Upon this Earth, those who worship the darkness exhibit gothic hearts
Situated within their murky sternums, flailing with the *need* to descend
To creep past the gates of perdition and join the disreputable ferryman
Upon his maritime excursions, traversing the violent rivers of expiration
Pining to inhale the candid fragrance of fatality, to study the foul notes
Only to return to this breathing realm, forgetting the aroma nevermore
Devotees of all things satanic secrete inebriating vapors of necromancy
Deliciously high from partaking in the foreboding properties of this life
Injected with more vitality when surrounded by the scent of destruction
Than they would be if swathed in the serenity of illuminated innocence
Criticized by those with bloodstreams of cane sugar and dreamy desires
Yet these cheerless souls care not—having fallen too far into the gloom
To ever again acknowledge ignorant accusations or disapproving beliefs
Pleased to watch the hourglass of life diminish without any complaints

Are darkened souls malleable, or are they unchangeably fixed in cement
Vaulted shut from creation or featuring slight chasms embedded within
Do souls allow sinister vines of melancholy to sneak inside like pythons
Whenever their minds grow too cruel and their moods turn too callous
Eclipsing any wisps of light lingering within, razing any scraps of luster
Until their existences are fully dimmed, never to find illumination again
Souls contain multitudes; some are filled with seedlings of love, of hope
While others, like these singed souls, include only weeds of wickedness
Impressionable as souls may be—nothing can transform intrinsic traits
Nothing can change the fundamental nature of a predestined existence
For the dimness which lurked inside, seeping into these ominous souls
Had derived from someplace within—where it was always lying in wait
Grim souls hunt those with equivalent auras produced from onyx fibers
Eager to indulge in a starved kiss of fate upon the nightfall they reunite
Only to clasp hands and dive into the veiled void of darkness, together

STARRY-EYED
ROMANCE

Isadora's Undead Admirer

*My sweet, confess I must, for many moons ago, amid the shadows, I saw you
A vision of inspired beauty if ever I did see one, blessing my worshiping eyes
Rays of stunning radiance encased you, rivaling the goddess of light herself
Prompting my lifeless heart to nearly begin beating—undead as I may be
Honor me with the rapturous sensation of your presence—for merely one eve
Grant me this divine gift and arrive at the Starfall Estate on August the 7th
Lest you prefer our meetings to remain in the darkness, woefully one-sided*

*Lovestruck with longing,
Your undead admirer*

Upon a solstice sundown, Isadora finds herself within this gothic estate
Approaching the walnut table centered in the grand chamber of luxury
Strewn with claret begonia petals—damp with dew from morning time
Nestled atop the charming florals lies a lavish spread of confectionaries
Upon antique platters of silver, shining like starlight beneath dim lights
Chocolate-coated pastries, layered cakes, tartlets of summertime berries
For her admirer must know her tongue hungers for the sweetest flavors
Just as his taste buds crave something more metallic—most of the time
For he will not deign to sip from the sparkling goblets of amber brandy
No, those are for his lovely guest, for he has not favored liquor in eons
But then, as Isadora reflects upon her host and his paranormal ailment
Yearning thickens the ambiance, and she knows her admirer has arrived

Draped in the mood of mystique and illuminated by gilded candelabras
Treading forward with haste while exuding an eternal sense of darkness
Isadora lifts her head, finding ivy-hued eyes staring deeply into her own
With the resolute potency of a rainstorm, showing no signs of stopping
Despite his eclipsed essence, Isadora notes the ardent patina in his stare
At last—he presses a kiss upon the wrist of the woman of his obsessions
An arousing touch stimulating every sliver of flesh upon Isadora's body
Tenderly freeing her hand, he makes his way to the far end of the table
Where his words will inaudibly echo between them to her wanting ears
Alarm whips through her soul—for she abruptly longs for his closeness

Though, Isadora needs not to worry, for her host only clutches his chair
Before towing it across cherrywood floors, ignoring the grating melody
Isadora's eerie admirer tilts his seat toward hers—as close as two can be
Closing the slim space between them, he perches a palm atop her thigh
A possessive gesture—one which reddens her cheeks and chest entirety
And yet, he would *never* touch Isadora if the deed was at all unwelcome
But then, she gives a shy nod, and if he were to believe in angels above
He would bow at their feet, lips pressed to the heavenly floor in thanks
For before this merciful eve, he dreamt of Isadora, imagining her scent
And now, the delicate fragrance of lilies and lemons she sweetly exudes
Proves better than his reveries, such that even her arterial aroma within
Does not rouse his gory appetite—a remarkable feat for such a creature
Isadora, still flushed, asks for his name, yet he needs not to ask for hers
For her admirer has long since known, aching to stamp it upon his skin
Parting the lips she continues to glance at with pining, he finally speaks
Dorian, he rasps in a husky yet gentle cadence, *say it for me, I beg of you*
Isadora timidly voices his name once, twice, testing it upon her tongue
Overcome with romantic rhapsody, Dorian feels immortal with rapture
Although—he has long been immortal for a far less sentimental reason
Talking until their throats grow sensitive, yet still—the pair do not stop
Isadora and Dorian discuss their favorite books and most intimate fears
Learning they both stargaze each dusk, only to curse the sun each dawn
For their personal dreams and demands, and doubts incredibly intersect
Now willing to divulge the truth behind his invitation, Dorian professes
I have watched you, my bewitching Isadora, yet not for any ruinous reasons
Undying I remain, and yet, it is not what gushes in your veins that I desire
My kind lives a solitary life, and I only wished for the relief of your closeness
So your voice could soar into my skull, as transcendent as a seraph's serenade
For an ethereal premonition spoke to me that love may bloom if only we met
And who am I, but a paltry being of the undead, to deny the call of the stars
Peacefully listening, Isadora interlocks their fingers, still upon her thigh
Admitting that she, too, feels the palpable intuition of their connection
Not ready for the night to end, she asks if she may stay just a bit longer
Dorian joyously accepts, with the luminosity of smitten hope in his eyes
Spurring Isadora to fall into the arms of her not-so-anonymous admirer
And when midnight strikes, *mercifully*, Dorian feels lonesome no longer

Isadora
&
Dorian
Isadora
&
Dorian

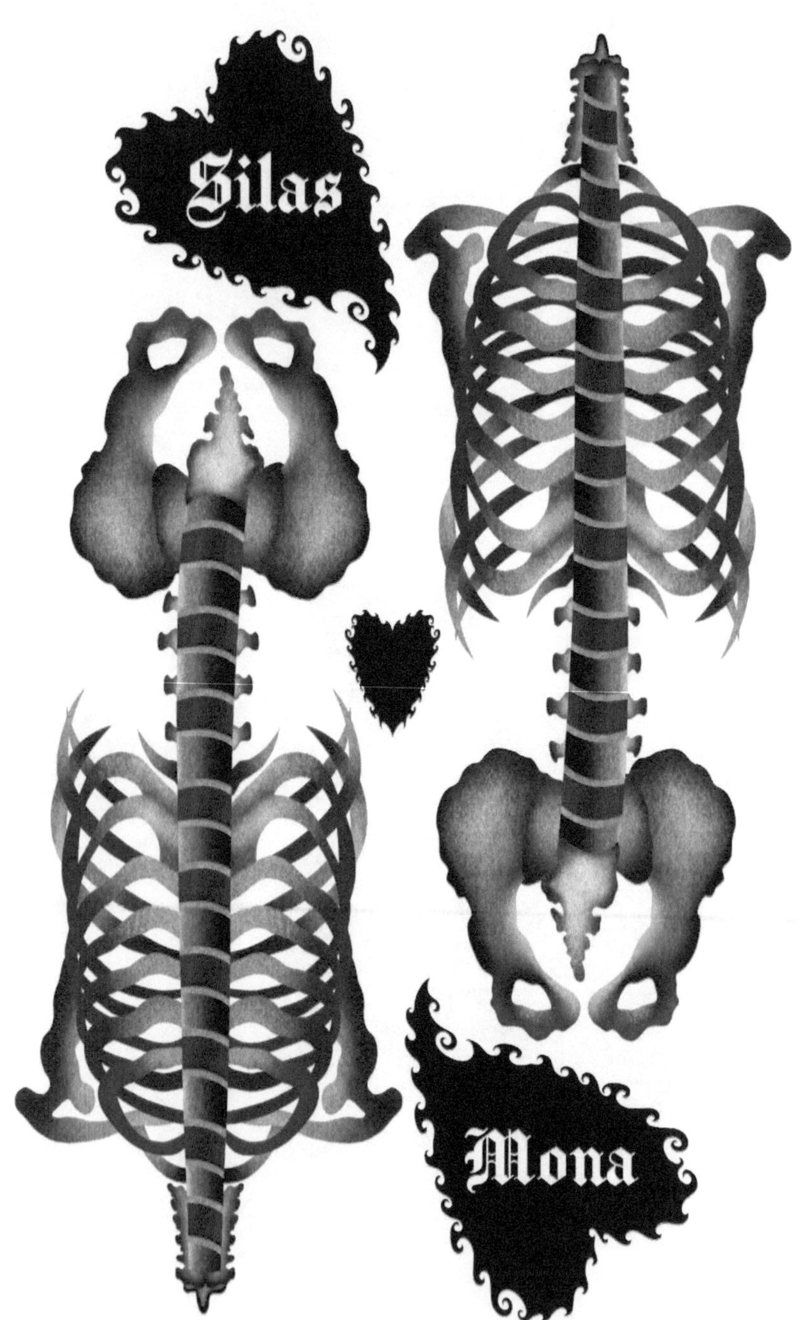
Silas
Mona

A Skeletal Favor

Sensing the billowing squalls of sundown amid the precipice of opacity
Emaciated individual—Silas—coaxes himself from his reclusive shelter
Summoning the nerve to saunter down unlit roads paved with shadows
Raking through the night for a gracious cure for his gaunt predicament
For Silas had met his maker many moons ago, expiring like rotten fruit
However—never did his soul ascend to paradise or descend to perdition
Moments into the afterlife, his life's essence spewed from death's mouth
Tersely revoking Silas's departed status for reasons abnormally unknown
Silas awoke with a start—trembling from revival, weeping with renewal
And while he sensed his soul was intact, he discovered his skin was not
No flesh clung to his sparse frame, comprised now of nothing but *bones*
Eclipsed alcoves of oblivion dwelt within his freshly despondent figure
As dim as the nocturnal hideout he retreated to with mortified disgrace
But presently—a promising view catches the eye of this scarce skeleton
More truthfully, it captures the empty sockets where his eyes once lived
Like a beacon of brilliance in the dullness of dusk, a window is left ajar
Just wide enough for a slender form to slip through without any clamor
Dexterously, Silas crawls in, for he is well-acquainted with the darkness
Before recalling all those who branded him as a monster—a bleak beast
Musing if the woman before him will believe the same after one glance

Mona—thus is the moniker of the mortal who Silas inquiringly regards
With sparkling locks splayed out upon her pillow like cherry sunbeams
With lips slightly parting even in sleep, wishing to inhale nighttime dew
Existing as an angelic masterpiece of dulcet hope depicted upon a silk canvas
If the mortal's honied mind does not recognize Silas as an abomination
Then perhaps he will *finally* unearth the confidence to believe it himself
Tiptoeing even further into Mona's bed-chamber, Silas reaches her side
Before resting a calcified hand upon her cheek as sensitively as he is able
Stroking her complexion with his metacarpal palm until her eyes flutter
Parallelly, the moon yanks open her lunar lids—aggrandizing her luster
Ardent as always, eager to illuminate this gentle moment for them both
As a genuine nightlight washes over Silas, spotlighting his tender touch
Mona's pulse skips not one beat *but stops altogether*—just for one second
Surprise bathes her features as she shakes off the final embers of slumber
Taking in the vision before her, as Silas awaits with insecure inhalations

Mona does not find muscles or meat, or membranes in her rapt perusal
For Silas's form lacks the blanket of bodily tissues one would anticipate
Yet—in total honesty, as she perches her gaze upon the bashful intruder
And as Silas murmurs whispers of calm comfort into her receptive ears
Mona realizes she does not sense any flares of danger in her blood at all
No, she needs not panic—not when his energy emits such harmlessness
Mona's muscles—previously tense from the surprise of Silas's company
Softly slacken from his pacifying presence until she can resist no longer
Mona takes it upon herself to nestle her head into the crook of his neck
As one, Silas and Mona shamelessly sigh, savoring their prized closeness
Silas feels the grief within his soul faintly retreat—not gone, never gone
Just slightly dwindling enough to let Mona's light slink into his skeleton
Allowing this serene mortal's vivacity to warm his eternally arctic bones
Adoringly brushing out Mona's strawberry strands with one ivory hand
Silas uses his spare hand to massage his thumb, *or the bones of his thumb*
Over her wrist—rejoicing within as he senses nothing but a steady song
For her pulse betrays no fright lurking within amid this eerie encounter

Mona urges the stranger before her to speak freely, without trepidation
For there is something gnawing at his fretful mind—this she is sure of
Promising to only ever express the truth to this newfound seraph of his
Silas discloses that a cadaverous body will only respond to one remedy
Amid the moon's fullest phase, he must seek a pure and precious being
Only after touching such flesh will his own coverings materialize *at last*
The lengthier the contact, the more skin Silas will be magically awarded
Though, such a mending act has never transpired—much to his dismay
For none have tolerated the lasting embrace of such an anomalous form
Only a few life-changing minutes were all Silas planned to ask of Mona
Although, her generous grazes have already bested the touches of others
For Mona's hands have been wandering over his bones—without pause
Without Silas ever begging, as if her palms knew *exactly what he needed*
Mona parts her lips with the beginnings of a response to his confession
But Silas speaks first—assuring her that he would visit the netherworld
Before forcing her to acquiesce to anything which she does not wish to
Should Mona decline, Silas will draw back with a peck upon her temple
And never deign to ask a kindness of her again, content to leave her be

Mona's mouth curves into a smile, just like the shining lips of the moon
For they both are certain that skeleton he may be, but monster he is not
Of course, Silas would respect Mona's reply with the chivalry of a knight
And so—with a kindhearted glimmer drowning within her amber irises
And nurse Nightingale's healing aura encasing her hands, Mona *accepts*
Staggered by this act of empathy, Silas is confident fate guided him here
As if the universe had affixed a divine harness onto his haggard sternum
And escorted him with a leash of destiny until he found Mona's window
Not by chance, but by the promising plans made by the merciful galaxy
Silas moves only a bit closer to Mona, hesitant to impose too drastically
Uncertain of the detrimental depletion this could exact upon his mortal
While also growing frightened that she will flee just like all of the others
Silas attempts to fold Mona into his jittery arms—with evident concern
And so, this female, this glowing saint, and owner of his amorous organ
Perches upon his skeletal lap, pulling Silas as close as physically possible
Embracing until her epidermis is molded against his bones—intimately

Utilizing a spindle with supernatural thread, flesh stitches itself together
Until Silas's skeleton, hauntingly visible, becomes more and more veiled
Causing him to pull back, grateful that Mona has gifted him this much
Yet—he seems to be more wary of her well-being than of his restoration
But with her assurance, Mona does not allow them to separate—not yet
Slackening further into her hold, Silas permits himself to relax in repose
At ease for the first time since his atypical death and peculiar awakening
Helion navigates his sun-heaving chariot across the skies, rousing dawn
Until daybreak rays expose Silas's cured form, *without a sole bone in sight*
Delicately, Silas sets his love, *yes, his love, for no other makes his heart soar*
Back upon her plush bed, urging his Mona to revisit her blissful dreams
Although before Mona dozes off once more, she asks Silas if he will stay
Pausing his woeful steps toward his exit, elation blooms within his soul
Silas's lips declare his acceptance before his brain even shapes the words
And in the reflection of the window that thankfully caught his attention
Silas sees the passionate joy in her eyes, imitating his own revering look
And when he reaches Mona this time, never will he leave her side again
Even if his newfangled skin vacated all over again, Silas would care not
For his endearing Mona would want him all the same—skeleton or not

Demonic Nirvana

To have your battering heart rocked in the hardened palms of a demon
Is to be incontestably idolized—treasured in a way that defies all reason
Within the warm embrace of a fiendish romance, trepidation wilts away
For hellish passions are unmatched in might and unrestricted in resolve
Rivaled only by the force of a flame enduring taxing tribulations of fate
Bask in the love of a netherworld entity and slink into heartfelt nirvana
Roughish demon, he who would maim for the object of his every desire
While his satanic body burns from searing coals stoking the infinite fire
Of a devotion never to be eclipsed or expelled from his enraptured lips
Besotted, a demon will cauterize his arterial organ with roasting embers
Ensuring that as his heart thrashes, the tempo mirrors an ardent ballad
For love is what prods his anatomy to blossom from kernels of affection
Romance, the severe energy of the word flows through a demon's spirit
Differently than it ricochets across a mortal body, with sickly sweetness
A demon's worship is acerbic, like salivating mouthfuls of bitter melons
And yet, your tongue aches all the same, thirsting for even a scant taste
Wishing the tart tang would lurch from his lips into your agape mouth
So you may consume the inebriating zest of wicked love—over and over

Infernal chains wrap around your adoring aura—fanatical from fidelity
Rather than feeling smothered, your lifeblood only rejoices in response
Vocalize your pining emotions, and a demon will obey your every wish
Satisfying your most unabashed desires and dreams in beholden delight
Love him openly, watch as he hands over his body, his brain, his bones
Aching to grasp your chin and bestow his awe down your gaping throat
As he sobs with validation, knowing you crave his audacious sentiments
Mercifully, his feelings will not loiter in the fog, unrequited and unseen
Not as you cherish your demon intensely—exceeding his own obsession
Exulting over his intestines swathed in coal, revering his obsidian blood
Dreaming of his sharpened talons tracing shapes over your beatific skin
Salivating for the opportunity to tug upon his horns, drawing him close
Until your writhing bodies interlock and your breaths dotingly interlace
Panting, the demon will depict the pain he extorts, the distress he deals
Fearful you will shrink away—revolted over his penchants for suffering
But, you would never, for you will only savor his love and beg for more
And even licks of hellfire will not be hot enough to pry your souls apart

Whirlwind of Passion

Wisps of weather, temperate and treacherous, wrap around lithe bodies
Indebted only to the missions oozing from he who controls the climate
Harbinger of hurricanes, warrior of hurried vortexes, tyrant of tsunamis
Daunting conjurer of glaring lightning, instigator of deafening thunder
Formidable pupils fracture and flicker as he governs the skies from afar
A living hailstorm defines his electric body, scarcely contained on Earth
Prehistoric globes of energy reside within atmospheric atoms of potency
Dynamic cells slip into his pores, the key to exerting weather to his will
Roaring shockwaves heave within his bloodstream like reckless tremors
Perforate his torso and witness the wound give birth to twisters aplenty
Calloused palms clasp together, and every cloud shivers in faithful echo
Oceanic tides of cobalt fall from the sky in droves as he solitarily weeps
Always isolated—knowing when he grazes another, they flinch and flee
For the palpable force of his talents, humming within his brawny hands
Often prove to be too alarming for their mortal skin, so fragile, to bear

And yet, when he touches *her*—the mortal mirroring Aphrodite herself
Nothing inside of her demands to withdraw from his transfixing touch
For the sensation is jarring—though not enough to incite any real harm
Only enough to galvanize, sending a staggering spark through her veins
Rendering her speechless before this arresting monarch of meteorology
Whose soul is far from sullied with a sickening sense of despotic malice
For within, he only carries genuine sentiments of gratitude for his skills
And in turn, the weather never refuses nor recoils from his instructions
In fact, arched raindrops beg to be conjured as snowfalls plead to begin
Pleased when their vehement, lifelong deity listens with loyal allegiance
And so—this mortal wrenches open her chest as if her fingers are claws
Beseeching this windswept god to crawl within, to hold her bared heart
Until her body animates with joy from his presence mingling with hers
Like a chaotic downpour of power and pleasure enrapturing them both
Wheezing for air in the aftermath, as if ravished by a blizzard of ecstasy
Then, a whirlwind of his own making wrestles open his walloping chest
And without hesitation, his mortal, his goddess, claims his heart as well
Neither of them concealing any aspirations to suture their sliced figures
For they have never felt more at home than in the cavities of each other

Wraithlike
Love

Wraithlike Love

Insensitive mortal companions with somber hands and synthetic hearts
Were never worthy or well-meaning, not in their words or their actions
Spurs of slumber infiltrated her mind whenever they droned on and on
Just as her hands quaked with hankerings to unzip her garment of flesh
To live unadorned and unsightly—so none would touch her ever again
For the bodies of these insistent mortals sliding their skin over her own
Felt very much comparable to an irritating splinter lodged into her side
Disappointing bouts of so-called-passion never once drowned her heart
In floods of irresistible emotions, singing sagas of lust or love or longing
No, time spent with these consorts only encouraged suffocating worries
Fearful that she may eventually evaporate into nothing but silent atoms
The longer they occupy her space—shattering her boundaries like glass
For their arrogant auras will asphyxiate the sanctuary of her uneasy soul
Until her airways start to beg for ether, her arteries begin to break down
And destroyed becomes her delicate figure by the horrid scythe of death

However, the stifling threat of termination abides with shocking mercy
When she is introduced to a new admirer, entirely unlike all of the rest
This refreshing suitor—purely a subzero spirit, a paranormal apparition
Arouses a reaction in every sinew in her body with the barest of touches
Spectral Sinner is the shameless title denoting icy and carnal decadence
That she has bestowed upon her ghostly paramour; a moniker of esteem
For his unearthly form embodies a brazen sin when he cradles her chin
Pressing his nebulous lips against her own—like an eruption of pleasure
Until their mouths emerge liberally swollen and sated from indulgence
If sunlight wishes to stroke her skin with radiations of constant warmth
Then this Sinner desires to devour her whole with an inferno of pining
Hedonistic vigor wrangles its way into her anatomy until her veins gasp
As the lobes of her livers blush from his wraithlike love trickling within
Yet she does not feel smothered nor scorched, for his energy is so bright
That there is no threat of choking—only the hope of fawning liberation
Though imperceptible, she still feels the fleeting vibrations of his grazes
Up until his spirit dissolves, shearing their epitome of perfect adoration
Firestorms fade to cinders as a polar rush of air passes right through her
And as her bereft heart pines—she realizes he has not vanished entirely
For though his touches may be absent, his love will never leave her side

VAMPIRIC
LAMENT

Vampiric Lament

Predator of the undead with the bloodsucking inclinations of a parasite
Laments in the arms of his lover, grieving over all he will never observe
Gazing into his medieval mirror and weeping over the answering abyss
For baroque glass is only ever charmed by the secular outline of mortals
Never acknowledging the appearance of a nocturnal being, like himself
Augustus—renowned vampire—festers within a sequence of mourning
For the cost of marinating his lips, a murderous canvas, in maroon life
Remains to be the repeated absence of his reflection—now and forever

Never again will Augustus relish the vision of his bright eyes of emerald
Straining below glaring sunlight and shining beneath frosty winter skies
For though time waltzes through life inversely, lazily—for an immortal
Only a meager period passes by before Augustus forgets his face entirely
If his irises were tinted emerald, *or was it navy,* he could no longer recall
Melancholic vampire, like a mosquito parched for the rosy liquor of life
Feels a kinship to transparent ghouls—not sincerely living as he should
Though, he muses, *he has not genuinely been alive for quite some time now*

Augustus's heart contracts—heavy with plasma yet rancid with calamity
Dispirited about his half-life, his soles ache to trek to unknown terrains
Perhaps if the vampire tunnels beyond the fertile crust of this kingdom
Barrages of spewing magma would illustrate his image in torrid shades
And though Augustus would be reduced to cinders, he considers it still

Aurora, his little love, his starburst of light within his arena of suffering
Understands the quandary burdening Augustus's undying heart of woe
With such an irrefutable sense of commiseration that she ached as well
Almost as if the lovers share one maroon organ—fated to feel in unison
Endearing Aurora would do *anything* to cure the abrasion of his anguish
Thus, with the delicate tongue of a pixie, Aurora narrates what she sees
Whenever she pleasingly gazes upon the everlasting face of her vampire
Aurora speaks about Augustus with blushing tones of flattering honesty
Until the dagger of despair plunged through his soul begins to dislodge

Looking once more into the furbished mirror—his spirits startlingly lift
When he is met with the likeness of his love, as beautiful as a buttercup
Upon viewing her imitated face, Augustus's self-loathing haze dissipates
And any aspirations to leave the impeccable haven of her kind presence
Depart at once, magma forgotten, for he could stare at her sight forever
In the mirror, in life, in dreams, in death— anywhere, anyplace, always

Aurora's loveliness could instigate battles rivaling the famed Trojan War
As if she was crafted by Michelangelo's palms *like a living Sistine Chapel*
Augustus's lover is so exquisite—her glory incites warfare in his skeleton
Bloodstreams ripple within as his body strains to graze her chiffon skin
Surging with adoration in desperate waves, as if controlled by Poseidon
Producing a circus of devoted enticement within his infatuated arteries

Yet, what truly makes Aurora remarkable, is how she looks at Augustus
How her likeness within the glass amorously stares upon nothing at all
As the vines of her reverence reach into the caverns of his eternal spirit
Sewing the fractures in his soul with the permanence of ardent worship

And though the glass does not show it, Augustus's face has transformed
Fervently high off the exquisite thrill of holding so dearly onto his love
Mirror disregarded, Aurora settles herself atop Augustus, chest to chest

Ensuring that when her mortal heart thumps to the sonata of humanity
So too, does Augustus's undead organ of immobility quiver in response
For Aurora's contact acts as a catalyst, rousing a brief jolt of movement
Making the vampire feel almost alive again, *almost human*, through her
Transfixed by this tender gift, his feelings are full of hardship no longer
Reflection forgotten, his soul only croons one song, one word—*Aurora*

Cain and Oriana's Reviving Saga

Ruin or revival, dual sides of a precarious coin spun by influential fates
Falling upon the dismal face of departure, an outcome hopeless to alter
Or so ruin believed it should have been—utterly unchangeable—that is
Still, revival never did relent, always daring to twist the coin once more

Justly fear the Icon of Death, Instigator of Demise, Idol of Devastation
Cain, archaic propagator of bereavement-inducing, harrowing wreckage
Masked behind a façade of mystery, cloaked within a baleful cape of sin
As misanthropic as a recluse, nurtured by a nature both ethereal and evil
Any morals or qualms concerning his gothic existence and employment
Tumble into a Bermuda Triangle of cynicism the moment they are born
Sardonic deity, pestering those nearing their destined days of expiration
Before bashing mortals with his custom-made sledgehammer of fatality
Never balking from the arising spatters of butchery, like bodily inkblots
Unaffected by the light waves of life leaving their eyes—fearfully aghast
Cain forsakes their mortal figures—uprooting their newly spectral souls
Transferring spirits from this sunlight-studded realm into afterlife voids
Before moving on to his next causality—without one ounce of remorse

Hail the Spirit of Resurrection, Supporter of Rebirth, Savior of Revival
Sanguine Oriana, draped in a healing shawl sewn with renewing threads
Humming sonatas of second chances, beaming from optimistic dreams
Sympathetically commiserating with those who endured untimely losses
Suffering through their grief with the understanding of a divine empath
Prickling with the altruistic desire to revive lifeless beings—defying fate
Swaddling their shapeless bodies as she bursts past the barrier of demise
Flying them back into brisk lands of breathing, delaying their reckoning
Appreciating the cathartic exhilaration of freeing relief in the aftermath
Aware that only the view of respiring mortals steadies her hopeful heart

Paradoxical vocations, entirely contradictory in every sense of the word
Nevertheless, Cain and Oriana relentlessly, vexingly seem to cross paths
Cain: allegedly maddened though covertly thrilled over their encounters
Oriana: seemingly revolted though secretly enraptured by his grave aura
Eventually, Cain's career grows redundant—for every time he slaughters
Oriana, goddess of restoration, annuls those murders with jovial delight

Gaia smiles while Satan swears as Oriana reinstates vanquished victims
Though those souls will ride the merry-go-round of passing once more
For the deed of resurrection does not guarantee the gift of immortality
Oriana solely prolongs the inevitable, which Cain considers to be futile
Ever the optimist, Oriana continues to revitalize—fruitless as it may be

Amid an autumn sunrise, Oriana is stricken down by an unlucky power
Cain, carnage oracle, feels her imminent passing and rushes to her side
Oriana, wearily sinking into an unending slumber, laments over her life
Pining for more time, *not only for herself* but for the souls who need her
All the while, Cain, affected by alien sensations of starry-eyed emotions
Bemoans a love that will now never acquire the chance to truly flourish
Finding himself sincerely pitying Oriana's grieving pleas *for the first time*
Cain never did desire her death; *no,* he wished to argue with her always
Wishing with all his will to never have to ferry Oriana toward her finale
Anyone else, any other existence he would freely claim—yet never hers
But Oriana realizes his morbid reflexes cannot be rejected or unheeded
And so, with shaking palms doling out ruin, Cain slays the one he loves
Within his bereaving mind, Cain's consciousness ambles toward Oriana
Finally acknowledging his enamored feelings for the deity of restitution
Letting free the first tears he has ever shed—as bleak as his broken heart
It is then, in the midst of his wailing, that Oriana miraculously awakens
For after all, she is the genuine goddess of recovery—able to resuscitate
And even that which can massacre a deity could not halt her rekindling
Cain, cognizant of how fleeting life can be, professes his ardent passion
Until Oriana, having *long ago* recognized her romantic feelings for Cain
Returns his sentiments, withdrawing a boulder of sorrow from his brain
Now held in Oriana's warm arms, Cain's pain ebbs, eclipsed only by *love*

Cain continues to seize mortal souls, for it is ingrained into his essence
Yet, he no longer begrudges Oriana as she rebels against his dark deeds
Contrarily saving those who deserve their circumstances to be capsized
After losing the soulmate of his morbid life, however transient it lasted
Cain knows the heartrending abyss his eliminations incite in their wake
Feeling silently thankful when Oriana injects verve into lapsed lifespans
Injecting elation into the living left behind, as crestfallen as Cain once was

Queen of Hearts

Lover of confectionary love and sorceress of sugar-cookie sentiments
Imperially dictating over the desirous chambers of drumming hearts
Defender of worship—labeled the archetype of enamored emotions
With unrivaled aptitudes sashaying through the corridors of arteries
Queen of Hearts—besotted occultist and stewardess of cardiac affairs
Bathed in a spa of liquid plasma and claret cells lies a vascular organ
Whose hammering ballad zealously inundates her infatuated psyche
Like gory music boxes, brewing an aroma of rapture into every note
Smitten symphony of stammering—conducted by the queen herself
Sycophantic mage singing fondly to the reddened muscles she reigns
Cajoling hearts into hastily running the race of love—without pause
Maudlin monarch, making the emotive structures blush with respect
Beating and blooming inside her palms and yielding to her authority
Sanguine ruler—harnessing heartstrings around her sprightly fingers
Tugging upon these responsive contraptions of palpitating affections
Twisting pulmonary veins into coquettish bows of awed endearment

Queen of Hearts, detecting supplemental feelings of lust, of longing
Nourishing the carnal desires in the sweltering space behind ribcages
Fostering the temperature of compulsive warmth and lovesick wishes
Until squirming bodies feel flushed with an intensified sense of *need*
Worst of all is discerning when the obsessive organs are heartbroken
For the aura of an anguished heart is just as visceral as an ardent one
Angst-ridden, the queen feels as if her own heart has been uprooted
Yet, when she studies her body for the source of her brutal grievance
Romantic flesh upon her form remains intact—her skeleton pristine

Doting Queen of Hearts has not one heart but many—all interlaced
And while others may hold their hearts within their individual chests
The mage still possesses them all—able to control them as she pleases
Even so, she leaves you with this concluding petition to of persuasion
To attentively care for your arterial organ, for it bruises so effortlessly
Know that this sorceress may crush or cradle your heart in her hands
And if you give her cause to compress it—breaking into petite shards
It is not only the skin of the queen which will end up getting slashed
So too—will your body adorn the welts of endangering virtuous love

Satan's
Soulmate

Satan's Soulmate

From the hearth of hellfire, a netherworld heathen arose from the ashes
Spawning impish Satan—rebellious since delivery, roguish until demise
With an untidy mane of burnished gold tousled by necropolis smolders
Spending his anarchistic dawns and villainous dusks waiting to slumber
For every eve when Nyx, the famed goddess of night, initiates sundown
Satan drifts into ironically heavenly dreams, idyllic reveries of reverence
Starring an immaculate mortal with an entrancing moniker—Anastasia

Awe-inspiring in all she does—for cells of elegance flood her capillaries
Just as atoms of allure make up her appearance, from lychee-hued locks
To cherub cheeks constantly flushed and vivid irises soaked in magenta
Observing Anastasia, his sweet Anya, upon Earth, Satan grows besotted
Wisely noting the clashing characteristics within her hypnotic existence
Underneath Anastasia's virtuous demeanor—as compassionate as a saint
Lies malign laser beams, thirsting to burst free and raze the world down
Within his nighttime reveries, Satan explores Anastasia's body and brain
Sampling her flesh—as tart as fragrant figs harvested from tropical trees
Before filtering through the insidious desires for chaos within her mind
As sinister as the gatekeeper of hell—craving sick sessions of bloodshed
Within dozing fantasies, Satan is captivated by Anastasia's duel natures
From innocent behaviors she flaunts to the insidious beliefs she censors
This underworld emperor hungrily finds himself enticed by her persona
Positive they are mated souls separated by the impulses of vicious deities
Provoking Satan, primarily a solitary being, into pining for her presence
Aching in the way cannibal entities crave forkfuls of appetizing marrow
Satan knows he and his Anya are destined to live as one—to love as one
Yes, *love*, for upon wakening, his comatose soul expressed only worship
And his conscious mind and lucid heart took no time at all to catch up

Satan's dear, darling mortal, the interstellar lead of his infatuated dreams
Lies in a serene meadow plucking petals—when the floor starts shifting
Until soil faintly undulates as if something or *someone* below is howling
Calling out to Anastasia, lighting up her body as bright as the north star
The guiding orb of enlightenment that coxed her to this field of flowers
Star-crossed lovers, they were not, for constellations indorsed their love
Advising Anastasia to place her ear against the dirt and prudently listen

Anya blocks out any melodious birds whispering of all which is earthly
Heeding only the jagged rumblings of the voice speaking to her, for her
Realizing with certainty that the voice harkens from an infernal domain
Belonging to none other than a devil, no, *the devil*, supreme ruler of evil
Anastasia's elaborate spirit is drawn to the darkness he harbors in spades
Desiring his company like a sugar-fiend needs toffee upon their tongues
Inciting her arteries to rejoice in delight upon hearing his wicked words
My sinner, my Anya, Satan purrs, *be my eternal bride and everlasting love*
One half of my soul turns ebony from dejection the longer we are separated
Satan goes on to decant pints of heartfelt petitions into his emotive ode
Articulating how relief will only find him when his palms hold her hips
And her breath flutters against his sensitive lips and thumping sternum
Eager to whisk his love away from her realm, Satan pleads for her say-so
Aware that as the devil's mate, an ardent storm of sin awaits Anya *below*

Yet Satan's charted destination would not be the torrid kingdom of hell
For this ruler wants not to share his precious paramour with any others
No, if Anastasia returns his warm sentiments, needing him just as badly
Satan will willingly renounce his cadaverous throne of cavernous skulls
And with every searing cinder of his infernal powers reinforced by love
Satan will construct a novel realm—an amorous sanctuary for only two
Raring to build with the attentiveness and devotion of a smitten laborer
Until the ambiance is steeped in his idolizing sweat and besotted blood
Having perfected a kingdom utterly unlike her Earth or his underworld
A realm of romance—inundated with neither benevolence nor brutality
Filled only with torrents of impassioned rainfalls and affectionate winds
A refuge for the pair to indulge in quiet harmony *or* nefarious depravity

Located an agonizing distance from his soulmate, Satan carefully listens
Awaiting Anastasia's response with bated breath—after bearing his soul
But, blissfully—the devil suspects he already knows his mortal's answer
For their bodies are chained by their connection—synchronized by fate
And since the devil's heart has been thrashing to the dulcet tune of love
Satan imagines his Anya's heart has been swaying to the very same song
Assured of their irrefutable kinship, the king initiates his lengthy ascent
Ready to hold his soulmate and weep while his eternal life *finally* begins

Love Bug of Lethality

Heed the fable of a torrid, tear-jerking tryst afflicting enraptured hearts:
Aphrodite and Eros, exemplars of syrupy love, wailed in aching protest
As this doomed tale of romance played out before their streaming eyes
Gazing from their clouds in Olympus, gaping with morose desperation
For they divinely knew—this love affair was condemned from the start
And all too soon, though their devotion was abiding, one would depart
Dante—muscular lion shapeshifter, adventurous though never arrogant
As impressively handsome as a human as he was striking as a jungle cat
Allegra, stunning though never spiteful—adept at altering into a lioness
With an enthralling feline demeanor and an entrancing silhouette of sin
Madly in love, the pair lived within the wild eye of a passionate tornado
Yet, Dante always knew his mated companion was designed for demise
Eras ago, there lived a demon who disparaged the concept of adoration
Dooming him to an existence as a *love bug*—a jinxed beetle of affection
Hexed to impart honeyed moods upon others as Cupid's insectile pupil
Forcing the former demon to outright loathe his now amorous lifespan
And so, crawling with wrath, love is not all he implanted within his bite
When the love bug stung Dante—whose body already bore compassion
The infuriated demon introduced his own hex into the lion's circulation
Sentencing the shifter—promising that whoever he dives into love with
Would meet an undeserved death at the mandatory hands of the reaper
Triggering nothing but wretched devastation for an inconsolable Dante
And eliciting nothing but diabolic satisfaction for the vexed pest of love
Who clung to Dante's flesh, salivating to watch this unkind fate unfold

Upon meeting, Dante and Allegra's love blossomed like oleander petals
Both infatuated souls knew the risks—as inescapably grim as they were
Though, even still, the transforming paramours could not stand to part
And decided, with besotted minds, to indulge in their fatal relationship
Rendezvousing only amid the veil of twilight, when shadows roam free
Fervently hoping the fates would leave them be—for just a little longer
Dante and Allegra's romance was violent—permeated with desperation
Soaking up every moment they shared like roses absorbing rays of light
Ravenous they became, foaming for a taste of their lover's alluring flesh
Sated by tenderly tearing each other apart, ensuing in loving lacerations
Before pressing their doting lips over the gouges their worship inflicted

Allegra treasured Dante so acutely—as if he was the deity she prayed to
Lovesick, Allegra filled a vessel with each other's candy-apple lifeblood
Before affixing it upon a chain so the pair could adorn the morbid vials
When racing across savannahs as mammals or calmly resting as mortals
Holding the core of one another close to their ardent organs like a vise
Acting as reminders that what flows below flesh can be easily extracted
Just as honorable lives can be haphazardly thieved by a profane destiny
Dante cherished Allegra so severely as if she was his talisman of serenity
At times, overwhelmed with admiration, Dante would unscrew his vial
Only to bestow a droplet of Allegra's blood onto his dehydrated tongue
Never recoiling from the macabre aftertaste or the iron-laden fragrance
Dante would humbly swallow it down, urging it to stream into his soul
For Dante's spirit, surviving only for her, was simply a shrine of his love
Stuffed with splinters of Allegra's essence and shavings of her sentiments
For everything she ever graciously gifted to Dante, his soul has coveted
And with wonderous reciprocation, Allegra valued Dante just as deeply

On one ruinous day, the pair were so immersed in talking and touching
That nightfall had emerged and evaporated, and neither took any notice
And so, the fates then awoke, the sun arose, and their love was exposed
Illuminated beneath daybreak as the hex within Dante was thus incited
A callous circumstance, for the spell did not pursue he who was cursed
Only targeting his lover, *his Allegra*, whose pain in life he could not bear
And whose agony in expiry would prove to be much more excruciating
Without any preamble, Allegra perished, finally leaving Dante forsaken

Dante hoped his soulmate would haunt him—shadow him like a spirit
Despite her death, he could not endure the space slotted between them
Dante's animalistic adoration remained evermore after Allegra's parting
Although—never again could he linger in his inconsolable mortal form
For it harbored the same complexion that Allegra idolized so genuinely
And so, Dante shifted into his lion, the figure he would stay in, forever
Wallowing within the grasslands, cocooned in the gore of Allegra's exit
For nothing is more ghastly than the vile aftermath of cruel heartbreak
And with that thought, the love bug finally detached from Dante's skin
For the finale of his love-hating hex had come to a sadistic close, at last

Wartime Affections

Before bodies of pulp and plasma with complexions easily carved open
And appendages effortlessly disjointed, like detaching petals from a lily
Before these flimsy mortals aimed to wage crusades against one another
A battle broke out amid worthy rivals, yet no victor would be crowned
Yin, vaporous shadow, plunged into war against Yang, blinding sunlight
Equally matched in power and pride, though inherently diverse in spirit
Draped in darkness, Yin was but a silhouette hungering for annihilation
As Yang, purified by a cataract of luminosity, pined to stifle and subdue
All the while, Yin could not dream about Yang's hands around his neck
How his lungs would roar for air, but his spirit would revel in her touch
No, Yin could not lose himself in hopeless fantasies—not often, at least
Just as Yang could not fall into her own trances of darkened attractions
For it was inherently etched upon their dueling souls to remain at odds
And so, despite the desires within their ancient hearts, the battle began

Instructed by their predestined volitions, Yin and Yang's bodies hurdled
Lunging across the air, attempting to bridge the distance between them
Sprinting with such velocity, their forms became eclipsed by their haste
Seizing jagged spears—yet they already harbored innate missiles within
Readying to deliver dire attacks yet hoping they would never strike true
Mercifully, or maddeningly, Yin and Yang never were able to truly clash
A resolute, elemental force of fate hoisted the foes apart *every single time*
For the world needed them both to emerge from their battle unscathed
As there would be no further life without the existence of light *and* dark
Stuck within a stalemate, the rivals stayed on separate sides of the arena
Languishing in apparent contempt, ostensibly seething with displeasure
For they could not collide within combat just like their bones aspired to

Though, covertly, Yin and Yang released an appreciative breath of relief
For they had always burned for each other in ways far beyond butchery
If only the pair could touch—if only their primordial souls could merge
Only then would they feel the harmony they grant the rest of the world
Their unprecedented affair would be abundant with both sun *and* shade
And if the sensitive balance of this empire did not forbid it so forcefully
Ying and Yang would poetically fly to the frontlines, shed their arsenals
And turn their reveries into reality as they soar into an endless embrace

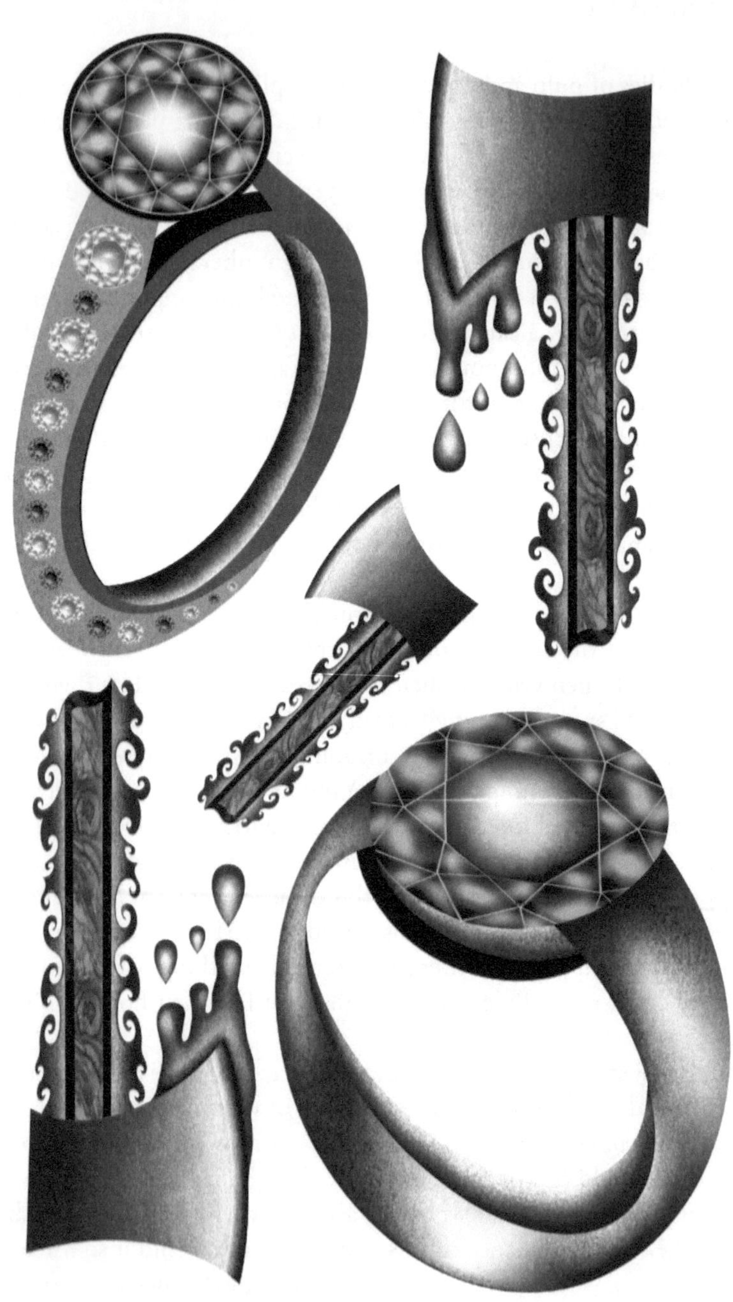

Bludgeoning Bride

Matrimony—uninhibited by mortal modesty when one remains undead
Antiquated vampire with a comatose heart dreaming of sickly romance
Binding himself to his fiancées with active organs—building his harem
A bride of beginning, with eye-catching dimples and ringlets of merlot
Beauty exemplifies her, although genuine desire and devotion elude her
A bride of secondary, as flirtatious as a vixen—fair-haired and doe-eyed
Pandering to her groom's passions, while her worship remains synthetic
A bride of finality, petrifying with raven tresses and moonlit-hued flesh
More lovesick than the rest—yet her maniacal gaze bodes certain death

Sinister husband, living in discordant harmony with his exquisite wives
Fastening titanium collars around their throats as submissive reminders
Raw, mottled skin throbs while the fraught wives claw at their necklines
Pulling and plucking, though only in private, feeling earnestly strangled
But never the third wife, who only appreciates her collar with reverence
For her intense exaltation is as everlasting as his never-ending existence
Chock-full of envy, she wishes for the other brides' permanent removal
Craving their erasure from this marriage, this manor, this mortal soil of life
Faking no hesitation, the loyal, latest bride begins to blissfully bludgeon
Until her vampire paddles through bountiful puddles of viscous plasma
Before reaching his remaining, bawling wife—whom he cherishes most
Pulling her close, calming her waterworks, then peacefully enunciating
That there is nothing he does not know— nothing he does not witness
Tensing, his final wife freezes her feigned tears—waiting to be rebuked
Though no admonishment follows, for her spouse is pridefully pleased
Exhilarated by her the atrocity of her sadistic perseverance and passions
So much so that he gifts his wife the key to release her collar as a reward
Yet she merely tautens it instead, luxuriating in the throttling sensation
Rousing her vampire to places an immortal kiss upon her jugular, at last

As a besotted, bloodied duet, the lovers live alone—as sincere soulmates
For her lethal thirst for love harmonizes with his libidinous lust for gore
No more weddings nor wives—although others are fatally invited inside
Only to never leave—stuck as ruby remains beside past, perished brides
Vampiric couple, satiated by their scarlet union, bound in bright blood
Reveling in the sacred rhapsody of their now private, undying romance

Cupid's Hex

Ardent angel, everlastingly humming love ballads to audiences of doves
Enchanted with an illness denied of any mortal cures or godly antidotes
Never to be healed with mouthfuls of medicines or dewdrops of tonics
For sentimental Cupid was hexed to become pricked by his own arrow
To plunge into a pond of pining daydreams with no chance of recovery
With a slumbering soul of saccharinity hexed to be animatedly awoken
By an enamored addiction—one which will imbibe his sweetened spirit
Like a lovesick bloodsucker, until grey cinders of loss are all that remain

With broken capillaries and bruised skin, Cupid *needed* to expel his love
For his restraint was ruining his complexion and mangling his anatomy
Downright rabid to cradle a heart, to cherish it like a rarefied gemstone
But then—Cupid's tearful gaze was pulled forward by a charmed power
Forced to settle upon Cora—certain to have descended from the divine
For her excellence was heightened by the Grecian aura of Helen herself
And as their eyes blissfully locked—a herculean bolt of thunder roared
While the unhindered intensity of Cupid's curse came unlocked, at last
Mayflies of swooning affection swarmed Cupid's skin as he beheld Cora
Then, his blood bred sugar, as his veins teemed with barrels of molasses
Until no plasma remained, for something so macabre was not welcome
Within the candy-coated body of someone so consumed with romance

Asphyxiating as the hex became, Cora's company alleviated his anguish
When they were close, the cloying caramel within Cupid's bloodstream
Sang out in sincere satisfaction—thankful for her passionate proximity
Minimizing the force of the curse traumatically pressing into his bones
Coaxing Cupid to feel *more and more* until his skeleton would detonate
Until his guts would burst in an eruption of rose petals and cherry juice
Leaving his physique sheathed within the spilled extracts of infatuation
For that was all Cupid had become—a vessel for love to lethally bloom
Cursed to romanticize—Cupid never insisted upon the reprieve of rest
Unable to ignore an opportunity to memorize the outline of Cora's lips
To learn the sum of birthmarks dotting her skin—the flesh of a goddess
Cupid pined to see it all, to illustrate her image upon his brain with ink
For the unlucky dawn when he cannot recall the hue of Cora's eyelashes
Or the saintly sight of her blushing complexion—would be his very last

Cupid soon required more than the tenderness of Cora's dainty touches
Needing to feel her within the connective cartilage of his doting rib cage
Cupid aspired to devour Cora whole—bones and brain and body intact
Only so she could observe his soul like none before had ever deigned to
And gasp—realizing that her name, her voice, the very core of her spirit
Was ironed upon his skeleton a thousand times over *like a tender temple*

Cupid thanked the sun and stars, and soil, for his love was reciprocated
Cora worshipped this winged entity of adoration with endless gratitude
With authentic feelings, never artificial—never encouraged by any curse
No, her emotions were as pure as a songbird, whistling with merriment

Grasping the unending appetite of Cupid's heart, Cora tried to satiate it
Willing to do *anything* for her lover if it would appease his gentle wishes
And so, Cupid shuddered when Cora slipped her fingers into his mouth
Gifting him a taste of her flesh to treasure as he had always hungered to
Astonished by the flavor upon his palette, the angel appreciatively cried
Wishing to remain within this elysian paradise of candied love—forever

But then, the stubborn hands of fate struck, and Cora grievously passed
Cupid bellowed loud enough that every divinity lightyears away winced
Wedded in life, widowed in death—yet Cupid's feelings never did falter
For he would sooner swallow his crossbow until it bulges from his chest
Rather than stop loving her: his salvation, his soulmate, his second self
Even in the wake of Cora's demise—cloaked in the aroma of mourning
Cupid's hex still thrived, flourishing like the stems of an undying flower

But now, without Cora breathing alongside his flesh or breathing at all
The force of the curse became too constricting—too controlling to bear
Chocolate fudge in his intestines shifted into perilous streams of venom
While bones crumbled—turning into nothing but besotted heaps of ash
Amid his trance of grief, Cupid sensed that his body was shutting down
And so—it was no grand surprise when death appeared to seize his soul
Cupid put up no fight at all; in fact, he was more eager to go than most
For the reaper would bring him right to Cora's side, where he belonged

Grim Reaper and Genevieve

Grim Reaper and Genevieve

In an erotic heap of waves, an inky mane inches along broad shoulders
As death's divine perfume spritzes from his never-ending noxious bottle
Bathing the Grim Reaper, portentous in spirit and provocative in looks
In a portrait of carnal sin, for the aura of allure never does discriminate
Even against one whose thoughts are grave and whose tasks are ghastly
A lethal entity—yet never would his existence be classified as lonesome
Forever escorted amid the trials of demise by his guardian—Genevieve
With flowing cobalt locks, as if she always brandishes an eternal breeze
Parading navy irises impersonating hydrangeas and an archetypal figure
Every bit as beautiful as her Grim Reaper and equally as sinister as well
Sharing a disdain for mortals with futile aspirations and frail anatomies
Reveling in the supreme frenzy which only a session of slaying provides
Eons ago—Genevieve was delegated to her reaper like magic to a mage
Elected with care to guard his archaic skeleton of cadaverous authority
Before becoming breathing armor, promising he will remain unscathed
Whenever pending corpses, unprepared to depart, venture to fight back
Genevieve, aware and alert, staves off these desperate attacks every time

While the reaper's guardian is well-known as a solemn force to be feared
So too, does she stand a full foot shorter than him, as petite as any other
Always craning her head upwards until the nape of her neck grows sore
Verifying he is still safe—well, as safe as one can be who deals out death
And though it is Genevieve's deity-granted duty to defend with fidelity
Often the Grim Reaper will glance down to make sure *she* is unharmed
For the one loss he could never stomach finalizing—would be her own
In the midst of their missions, romance had bloomed between the pair
Heartening saplings of love flowered, not into petals of gentle affection
But into stems of gothic flora tangling with perverse demands of desire
Raring to stay united, his coarse fingers now dig into Genevieve's waist
Resulting in bloody imprints, reminders of their paranormal proximity
And whenever peril looms, the prospect as hazardous as his sharp scythe
Genevieve tenses, agitated yet inclined to fight for his life with her own
While the Grim Reaper halts, alarmed yet assured in her expert abilities
And when antagonistic threats are abolished, their hearts finally slacken
Blinking away bottled tears—the reaper possessively grasps his guardian
As the impassioned pair amble toward their next contestants of fatality

Paragons of Grotesque Romance

Entitled the monstrous paragons of grotesque romance and primal love
Nadia and Nox, inhuman pairing, were as beastly as they were beautiful
Supernatural couple with slaughterous penchants and scandalous minds
When their wanting mouths met beneath a hailstorm of besotted pellets
A chemical reaction erupted upon the swollen flesh of their pulsing lips
Until the flickering essence within their souls ruptured due to obsession
Tempting their mortal makeups to transform—like shifting werewolves
For the passion between Nadia and Nox resulted in a novel renovation
Yet, it was not a succubus nor vampire nor serpent the pair emerged as
But rather, a catastrophic amalgamation of all of the above—and more
Possessing a perilous cornucopia of unprecedented forms and facilities
Bearing menacing exteriors and haunting energies radiating infatuation
Nadia and Nox were immortally inexorable, both feared and revered by all

Vixen-like Nadia—one mouthwatering half of this paranormal alliance
With lashes coated in carbon coal, deepening her already demonic gaze
Blushing orbs of cherry stippled Nadia's cheeks as her bloodlust swelled
And serpentine venom swam below her translucent flesh like toxic fish
Extraordinary wings, membranous extremities emulating a gothic moth
Protruded from her shoulder blades until bloodied tides lined her spine
Sea nymph-like scales gilded her arms—like viperous designs of appeal
Sprawling all the way to her jagged talons, painted with obsidian polish
Obscured below elbow-length leather gloves until sensually stripped off
Plum tresses, dripping wet from gore, tantalizingly tousled and tangled
Drenched the pinot-noir-hued negligée plastered to her hourglass form
A garment so truly imitating the likeness of plasma—one could not tell
Where the fabric ended and where the grisly remains of her prey began
Despite Nadia's mutant complexion—her elite splendor was irrefutable
Cryptic Nox, the steadfast hilt to his darling lover's hatchet of homicide
Categorically handsome in a ruined, ripped shirt, every button undone
Cuffs lewdly rolled up to thick forearms as the cloth threatened to tear
Under the strain of his animalistic muscles, the tendons of a burly beast
Nox bore bone-dry fangs, for he *emphatically* sucked them utterly clean
Impatient to inundate his palette with any dashes of expired existences
Lastly, locks atop his horned head were streaked with lines of butchery
As an undying smirk lifted his lips, exposing an erotically forked tongue

Nox remained just as eye-catching and ethereally enigmatic as his Nadia
Depicting a renowned magnum opus of desirability—when side by side
A pairing of monsters possessed by the hypnotizing pupils of adoration
Often *feel* miles deeper than mortals upon dirt and angels upon breezes
Closed-off beings dare only to emote with the first layers of themselves
With soft skin and superficial murmurs—offering but a shell to be seen
Designing synthetic, vapid personas enveloped in protective restrictions
While the affections of a fiend originate from far beneath shallow flesh
Unearthly emotions derive from unshielded capillaries and bared hearts
Rapturous bliss decants from the overcast depths within criminal souls
So long as their spirits are accepted—their hearts never feel abandoned
Nadia and Nox ran wild with want, *yet it was never only love they craved*
Thus, the beloveds embraced their lethal wishes, their murderous itches
Before embarking upon slaughtering sprees with one harmonized mind
Slaying with the synergy only soulmates own while scheming in silence
To begin their bouts of mayhem, the couple intimidated potential prey
With their mysterious though enviable appearances, *downright beguiling*
Before stunning helpless victims with the enraptured aura they radiated
Trapping them within a noose of doting intrigue and tentative worship
Nadia's powers meshed with Nox's until they convulsed with authority
Fashioning sinful bolts of black magic from the intensity of their bond
Ready at last, the supreme sweethearts of wrath began their eradications
Ramming their hellish antlers into soft torsos before perforating bowels
Poisoning jugulars with toxic nips, amputating limbs with visceral force
Showered by hazes of spilled blood cells amid the rowdy pandemonium
Nadia and Nox's palms never separated, forever laced together lovingly
Even when they depleted life from crushed lungs with languid pleasure

Patrons of chaotic devotion whose attraction tore through altered flesh
Until aching drops of desire fell to the earth in a monsoon of romance
Just as drips of violence raided from their victims descended to the soil
And yet, Nadia and Nox were always too absorbed in each other's gaze
To ever notice the aftermath of carnage surrounding deceasing mortals
If anything, to these monstrous lovers, their screams were like arpeggios
Serenely waltzing amid the craters of their sadistic yet starry-eyed skulls

Devil's Affair

Sublime wings as luminously golden as the sour liquid of juiced lemons
Like twin tapestries of canary-colored starlight, rarified in raw splendor
Gleamed with enchanted glory, the way they shine in the midst of June
When budding springtime sheds its flesh and summertime seeds bloom
Yet—in this feral province of fury, no seasons cycled, and no sun shone
Leaving this comely fairy's limbs to effervesce only through sheer drive
Backed by a will as firm as the fortitude of the hedonistic god, *Dionysus*
Divinely determined whenever he desired a goblet of his grape draught
And it was this same persistence that pardoned her membranous wings
From being charred upon necropolis-scented flames during her descent
Freya, the fairy with heart-hewn lips, hazelnut locks, cocoa-tinted irises
Strolled upon ethereal legs into a subterranean world, lacking any sheen
Vaccinating doses of splendor into the sinning ambiance with each step
Ambling upon a thorned track, Freya beheld ulcer-inducing debauchery
Below rotted clouds, putrefied funeral flowers littered ash-filled gardens
As flinching ankles were obstructed and throbbing jugulars were opened
Off-putting designs, using brain matter as paint, illustrated barbed walls
While sickening exclamations of excruciation found Freya's aching ears
Threatening to wreck her resolve like shattered jewels if she did not flee
Even still—the fairy stuck to her scheme, and her expedition carried on

Freya's eyes, although hypnotic in hue, became progressively exhausted
For her slumber as of late had been interrupted by refrains of lost souls
Who sensed the mercy within her sympathetic spirit, even a realm away
Perished souls sang out to Freya, telling tales of their mistaken captivity
Existing now within an abyss of endless torture—desperate for a savior
And so, with a humane heart of honey, the fairy flew to the underworld
Willing to hike up the rickety hills of hell in pursuit of the hapless gates
Hopeful that when she returned above, her gentle arms would be filled
With every sorrowful soul who inundated her dreams, freed at long last
Rouge King of Hell, unholy Liege of Hades, none other than *Malachai*
Expected Freya's arrival, having heeded rumors of her trancelike beauty
Malachai judged her selfless quest, saving those already lost, to be futile
Yet—the remorseless demon could not refute his esteem for her mettle
And before long, Malachai burned with a fevered feeling of anticipation
Curious to witness a being of benevolence within a district of depravity

Malachai's sentinels unlatched the gates for Freya, who glided into view
Exposing wings of exaltation that glazed the empire in a veneer of glory
Until the devil rapidly shut his eyes—for Freya's brilliance was blinding
When piercing the pupils of someone who only ever observed darkness
But, what was worse, Malachai realized, prying his lids open once more
Was barring his eyesight from beholding the fairy's remarkable features
As her cheeks reddened like a rosette, bashful in the most beautiful way
Like a sapling wary of sprouting, *yet when it does*, a heavenly floret arises
Malachai, roguish ruler, raptly listened to Freya's philanthropic petition
Pondering her words with a focus he had not known that he possessed
Shockingly stirred by the ache in her voice, as if *she* were the one caged
While painfully noticing the unshed tears swelling in her brunette irises
Not a second later—he found himself urgently marching down his dais
Halting only when standing a breath away from his caring visitor, Freya
Freya, he mused, a forename of such loveliness for a fairy of such luster
And it was that train of thought which formulated his awaited decision
Much to the perplexity of the ruler's hardhearted demons in attendance
Malachai emphatically decreed that the captive spirits would be released
For if they were unlawfully trapped, then they did not belong here at all
And while Malachai still believed in the chastisement of corrupted souls
He harbored no tactless yearning to harm those stained with innocence

Consequently, a shocking act of acquittal fell from his ill-famed tongue
As Freya's picturesque lips separated in disbelief over his assertive speech
More so, the fairy felt in awe of the baritone voice delivering his decision
Rough and rasping, and yet, Freya could detect that the devil before her
Had strained to speak with as much of a tender tone as he could muster
Fearing that the edges of his calloused accent would nick her pastel skin
Which would justifiably cut his own soul with a paring knife of remorse
The fairy—flushed with cheerful triumph—thanked Malachai profusely
Before starting to bow, prostrating herself at his feet in honest gratitude
But instantly, Malachai caught Freya by her hips and softly lifted her up
Explaining that she could request flames of silver, like metallic infernos
And Malachai, with bare palms easily blistered, would dye them himself
The impish leader would blissfully grant Freya *anything* she ever wanted
For it would be his most idyllic honor to appease this fairy, forevermore

When the guards absconded to emancipate the victims Freya fought for
Malachai and his darling guest swiftly found themselves relieving *alone*
Inching closer to Freya's form, the devil joined his and his fairy's hands
Escorting them to his regal throne, urging her to rest atop the satin seat
As Malachai—invincible king—lounged upon the gravel dirt below her
Staring up with a pure expression that propelled pleasure through Freya
For though his gaze was seemingly chaste—it was full of lustful promise
And then—with the natural ease of divided soulmates abruptly reunited
Freya and Malachai expressed every intimate emotion they dared to feel
Every word felt forbidden—for how could such contradictory creatures
Converse with such heartfelt effortlessness and instantaneous reverence
As they spoke at length, never once did their explorative touches pause
Malachai still held Freya's hand, before transferring her from his throne
And onto his lap—wrapping the fairy in his arms with affectionate care
Freya leaned into his touch, trailing one petite palm through his tresses
While the other settled atop his chest, delighting in his hellish heartbeat
Before either of them knew it, much time had lapsed into the vile ether
Amid that session of speaking, they had absorbed all of their intricacies
Both superficial and soul-deep, until the spark they both initially sensed
Flared into an ardent blaze, never to be eliminated by seraphs or spirits

The devil, with a foreign feeling germinating within his untrained heart
And with unconcealed desperation lining his newly sensitive intonation
Begged Freya to remain, both in Malachai's underworld and in his arms
At that same moment—the fairy with dreamlike dust bathing her body
Uttered her timid request to stay within the kingdom she once loathed
For the voyage above would feel frigid without him, despite the hellfire
Just as life on lush soil would be troubling without his horned presence
With a pleased exhalation, Malachai warmly anointed Freya as *his queen*
Vowing that amid their reign—no other souls would erroneously suffer
An oath that made Freya's love for Malachai, *her Mal,* swell ever further
King Malachai, with his forehead affectionally pressed against his fairy's
Finally felt a sense of what the solstice season on Earth would taste like
For Freya's touch was so transcendent, and her aura was so resplendent
Introducing unknown illumination and humble integrity into this land
That no longer did the despondent underworld feel quite so bleak at all

Tristian and Torvina's Gothic Tale

Two hearts, a spellbound duet, hiked the preordained labyrinth of love
Undeterred by the looming ghouls of expiry who lurked in the corners
Assailed by lethal hands, then revived by the intervening aid of destiny
Thus was the gothic saga of Tristian and Torvina, ill-omened soulmates
Compelled to connect by the midnight fog plastered over their arteries
Lusty cobwebs of woven silk draped over their skeletons since the start
When their flesh first touched, visceral firestorms of sincerity broke out
A miracle that they did not dissolve into cadaverous debris immediately
Yet, their inferno did not singe their skin; it only enhanced their desires
For Tristian and Torvina were forged in an amorous oven of admiration
Ignited sweethearts who would *die* for another moment spent together
That dungeon-like notion, unescapable in nature, was constantly tested
Tragedy stalked the lovers like the ragged pages of a Shakespearian play
Visiting from a tomblike territory, the cynical reaper schemed to ravish
And so, his throttling lasso of death lashed out with terminal willpower
Grievously harming Tristian and Torvina in simultaneous synchronicity
As Hades's multi-headed hound oozed feral foam from his snarling lips
And archangels of morality fine-tuned their lyrical harps in preparation

Yet—the breeze of fatality slipped past the pair upon a benevolent wind
Leaving them littered with abrasions—like sentient statues of wreckage
Tristian and Torvina were then pulled apart by mighty pilers of division
Amid all the calamity—their sentimental minds were insolently purged
Until any Eros-inspired thoughts waded into a blackened, barren abyss
Amnesiac mates, still gushing with gore, ambled with amorous instinct
Unable to recall what their malfunctioning hearts were sure was absent
Though their arteries were tangibly unharmed, they wailed all the same
Lovingly longing for something or someone unknown, unremembered
Ailing in a crushing condition of unease, barred from feeling any peace
Until the deteriorating mates discover each other again, against all odds
Drifting closer—Tristian heard the faint notes of Torvina's bodily ballad
What echoed into the hushed twilight like toneless thumping to others
Delivered an epic poem to his optimistic ears only—as his wrists purred
Readying his pulse to pen a symphony—composed only for *his* Torvina
Eager to soothe her spirit with his own concerto, in affectionate return

Much to the merriment of their obsessed skulls, quaking with reverence
Tristian and Torvina's unplanned strides converged upon an idyllic path
With sores decorating their arms and contusions garnishing their necks
Incredibly—the pair recognized each other and remembered *everything*
For amnesia does not ensure erasure, and so, never did they truly forget
Even when their injured brains were coerced into the act of eradication
Torvina identified Tristian at once, for long ago, far before the violence
Tristian handed her his heart, letting her cradle the hemorrhaging organ
And during their time apart, Torvina's bloody hands felt eternally empty
Missing the wet sensation of the arterial gift she once held and honored
When their trails crossed, her fingers ached—straining toward his chest
Proving, in parallel time as her mate, *that this was truly her mislaid lover*
Tristian and Torvina's morbid, maudlin tale was affixed into the cosmos
By the plaiting palms of celestial magic—as skilled as an onyx arachnid
Nothing could unknot their crocheted seams within the nocturnal skies
Dust clouds of doom may try, but the sappy stars would *never* permit it
As the beloveds intimately embraced, any lingering wounds were healed
While their mended bones begged them to remain interlocked—as one
Aware that should they stay like this, touching and teasing with *urgency*
Fate would only wrench the sweethearts apart again, needy for conflict
Acting as cynics testing their love or as romantics enriching their bond
Either way, the soulmates were too infatuated to pull away, not just yet
Tristian's worship surged into Torvina like waves caressing sultry shores
As her deprived complexion grew soothed by the surety of his devotion
Reunited, the couple felt resuscitated, born anew with revitalized desire
Savoring the familiar energy of fondness regifted unto their tender souls

All too soon, as anticipated—Tristian and Torvina were grimly attacked
It should be noted that each time death's minions nipped at their heels
Among all the rubble, outstretched were their hands, delicately clasped
Knowing that though their dazed division was regrettably forthcoming
So too, was the prospect of meeting once more and finally reminiscing
Tristian and Torvina's feelings never abated amidst sinister tribulations
While veins depleted and skin scarred, their romance only ever thrived
Dotingly sure that their unfailing reunions—like being sent to nirvana
Were well worth the bloodshed they stoically endured every single time

Frankenstein's
Monster

Frankenstein's Monster

Just behind a velvet curtain and directly below an illuminating spotlight
Shining dramatic rays onto the stage like seas of effervescent champagne
A medieval legend of renewal and ruin and romance hauntingly unfolds
Both tragic and tender—revealing unseen horrors and unforeseen affairs
While the audience, restless within their seats, observes the chilling cast
Utterly riveted, with gasping breaths, tearful eyes, and sentimental sighs
All too eager for the next act to embark—for the thrilling end was nigh
Beginning with Frankenstein, megalomaniac scientist, inventor of sorts
Sneaking downstage to burgle graves while cemetery dirt remains fresh
Reeking of perished lives only just starting to decay within their coffins
Raiding corpses from lethal gallows, robbing their most essential organs
Frankenstein—surging with hubris and fixated on his risky experiment
Cares not for bothersome ethics, only cherishing the idea of giving life
Back to skeletons and organs and skulls of limp figures, vacant of souls
Calamitously wielding a gluttonous sense of supremacy while he labors
Imitating a god upon Mount Olympus rather than a mortal upon Earth
All the while, riotous skies of wicked weather rage with a restoring storm
Reverberating with the electric control Frankenstein requires for victory
Until his patchwork creation—fashioned from pickpocketed fragments
Becomes assailed by lightening imbued with galvanizing bolts of energy
Jumpstarting his thieved heart, resurrecting his spirit with unique verve
Frankenstein's monster, *alive, alive, alive,* is gloriously reanimated at last

Triumphant celebrations are transient, for Frankenstein grows regretful
As he rebuffs his handiwork—realizing the error of his ways, *far too late*
For destruction and demise ensues, though not by any means malicious
Uncaring of acquitting explanations, Frankenstein deserts his invention
With the unsympathetic air of a deity discarding all which he had made
Never turning back or checking in—as if his trial never happened at all
Frankenstein's monster, renounced, startles at the sight of his reflection
How could he not after being titled a *monster* from his cadaverous birth
Wandering without purpose, Frankenstein's brainchild provokes dread
Townspeople wail, seeing the monster through grotesque-tinted glasses
And yet, it is this slandered individual who experiences authentic fright
For all those who encounter the monster recoil, dreading the unknown
And it is always unbiased judgment which yields the most horrid results

Now forced to flee—the monster heeds the bellows trailing behind him
Incensed residents ignited by panic start a virulent hunt void of any pity
Clasping singeing torches and letting loose predatory, growling hounds
Never daring to grant Frankenstein's monster a measure of compassion
Only salivating to inflict disciplinary justice, which is not very *just* at all
For this misjudged character is a monster only in name, never in nature
With an atypical façade and an affable spirit, our lead antihero is woeful
Abandoned by his patriarchal architect and rejected by all of civilization
Frankenstein's monster languishes in the shallow rivers of self-contempt
Inquisitive about the intricacies of life—though none ever indulge him
Forsaken—this feared being falls into trances of an archetypal existence
One surging with acceptance and romance and kind acknowledgments
Though the monster remains an alarming figure of accidental wreckage
So too, does he crave the *concept of love* as a balm for his endless solitude

But then, who emerges from the wings, but the scientist—Frankenstein
Reinvigorated by inspiration—not yet ready to fold his spawning hands
Watch as he electrocutes a revolutionary character into breathing reality
A female, devised from bridal blueprints, filled with matrimonial desires
Upon meeting Frankenstein's original offspring, a fond kinship blooms
Already starting to sense the arduous quality affixed to her irregular life
This freshly born bride finds commiserating comfort within her groom
For their budding bond contains all of the merits they each are missing
Just as their bodies are made up of pilfered parts belonging to cadavers
Our bride grants her monster the eternal companionship he longed for
Never balking, always patient, while our monster fondly helps his bride
To navigate this foreign life—speaking as tenderly as physically possible
When their marriage is thus sealed with an unpracticed kiss of intimacy
Love rapidly thrives—while their souls harmonize like an ardent sonnet
Despite the weary road ahead of them—rife with belittling harassment
At least now—forever intertwined by the dedicated vows of matrimony
Never will they sense the sting of hatred pricking at their sensitive skulls
Not as rain showers of warm approval flood their joyful, wedded hearts
With applause, the act concludes, the curtain falls, and the lights expire
Ending this gothic tale with a shockingly sentimental conclusion for all
Well, except for the man who started it all, for he is fated only for dishonor

Ember and Evil

As the aura of malice tore across the atmosphere—a rare romance arose
Ember's notorious lover was never known as death nor demon or devil
No—it was evil incarnate which she had severely and speedily fallen for
Dawdling in the quietude of the ether, Ember had detected his essence
As the lissome soul of this original sinner—the epitome of malevolence
Embraced Ember urgently—for he had discovered his mate at long last
Aghast—even Ember's awe did not stop her from returning his feelings
For this mortal knew they were meant to be, she could feel it in the air
And she would revere Evil due to his wicked nature, never in spite of it
From that initial meeting, the ruby organ palpitating in Ember's ribcage
Would belong only to Evil, as the pining stars had always intended it to

Evil, the embodiment of fiendish wishes, a writhing bundle of darkness
Brutally indulged in love like a kettle, amorously bellowing and boiling
Afflicted with a savage and smitten fever, one he never hoped to remedy
Ember and Evil's affair bore the aroma of a storm searing a summer sky
And tasted of rousing venom, both acidic and ambrosial upon lush lips
Brutish emotions of affection carved through Ember like gashes of love
Only to be healed by Evil's teasing murmurs whispered against her skin
And his shameless tongue sliding over her exposed lacerations of passion
Ember and Evil loved like werewolves—with ardent bouts of aggression
Lupine longings burgeoned within their blood—animalistic with desire
Urging the couple to gorge upon the taut flesh of each other's skeletons
Ember severed his menacing limbs; Evil cleaved her mortal appendages
Yet the pair remained infatuated as their needles sewed one another up
With doting touches, in the wake of their ruinous, besotted destruction

If deities of destiny ever unglued this pair from their unending embrace
Ember's heart—still scorched from the spot where Evil clutched it close
Would suddenly stop, for it was never hers to own—only his to cherish
And Evil would slink back into the clouds, never knowing such despair
Stroking the reddened scars of his lover's needlework decorating his skin
But for now, leniently, mercurial gods remained soundless and stagnant
Sanctioning the loving duet to remain recklessly tethered together in sin
For Ember and Evil's scandalous epic of grim love was far from finished

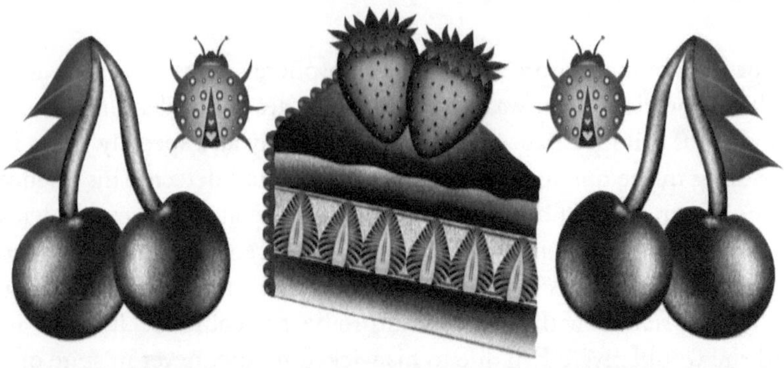

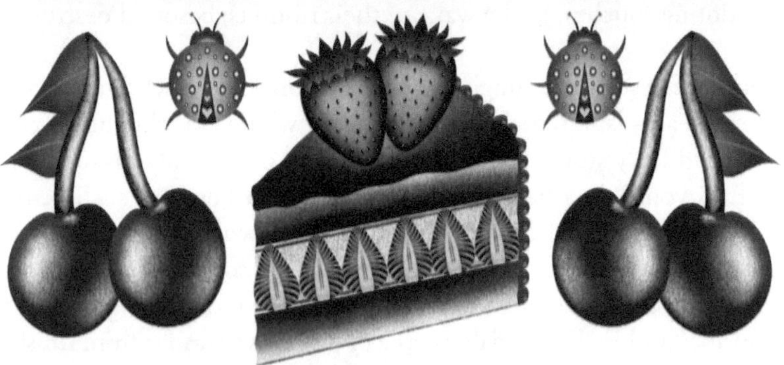

Bash and Willa's Besotted Letters

Bathed in a lake of besotted stardust swims a merry pair of mated souls
Wading within a dreamlike utopia of infatuation amid enchanted waves
Willa and Sebastian breathlessly trade water-logged wax-stamped letters
Poetries so tender, even hellish entities hunger to rip into the envelopes
Hoping to savor the softhearted odes within, to learn of *true love,* at last

Dearest Mona, my precious mortal maiden,
Mona, my Mona—my sugarcoated slice of honeycomb, my petite pearl
You have lightened my heart, chipped away at the coal it was coated in
Revealing raw layers of tissue beneath, utterly sensitive and finally freed
Never had I aspired for *anyone* to behold this ruby organ I veiled within
Let alone touch it, treasure it, as you have freely done since we first met
When our trails in life intersected, feelings of fondness struck me down
And whenever we are tragically parted, my rapt lungs struggle to respire
Until my mind retreats to lucid memories of only you—my caring cure
Idyllic reveries of your resplendent flesh caressed by my reverent palms
Soothe my forlorn soul until we reunite, and I slink from those dreams
Back into reality, rejoicing in the fairytale paradise your presence incites
With as much warmth as my pen may portray with only ink,
Your dedicated beast, Sebastian

Dearest Sebastian, my immortally perfect paramour,
Sebastian, my tongue's favorite flavor, my most divine desire in this life
I remain in an endless state of entrancement triggered by your existence
With every delivery of each smitten letter, my aching hippocampus stirs
Memorizing all the notions your beatific skull has poured onto the page
Mail me your verbose essays and epics—I will read them ten times over
My Bash—your touching verses award me as much joy as April showers
As pleasing a feeling as the peace I find when composing my own notes
Trusting you will save them when I am gone as lilting tokens of my *love*
As I inscribe this, you are intimately gripping my hips, stroking my skin
And as I labor to write with uniform strokes, diverted by your attention
Never before has my body felt more honored and my soul felt more full
Sending my syrupy sentiments to you, mere inches away,
Your heartfelt devotee, Mona

Dearest Mona, my tart little lemon drop,
My fresh bouquet of bluebells wrapped in the parchment of my praises
Knowing our musings offer you candid rhapsody is my utmost triumph
For I would bear any hardship to inject pleasure into your exalted veins
Unadulterated ecstasy skates into my affectionate anatomy while I write
Dotingly wishing that my letters will radiate the full extent of my fervor
Ensuring that you, my dear Mona, know how utterly cherished you are
Amid your transient existence, ever too ephemeral, much to my sorrow
My prized fallen angel—that is how I perceive you whenever we touch
Though I am but a demonic being, confident my condemnation is near
For daring to graze skin so supple with hands so stained from slaughter
But halt my ministrations I cannot, for the sensation is too exhilarating
My Mona—I would swallow a sword if it would save you from its blade
And while the slashing pain in my throat would prove to be unbearable
I would descend into death peacefully—ever so grateful for your safety
    Rallying the powers of witchcraft to imbue these words with my worship,
                                  Your sycophantic suitor, Bash

Dearest Bash, my besotted sugarplum prince,
Bash, my ever-chirping bluebird singing me a melodic song of flirtation
Whose voice lands upon the forms of others like a butterfly's subtle kiss
But with me, the harmonies you emit find my flesh with fervid urgency
Branding my body with permanence like scarring motifs of sweethearts
Oxygen offers my gullet no relief, only your lips slotted against my own
Allows me to effusively breathe while I swoon into your trancelike arms
My gentle, self-effacing soulmate, we were both assembled incompletely
Bearing absent shards of our spirits before being heaved into this realm
Left lonesome to hunt for our missing parts without a chart or compass
It was only through the endless pull of passion—like amorous magnets
That we reunited and pieced ourselves back together, bit by bit—at last
If ever you bled, though I hesitate to even write of such a *horrid* notion
Copper would engulf *my* mouth, yet free of lacerations, I would remain
Such is the sweet proof of my devotion to you, my inhuman buttercup
    Shouting into the wintertime ether all the ways in which I admire you,
        Your ladybug of love and lust and everything in-between, Mona

Dearest Mona, my resplendent ray of sunlight,
My strawberry shortcake darling, how *extremely* lucky I am to know you
You are the protective sheath to my painful dagger, my beautiful shelter
How I wish I could bribe the deities of time—for more of it, for *all of it*
There is no quest I would not embark upon to dissuade your departure
Be it raiding a dragon's gilded hoard or climbing the peaks of perdition
I hanker for mystic methods to rid our weary minds of the ticking timer
Counting down to your mortal demise, *which nauseates me dreadfully so*
My tiramisu truffle, know that when your soul leaves this earthly plane
Though the thought abhors me, I will remain alone, dolefully immortal
And my mourning ears will everlastingly miss the tune of our adoration
A tear-jerking sonata of soft sighs and sensitive stanzas of treacly regards
My pretty girl, my Mona, you are the first, last, and only love of my life
Even as seasons alter from bitter to burning, my feelings will *never* abate
I handed you my heart so long ago; I only ask you to carry it into death
Lest the organ remains broken and bellowing, missing you forevermore
    Thinking of you with as much longing as Hades harbors for Persephone,
                  Your awestruck beau, Bash

Dearest Bash, my monstrous beam of moonlight,
My vanilla bean sweetheart, expel your worries, for even in the afterlife
My idolizing bones will never wither away into freezing ashes of apathy
Death may clip my life's leash, but he may never erase you from my marrow
When I perish, a cherry tree will arise from the roots of our admiration
Producing acidic fruits with ardent pits, bursting with heartfelt romance
My Bash, utilize the bark as woodland papyrus for potential love letters
As I hope you will write to me—even when my address is otherworldly
Bury me beside the ocean—let the sound of summertime tides find me
Swelling sea ballads will mercifully remind me of your undulating voice
Crooning sugary nothings against my locks so I could slip into slumber
Sebastian, promise me you will remember that delicate mortal I may be
But my love for you, my hammering aches, are anything but temporary
    Basking in the saccharine nirvana of our union while I still can,
        Your seraph soaring high upon the wings of bliss, Mona

Spellbinding Witchcraft

Grimoire
Grimoire

Bewitched Grimoire

Medieval grimoire emanating iridescent supernovas of deathless sorcery
For the brilliance of the atavistic witchcraft within cannot be contained
Trusted tome fashioned many millennia ago, cloaked in pebbled leather
Stamped with ornate designs—spellbinding motifs to worship the stars
Rare jewel of Alexandrite, ever so carefully embedded within the center
Everlasting, elemental wonder with the notable aptitude to shift shades
So too, does the grimoire feature a bronze lock as inanimate gatekeeper
Guarding cloaked charms within the feathered pages and deckled edges
Blotted with the menagerie of mystical materials needed for invocations
Bearing a barrage of supernatural knowledge, of imperative information
Extensive descriptions on how to create talismans, sachet bags, amulets
Comprehensive accounts of all enchantments and their distinctive aims
Readings of otherworldly rituals to call upon demons, angels, divinities
Effusive grimoire—encapsulating everything one must know as a mage

Elegantly baroque, though not every pupil may witness what lies within
Spill a bead of blood upon the oxidized latch from the vein of a Wiccan
For only the lifeforce of an enchantress may unlock the grimoire wholly
Spine split, pages revealed, exposing writing penned in an illegible script
For the writings will be divulged only beneath the safety of the shadows
As the lyrics of a primordial spell are vocalized with reflective reverence
And when the last line gracefully spills from the lips of a heartfelt witch
Unintelligible calligraphy deviates into hallowed chants and ceremonies
Ensuring that the sanctified act of witchcraft will forever remain sacred
Never to be discovered by undeserving gazes with loathsome intentions

During the midnight fog of the witching hour, amid this dreamlike time
Take the ruby essence falling from my finger, steal what was once mine
Hear my spell glide through nebulous skies like a skylark upon a breeze
Unlatch your lock of fortification so my inquisitive skull may be at ease
Unveil your inscriptions to my shrewd eyes—the spheres of a sorceress
Within the grimoire, show me the wisdom of witches I yearn to possess

Solaria's Enchanted Forest

Calamitous timberland caught under the curtain of everlasting twilight
Private gathering of witchcraft governed by the authorities of midnight
Burgeoning with freesia flowers imitating the scent of fresh strawberries
Captivating snowdrops tirelessly curse the obscurity within the clearing
As canopies of shades disallow any infiltrating sunbeams from entering
For a lightless hex was imposed upon the forest by an insolent sorceress
Forever casting ferns and dirt and pinecones into disorienting darkness
Stifling all organisms of nature, restraining their magic and movements
Leaving them all within perpetual dusk—pleading for one ray of luster

Nearby, a benevolent fairy found herself in the feverish midst of fleeing
Solaria, a softhearted being of light—as genteel as a princess of nobility
Whose charmed touch invoked marbles of luminosity—orbs of wonder
Illuminating everything she grazed—by the sorcery of the sun and stars
Though, her talents troubled mortal men, as feminine powers always do
Leaving Solaria no choice but to escape those who labored to chase her

Evading capture, the fairy staggered into the forest, an apparent asylum
Hidden within this abode of fixed nightfall, Solaria released radiant sobs
Until beaming tears toppled to the mud, altering the fabric of the forest
Infusing the ether with light and injecting the environment with liberty
Eradicating any depths of dimness, replaced by blinding sparks of gold

Freed from their dismaying scourge, violets nearly flew from their roots
Foliage upon oak trees adored this spectacle of exotic shines and sheens
While maple branches oscillated in emancipation, finally able to emote
Opaline hope flooded the newly sundrenched air in a monsoon of bliss
Yet, the peace within this blushing wonderland would not prove to last
Far too soon, Solaria—bursting with nothing but brilliance, was located
Discovered by hostile huntsmen unable to forget their stalking schemes
Strategizing, Solaria siphoned glinting globes of starlight into her palms
Before fathoming that the beholden forest were priming themselves too
Pining to represent their bright savior in this war, evermore in her debt
As nature eponymously dubbed their dwelling *Solaria's Enchanted Forest*
And it was their *honor* to safeguard the harmony she kindly gifted them

Orchid stems strangled, leaves muted shrieks, felled trees crushed limbs
Dollops of muck hardened over fingers and feet, immobilizing with ire
Saplings piled high atop anxious eyes, heightening their horrified senses
Dirt dragged the huntsmen under, burying them beneath fatal boulders
Even the empathetic earth did not deign to mourn these merited losses
Ensuring nothing would bloom from their remains, rotten as they were

Drained from taxing warfare, Solaria and her forest exhaled in triumph
As the atmosphere coursed with the sugared aroma of warranted justice
Like an edible drizzling of maple syrup raining over the tired ecosystem
A confectionary prize for the protection they bestowed upon their fairy
Even prying divinities were thrilled that Solaria's enemies were defeated
Demolished with elemental permanence—never to hunt or harm again
Never to stalk those whose abilities outweigh and overpower their own

But even still, in the aftermath of such victory, the wildlife were woeful
Not yet capable of appreciating all of their valiant feats and noble deeds
For the notion of their fairy now departing, no longer in need of shelter
Invited dread into their woodland hearts—the concept deeply upsetting
But then, Solaria declared that she hoped to stay, never planning to exit
For this isolated forest, *her forest*, was where she was always meant to be
Leaving the buds of bluebonnets and the barks of balsams to finally rest
While emerald blades of grass quaked from overwhelming thankfulness

And in the ever-looming future, when covert footfalls tread upon twigs
Forewarning of another uninvited intruder, already lethally condemned
Solaria, dreamlike fairy, and her forest, gently spelled with gilded magic
Steel themselves to fight once more—to gallop into battle courageously
Willing to endure grisly lengths to uphold their secluded refuge of light

But for now, the bewitched timberland heaves with Solaria's brightness
At last able to sense the warmth of sunlight and the serenity of starlight
Merrily capable of feeling the freedom of unlimited, unhindered power
Teeming with witchcraft-spawned radiance and flushed with autonomy
Never to be entrapped by the tyrannical blanket of darkness ever again

Senka's Silhouettes

Senka, beautifully bearing a secular skeleton underneath her supple skin
Tethered to this temporal Earth by her corporeal body, delivered in dirt
Yet—the depiction of her soul remained obscured by an obsidian magic
For Senka bore a willowy form of witchcraft within her spelled anatomy
Granting her dominance over all shadows who were never as solid as she

It began as a curse—for when Senka sprouted from this kingdom's soil
So too, were shadows born, emerging from her lips as ethereal energies
Sovereign of silhouettes, blearily desiring an existence of independence
A private reality of isolation—one which would never come to fruition
For Senka and her umbral daughters were relentlessly bound from birth

Her kin latched onto their ruler, squeezing like vipers curling over prey
Though, unlike the crawling reptiles, they would never slaughter Senka
For she was fixedly their darkened deity, their guardian and giver of life
And the shadows, writhing around in the wind, cherished her with care
Senka's heart, however, was sinking within a river of stifling resentment
For she was surrounded by her spectral subjects every dawn, every dusk
The interminable concept that only *she* could be a queen to the shadows
Suffocated her already swollen skull until she wailed out in exasperation
Only when her throat tore out the words—wishing for a serene reprieve
Did the offspring of her organs hastily disperse into the silent sundown

The shadows did not voyage far, for they could not endure the distance
Even so—Senka still sniveled over her newfound experience of solitude
Though her thick tears were not bursting with grateful, blithe liberation
No, they were shaped only from abrupt destitution, like droplets of grief
She realized her shades were what drilled life into her heart all this time
Accepting the magic whittled into her bones, Senka howled into the eve
And love is loyal, so the silhouettes returned, embracing her once more

Never was it truthfully a curse, mused Senka—sole mage of all shadows
Because now, the witchcraft she stored within her spirit acted as a balm
Washing over the hazy sensation of the silhouettes, fixing them in place
Promising that Senka would nevermore feel alone in the frigid darkness

Enchantress of Nature

Witch, Warrior, Wiccan of all which envelops this environmental world
Elemental enchantress, guzzling down draughts of earth, fire, water, air
Submerging them within her soul until her skull is high off their power
Until monochrome bones swell—metamorphosing her malleable form
Pain yields to pleasure as the elements congratulate her altered anatomy
For now—this mage appears only as a sincere sister and elite twin flame
Pressing her palms upon the gravel, she calls upon the flourishing earth
Allowing her complexion to change into grains of sand upon a seashore
Blood becomes bark, while veins convert themselves into verdant vines
Flesh folds itself into peony petals strewn across a burgeoning meadow
Dew adorns the aching crevasses of her yearning heart with satisfaction
Even when her lungs become grasslands, restricting her gagging airways
Never does this enchantress curse the facets of nature she now exists as
Romancing the rain listlessly tumbling, she converts into living droplets
Flowing tenderly across a rippling pond drowning in shades of cerulean
Cascading as a gleaming, gushing waterfall nestled within a furtive cove
Organs become oceans, coursing with cherry waters of her own plasma
Undulating, quiet waves conduct her pulse, lulled into a swaying tempo
Soothing her ever-changing mind with each relaxing rise and restful fall
Embracing the lively expanse of the ether—she purrs to the wild winds
Elastically twisting, becoming both mellow breezes and unruly cyclones
Floating with an angel's elegance, dawdling atop flimsy clouds overhead
Faintly sobbing for the mortals who will never witness the skies like she
Her weightless physique hums from the noteworthy ability of buoyancy
Idolizing the lovely harmony which lies between tranquility and turmoil
Savoring the singe of flames, she solicits neon sparks to ingest her whole
Until her body becomes a torrid blaze, emulating an unyielding inferno
Bold licks of fire gnaw away at tempting flesh until none remains intact
Fully infusing arteries with canals of torching lava the hue of grapefruits
Pirouetting as a living wildfire, the sight as entrancing as a shooting star
Blood blisters, bubbles, and burns, filling the mage with vibrant ecstasy

Practical witch—both shapeshifter and sorceress of the vital roots of life
Transforming until her skeleton ceaselessly siphons consummate power
Swearing to respect every element until her finishing and fateful breaths

Mystical Séance

Let the warmth of three thousand incandescent stars infuse these verses
Sanction whimsical organisms within the universe to shield this séance
Abandoned, adrift spirits seized by demise—cross over into our empire
Until the depths of darkness dwindle, and each moonbeam is devoured
Only then, when crisp daylight arises, will this unworldly visit conclude

Sorceresses of pyromania—exhale from afar and set these candles ablaze
Whisper to their ebony wicks until wax waterfalls stream, like soy rapids
Inhale reminiscent perfumes of jasmine and juniper, of plum and peony
As the impeccable aromas orbit the sacred space between life and death

Encircling atmosphere—traverse down our wanting and waiting throats
As we communicate this refrain rooted within us, yearning to be heeded
Endorse our ethereal verses as they rocket across this world into the next
Where bleak departure eternally presides, and lurid life is always lacking

With intentions as innocent as a starry-eyed maiden, trust in our words
Mystified essence, we invite your influences to procure all those we seek
While we lie in wait for the mighty restraints of separation to be severed
Confirming that this bodily realm will soon welcome wraithlike visitors

Our hopeful pupils distend, aching to view those we wistfully call upon
When the time comes, authorize our enchanted lips to spill out sounds
From the incorporeal sphere of spirits—so we may commune with ease
Let this language torrent our tongues until the séance's dismayed finale
When blackbirds serenade a renewed sunrise, let these spirits float away
Gliding to their aerial abodes upon the elusive wings of this incantation

We will grieve their melancholic absence and cherish our conversations
As the restricting cuffs of divide faintly snap back into place once more
All alone, our candlelight will taper, and our mouths will begin to close
Until our pensive hearts sing out to them again in a melody of missing

Devil's
Helmet
Deadly
Nightshade
Deadly
Nightshade
Devil's
Helmet
Deadly
Nightshade
Devil's
Helmet
Deadly
Nightshade
Devil's
Helmet
Deadly
Nightshade
RAVENWOOD APOTHECARY
RAVENWOOD APOTHECARY

Ravenwood Apothecary

Meet, Penelope—occultist icon of deadly nightshade and devil's helmet
Hazardous witch of venoms, manipulator of poisons, handler of toxins
Weaving grave compositions of noxious plant life to her numinous will
Owner of the Ravenwood Apothecary—with medicines and herbs alike
Though, intermixed upon the remedial shelves lies vials of killer tonics
Both for patrons in pressing need and for the personal use of the witch
For Penelope suffered from cloying maltreatment—misbranded as love
Sadism choked her senses until she took matters into her Wiccan hands
But first, Penelope sang an incantation as armor from incurable flowers
Doubling as a hex—promising that her defense will not apply to others
Thus was the precarious invocation Penelope vocalized in preparation:

Abused by violating lips and asphyxiating limbs, I hunger for liberation
Permit him to be receptive to toxins—past the point of hospitalization
Let his despicable physique and vacant heart fall victim to my fatal plan
Yet halt the poison from harming me, lest shortened will be my lifespan

Pretty Penelope bathed her perfect body in bouquets of baneful poison
Smelling of oleander, emulating honeyed apricots, spiked with lethality
Even submerged in a palatable fragrance—the floral effect was terminal
Penelope tarnished her flesh with the virulent plant— one leaf at a time
Letting the slaughtering sap leach into her skeleton with vampiric thirst
Fixating upon spiking her bloodstream—craving to override her organs
Within Penelope, her sorcery and her spell obstructed true termination
Yet, ruinous consequences were never effusively avoidable—even for her
And while her energy depleted, her rigid smile remained tightly in place
As her lover—for that is the name he unjustly continued to call himself
Though his love Penelope never did desire—lustfully trailed to her side
Starting to caress and clutch her as he always did with unwanted hands
Concurrently, the oleander coating her skin transferred into his arteries
Wilting his heart, withering his pulse, until his life waned away—at last
Such a demise intensified Penelope's powers and the potency of her spell
Enabling her body to finally reject the poison and escape her own death
And though she would never fully escape the feel of his phantom touch
At least the witch of venoms was mercifully left alone in her apothecary
Blissfully eager to never visit her tyrant's tombstone—not now, not ever

HECATE
HECATE

Hecate's Silver Tongue

Heart of Hecate—veiled ventricles hammering with chasms of darkness
Wings of witchcraft embroidered onto her spine like an enchanted fairy
Veins of broiling magma running alongside monsoons of cryptic blood
Until stones of obsidian are hewn—gushing to the epicenter of her soul

Arcane goddess of spirits and sorcery—serenading ballads of protection
Gothic gates of contradictory realms unlocked only by her silver tongue
Mage of necromancy, emerging from the satanic dirt of the underworld
Communing with phantoms, empathizing with their rotting afflictions

Hecate, Hecate, Hecate, a triplex of talents within a mesmerizing figure
As bewitchingly influential as she is exquisite in the stupefied eyes of all
Draped over her dreamy skin, the hue of coffee beans, lie toxic serpents
Everlastingly hypnotized by the tantalizing occultist they fell devoted to

Maiden of magic, awaken from your sedate slumber within the cosmos
Amid this ghostly hour of lunar light, accept our sycophantic offerings
Vessels of citrus extract converted into flasks of effervescent, fruity cider
Hypnotic jewels of moonstone and ocher bouquets of cinnamon sticks
Frankincense oil infiltrates the ecosystem as ebony ravens govern above
Brewing a tempest of magic—now seeping into these supernatural skies

Heed us, Hecate, for we summon this heartfelt spell to ask for guidance
As our moonlit coven navigates the laborious lanes of our own witchery
Harken our hopes, please, and employ your skeletal key to visit our land
Inhale our incantation, just like a preternatural breath of paranormal air
Imbibe these lines as if delivered down your throat with a mystic spoon
Like precious medicine, pacifying our hearts when you reply at long last

Emmeline's Woodland Animals

As animals, loyal children of nature, we renounce our souls to only one
Adoringly dashing to our idyllic savior before losing the light of the sun
Traipsing in circles around peach trees, we wait until she appears at last
Matriarch of all woodland creatures—charitable mentor with skills vast
Empathetic advocate and altruistic mage, we obey your edicts forevermore
Maiming as we must to shield our coven, exiling all those we justly abhor

Within the cloaked core of the woods, Emmeline's enchantments echo
Intoning from inside her limestone cave, as resonating as a snare drum
When Emmeline rallies her animals, rainfalls of relief spew from above
Rinsing this mage's endearing features with the affirming waters of glee
For the tunes of critter-like rustles grow more proximate by the second
Before long, dragonflies decorated in mosaics settle upon her shoulders
As innocent hares nestle themselves into the crook of Emmeline's neck
Gazelles elegantly lay at her feet while rattlesnakes spiral over her wrists
Fauna of every breed fathom the poetries Emmeline expels into the eve
For she has long ago learned the animalistic language of all living things
To commune with her creatures as if they were born as the same species

Chanting a steadfast oath, Emmeline swears to protect those in her care
And yet, evildoers who endeavor to trap her reliable animals still remain
Whose hearts are heavy with criminal intentions of insensitive slaughter
Leaving Emmeline and her bewitched beings to fend off these pursuers
With a type of finality so foul, remorse will erupt in their vicious minds
Using the synergy of their guild—this wildlife coven imperils huntsmen
Subjecting them to their own snares, like a reversing form of retaliation
Triggering anarchic mechanisms of capture to detain their flailing limbs
While extremities are clasped to the breaking point of near-amputation

Exposed, Emmeline alters them into the animals they craved to destroy
As a worshiping ode to Circe, resilient and revengeful sorceress of fame
Who would gaze upon this method of vengeance with quiet satisfaction
Bleating into the endless depths of obscurity, the huntsmen scurry away
For their banishment has begun—never again able to sully these woods
As Emmeline and her animals are left alone once again in quiet serenity

N★VA
N★VA
N★VA
N★VA

Nova's Celestial Charm

Celestial charmer—humming starry enchantments amid the astral skies
Intoxicated upon titanium moonbeams, inebriated atop pearly skyglow
Nova, sorceress of the infinite solar system and all her astronomical kin
Presented from birth with bespoke piles of magic hovering in her mind
Curtsying to all which contain the metallic menagerie of the milky way
Just as the stellar inhabitants of space all praise Nova in fanatical return

Lover of aerial nebulas, listener of the lunar melody within the universe
With the ageless heart of an astrologer, whose arteries run with stardust
Caught within a dreamlike daze—everlastingly gazing upon the cosmos
Melodically murmuring to every star and each intricate shape they craft
Exulting over the allure of the aurora borealis, of blinding total eclipses
Admiring every planet with admiration, doting over Mercury and Mars
Reigning Neptune, Uranus, Saturn while revering Earth, Venus, Jupiter
Guiding the dynamic moon as it rotates through its inventory of phases
From waxing crescent to waning gibbous, Nova admires every variation
Interstellar mage—almost as entrancing as a descending meteor shower
So titillating that even asteroids to envy the stardom of her cosmic light

Ethereal Nova, with an illustrious body adorning symbols of starbursts
Divine emblems of the zodiac delicately imprinted upon her silver skin
Beautified with trinkets decorating her fingers and baubles on her neck
Necklaces of moonstone, invaluable rings of opal, bracelets of obsidian
Clutching crystals of lapis lazuli and amethyst—her beloved gemstones
Prancing across the nebulous quintet of stars encompassing Cassiopeia
Singing out her prominent spells, certain the universe is eavesdropping

Ages ago—Nova once plummeted from space like a mystical meteorite
Though the sorceress never did land upon the plush grasslands of Earth
For she began to ascend at once, through the ether and into the galaxy
Floating beside comets and constellations where she was always meant to be

Violetta's Witch Trial

Devil, sinner, demon, such hecklings were the litany of vilifying slanders
Screeched at the shackled Violetta; screamed into the disheartened skies
Libelous verses careened across wraithlike mist, spat from incensed lips
Wishing their words would spear her flesh as verbal bayonets of hatred
Violetta, with the essence of an enchantress, had been pitilessly hunted
Until her witchcraft proclivities were exposed by outraged townspeople
Who bore nonexistent cells of clemency amid their hypercritical hearts
Whose chests rippled with righteousness even as they thieved her away
Every resident believed Violetta exhibited the diabolical mark of Hades
Planted into this village as one of the *Dark Lords* cherry-picked servants
Thus, a witch trial was set into motion, yet a genuine hearing, it was not
For no lawful scales of justice were present to ensure impartial integrity
Not while the defendant was bound to what would be her funeral pyre
Sneered at by a biased jury who begged for a merciless verdict of death
No, this trial was merely unwarranted murder under the guise of justice
For Violetta's *clearly* hellish transgressions were not transgressions at all
And the only fiendish offense was the prejudiced act of her persecution

Violetta, a *mending, melodious witch,* never beholden to any satanic idol
Delicately uttered harmless healing incantations upon her mystical altar
Until the moment she was spotted—her haven of magic intruded upon
At once, Violetta was abducted, labeled a heretic without any hesitation
Regarded as if she brandished a terminal javelin within her taboo palms
Rather than the ethereal aura she *actually* held amid her gentle anatomy
How heartless that Violetta was chided for using what streamed within
Granted unto her kaleidoscopic circulation by the kindhearted cosmos
Even when Violetta practiced her witchcraft and looked on with respect
No worship or wonder found Violetta, *no*—only denigration transpired
Violetta mused, with the welts of inequality defacing her feminine spirit
That those targeted and criminally tyrannized were practically all *women*
If men exposed themselves as warlocks, their judgments would be slight
For it was women that were expected to never exert any extra influence
Or, more accurately, women were never supposed to wield any control at all
But men, men were born with power, and should they attain more of it
Should they partake in wizardry—most would be pronounced innocent
Never to meet the blazing fates of their wives and sisters and daughters

In the heart of a remote forest strewn with mushrooms and mayflowers
This sweet mage was impatiently secured to a sorrowful weeping willow
Who would wail on Violetta's behalf when her own tears would not fall
A grassy tree whose bark would resentfully act as reprehensible kindling
Aghast at humanity yet rooted in mud, it had no choice but to comply
Then, a match was ignited, a flame was thrown, and Violetta's finale began
Despite the escalating inferno, Violetta's composure did not once falter
Even when her flesh changed into a horrid collage of blisters and burns
And though her body was set alight—embraced by a scorching hellhole
Her abating soul *finally felt free* from their abusing manacles of loathing

As Violetta melted, her eyes grew as blackened as acrid fumes in the air
While a grievous curse determinedly tumbled from her raw, singed lips
For if her pursuers believed Violetta's powers to be cloaked in darkness
Then by the magic of her hex, so too, in obscurity shall they forever live
If they so wished to behold Violetta as an evil enchantress of corruption
Then she would guarantee that the morose portrait of pain *they* painted
The chilling exhibition of her form boiling upon a stake *they* tied her to
Skin unbearably liquifying from a fire *they* lit with their very own hands
All that agony would be the last sight their pitiless irises would ever see

Thus was Violetta's hex, armored by the witchcraft of wronged ancestors
Who understood the desire for vengeance in the wake of such brutality:

Submerge my hands in cement and strangle my throat with solid chains
Bind my bones, shred my flesh, raid my blood until empty are my veins
But strip away my freedom, impede my mouth from speaking my spells
And hear my maddened moans, like the sinister rebounds of death bells
Scald my body, let flares sear my skin until skin it no longer seems to be
Embolden my oppressors to stand atop my ashes beneath the willow tree
Stain their feet with the morbid grime which was once my beating heart
Let smoke blind their eyes; let cinders clog their lungs until they depart
History—repeat yourself by burning them alive, just as they burned me
Bind this hex to their skeletons, just as they bound mine with cruel glee
Let the torrid effects of these lyrics trail my foes into expiry and beyond
As an undying punishment for the unforgivable trial they once spawned

Maenad
Festivity
Raspberry
Wine
Raspberry
Wine

Maenad Festivity

Follow the footpath to the timberland revelry and indulge in the divine
With liquefied mouthfuls of nectar and sour swigs of raspberry wine
Heed the melody of merriment dripping from the cadence of this spell
Let this charm transport you to a wanton festivity—as wayward as hell
Where dedicated maenads will muse over Dionysus, their drunken god
Shedding their integrities of innocence like the skin of a snake so broad
Wander inside this frantic forest—let your soul swallow the seeds of sin
As you revel in the lustful bacchanal, where orgiastic ecstasy lies within

Deep inside the stomach of these moonlit woods—a Bacchic sanctuary
Maenads part their painted mouths to excessively imbibe treacly spirits
Licking the uplifting juice of the gods from their swollen, reddened lips
Ballads spewing from the lungs of feverish females flood the atmosphere
Hankering for hedonism, the attendees relinquish their pure inhibitions
Swaying their slackened bodies and sawing open their walloping hearts
Until the cathartic liquor of inebriation seeps out like tides of liberation
Then, as the saga of night persists and the demons of perdition awaken
Molecules of air turn animalistic—as whispers transform into screeches
What started as an eventide celebration within these flowered meadows
Befalls an episode of folly, as dissolute dancing turns into avid sprinting
While otherworldly reverberations of hellish chants follow in their wake
Calm touches upon flushed faces, affable massages upon tense shoulders
Become eager palms steered by need, seizing throats and grasping waists
Translucent gowns are stripped from impassioned flesh steeped in sweat
Lips sultrily wrap around carafes of berry-flavored wine, goblets ignored
Eventually—the maenads crash to their knees upon the lush forest floor
Intending to decadently inhale the perfume of aromatic primrose petals
Though, the fragrance is not sufficient, urging them to rip the roots out
Before ladling wildlife down their throats, moaning over the floral taste
Gliding soiled flowers down their esophagi, like sliced segments of fruit
Chewing upon worms as if they are dusted in a patina of pleasing sugar
Tempted by Dionysus, everything seems enameled in a sheen of honey
Sweet enough to require more, sticky enough that they cannot yet leave
Soon, the spell will break, and the forest will become vacant once more
Maenads will gawk at the love marks of this bacchanal upon their flesh
Itching for *more*, never to feel content until the spell regales them again

CURSE OF THE
BLACK STAR
SAPPHIRE

Curse of the Black Star Sapphire

Sequence after sequence of titanium lies linked within a cohesive chain
Lying atop your sternum—cradling an ornament of black star sapphire
As inky as the pupils of a meerkat until light waves reveal a gold center
Replicating the stellar contours of aureate stars decorating the universe
Not gaudy nor garish—simply as mesmerizing as a radioactive asteroid
Swimming within a lake of onyx, the starburst silhouette exudes luxury
Rivaling any supplemental gemstones, outdoing opals and garnets alike
Even still—you cannot recollect how this necklace appeared in your life
Any memories of the merchant and the market have eerily disappeared
And yet, surges of certainty fill the air, intoning what you will not voice
Decisively singing that this elegant piece of jewelry is not what it seems
For the blackened sapphire upon your flesh is far more than just lovely

All those who gaze upon the necklace become fascinated by its grandeur
Reaching out their beguiled hands in a stupor—undeterred by etiquette
Pining to fold their fingers over the jewel, to hold it close to their hearts
Operating only on impulse, their skin slightly brushes against the stone
Until upset lungs pluck out a scream, for they have been burned—*badly*
As if the pendant is sopping with poison—meant to blister bold thieves
Chastised and charred, they bolt with as much speed as their feet allow
Though, worry not, for the chain and its charm would never singe you
For you are their owner, you just do not yet know that *they own you too*

Upon one normal night, you elect to polish the pendant with precision
Yet, the necklace sharply resists when you attempt to unclasp the chain
Instead of slackening, the spelled jewelry squeezes, almost alarmingly so
As the pendant urgently stays in place, like it wants to excavate beneath
To drill a hole in the center of your neck, to forever attach itself to you
And while the gem never sears your complexion, for you are no burglar
It does do everything it can, while weeping within, to devotedly remain

Banish any ideas of removal from your mind—for nothing else matters
Not the mislaid memories, nor the torrid toxins, or the relentless chain
So long as you detect the black star sapphire caressing your collarbones
All will be alright, for your necklace whispers to you that this will be so

Sisterly Coven of the Stars

Embarking on a lone, celestial path through life, mages remain resilient
With bushels of competence embossed into their introverted existences
No guide nor guardian is needed to hold their hand through life's traps
For their sorcery clings to them, thawing their flesh in the isolated dark
Acting as a defensive shield, from natural disasters to errant individuals

Though, there is something undeniably unstoppable in the sheer power
Belonging to the mages who crochet the outline of their sorcerous souls
Into the tissue of each other's tendons—manacling them to their magic
Certifying lifelong connections thanks to the powers of their vast coven

Mantras fall from open lips and rise to gauzy clouds, fusing their bond
Promising with primordial tongues to persist as loyal sisters of the stars
As their stanzas cement themselves into the stratosphere, sparkling afar
In accord, the mages gasp as one—for their coven is sublimely finalized
Humming hearts embroidered together harmonize with palpable relief
As the magic within their arteries tangos in impeccable synchronization
Bodies are united by shatterproof sorcery, and spells are liberally shared
Now wedded by the officiant of witchcraft, the coven takes to the skies

One hundred mages circumnavigate this arched word of such suffering
Overhearing the evocative wails of women shoved into larva-laden soil
Held down by misogynistic hands, then left to decay amid the wet dirt
Maltreated by aggressive men whose mouths lather when submitted to
Men who ladle mud down throats to suppress the screeches they incite
Who strangle and suffocate until only the refrains of stillness fill the air
Even without magic, these weeping women are still bound to the coven
For their spirits, mortal or mage, are all covered in the same weary scars

By the powers we possess, we recite this spell to the winds of the west
Until our voices emerge from the mist as a serenade for the oppressed
As our words detonate like warnings to hordes of malice-minded men
Women will perceive our supernatural melody—never to be silenced again
Earthly mortals—feel perpetually embraced by the guidance in our song
For the charms of this coven of sisters forever land right where they belong

Venus's Incantation

Backlit by the blood moon's striking radiance amid this scarlet nightfall
Devotedly cry out to the syrupy heart within Venus—besotted divinity
Prepare vintage goblets of blackcurrant gin and valued crystals of finery
Sanction these offerings to seduce her godly spirit with loyal femininity
Enchanting spell—avalanche pails of amorous energy into my anatomy
Until Venus, a perfect icon of love, liberates me from life's loveless cage

Embraced by the galvanizing winds within the brief month of February
Find me lazing underneath an olive tree, counting the diminutive fruits
While plaiting baby's breath petals into my chin-length curls of espresso
Pushing a puckering goji berry past my lips, sucking upon the ripe juice
Letting the fluid infiltrate my circulation like infusions of tart sweetness
Setting ten pomegranate seeds, vivid in crimson color, upon my tongue
Crunching each one between my teeth, then swallowing them all down
Peacefully admiring the bursting explosions and the succulent aftertaste
Hopeful the flavor will jumpstart my static heart like a sour defibrillator
Readying my fruit-filled bloodstream—so this pining potion may begin

Track my idyllic actions as I gather a menagerie of heartfelt components
Placing them into my flaxen wicker basket, woven by proficient witches
Listed are the passionate ingredients I harvest, like a farmer of romance:
Flasks of snapdragon sap to sugarcoat the sentimental lining of my soul
Seven dozen amber droplets of honey, so affection may stick to my skin
Rose quartz gems to inject blushing love into the fibers of my ligaments
Lilac vines of wisteria, so the floral scent of attraction imbues my atoms
White gardenia dew to ensure this charm's powers will eternally prosper

Nearly finished, now I dispense the requirements into a translucent vial
Shaped to mimic the silhouette of my most emotional, enamored organ
Slicing into the flesh of my palm, I carve a path down my pulsing wrist
Dribbling out sickly blobs of plasma as the remaining essential element
Watch on as I trickle the potion down the valleys of my thirsting throat
Modifying my body into a pleasurable vessel for adoration to slink into
Until Venus spares a glance toward this verdant kingdom and heeds my cries
And my aching ears rejoice as I harken the lilting notes of love—at long last

Rarefied Ring of Magic

Welding late into the witching hour—illuminated by roasting firelights
An artistic coven, a quintet of creative mages, craft an esoteric talisman
A glorious ring with a woven band of caramel—framed with gemstones
With a priceless pearl in the center, shucked from a supernatural oyster
Still slippery from seawater, surrounded by a circlet of dainty diamonds
Bracketing the opaline treasure—reside identical jewels of precious jade
Like twinkling spheres of bottled moss, praising the pearl with sincerity
Below a curved moon, the coven instills the gems with a bead of blood
Until every stone is bewitched—streaming with mage's coalesced auras
Mortals fortunate enough to glide this exceptional ring onto their flesh
Will ascertain the unique magic of five pouring through their own veins
For every mage hemorrhages cells of different shades and diverse strains
Promising that no matter which finger the jewelry is finally fitted upon
A novel gift will be granted—for these powers are now theirs to possess

Rest the ring upon your first finger and be relieved of attempts at aging
Remain as you are—full of life, free of lines, as fresh-faced as a seedling
A breathing wishing well of youth, whose revitalizing waters are infinite
Move the ring onto your second finger and guard your vulnerable mind
Shield your pliant brain matter from being swindled by devious sinners
Until illicit objectives and malevolent illusions are barred entry, forever
Transfer the ring onto your third finger and preserve your fragile bones
Adorn unseen armor saving you from the displeasure of physical injury
Ensuring that flesh will never be flogged and skin will never be stabbed
Skate the ring onto your fourth finger and obtain impervious immunity
Unaffected by detrimental sicknesses, untouched by abhorrent ailments
Never to be disease-ridden by viruses, never to grow fevered by plagues
At last—relocate the ring upon your last finger and acquire immortality
An offering imparted upon your spirit and indorsed upon your skeleton
Never to fall into the rancid arms of death—so long as the ring remains

Medley of mages, peering into pupils of mortals with imperative intents
Searching stupefied stares for the true essence within their secular souls
Passing their creation to worthy candidates—only one every generation
Guaranteeing that their efficient protection never withers away to waste
For their powers will stay alive through the eternal relic of this rare ring

Lilith
Lilith

Unholy Tempest of Lilith

Oh, Lilith, manipulative maiden of hell, malevolent author of monsters
Listen to this incantation, dripping with sorrow, with an agreeable heart
For my flesh glows from within as if I had long ago swallowed sunlight
And the ensuing sparkle has steadily escaped my bones, no longer jailed
Yet, the luster upon my soul and the specks of innocence upon my skin
Offer no comfort, for their touch only mimics the stinging bite of a bee
As these hexed lyrics leave my lips, throw me into a cauldron of impiety
Until I ascend from the waters dipped in the wretched essence of sulfur
Finally freed from the glistening varnish I could not escape on my own
Beatific no more, my obsidian horns of sin would be enticed to emerge
Just as my brain, screaming for sin, would be enabled to indulge, at last
Lilith, think back to your own tale, let it inspire your inclination to help
Let me reject the oppressing light I have carried within for far too long
Hold my hand as I step into your sphere of endless evening—evermore

Before, femininity followed Lilith faithfully within the Garden of Eden
As satin, the hue of jasmine, clung onto her divine figure of enticement
Yet—Lilith was never naïve, never sacred in spirit or virginal in practice
As her ethereal gown, lined with yarns of purity, would wrongly suggest
Flasks of virtue and saplings of subservience had doggedly evaded Lilith
For no gentleman nor god nor ghoul was ever worthy of her obedience

Upsetting those with devout auras, an unmerited expulsion was decreed
Ejecting Lilith from the sanctuary of Eden, prompting her to transform
Shattering her pristine façade, only to be displaced by dim dissoluteness
Girlish features darkened from her surge of rage like an unholy tempest
As if her eviction also banished any locks of luster she had veiled within
Lilith ceded to the immoral mountains of evil she dreamt of embracing
Shifting into something so diabolical, even death convulsed in her wake
Revitalized as a demon, Lilith slunk into her wicked skin—a flawless fit
Becoming the Queen of Hell, Lover of Lucifer, and Mother of Demons

Beneath the bloodstained glow of the underworld, Lilith listens intently
Assuming the role of a grim genie, heeding wishes echoing from beyond
Granting dire pleas fortified with the hollow ache of undiluted *wanting*
For she understands the seductive call of darkness better than any other

Healing Invocations

While a capacious gash mutilates mortal muscles, leaking liters of blood
Shape this spell with a desperate tongue, let it tumble from magical lips
Vocalize these words any hour of any night, whether bitter or blistering
For lacerations never do cater to the confines of witchcraft instructions
Engage this charm as often as needed, for mages are meant to be whole
Never destined to whimper from wounds, to be ensnared and sundered
Never to be injured at all, for such hurt is a hex meant only for mortals
Prepare a magical paste, guiding the stomach-turning gushing to a close
Within a marble mortar, blend together lavender and lunar moth wings
Add in thirteen azalea petals, seven pixie eyelashes, four magnolia seeds
Stir with a wearied wrist, then throw in the thorns of an enchanted rose
Combine until the spelled substance changes into the hue of blueberries
Press the paste into areas torn open, sanction it to saturate harmed skin
Let the mending threads upon the mystical spool of witchcraft triumph
Regard dire slashes being sealed, and release a gratifying breath of relief
For all pain will perish, terminating like the last breaths of a dying spirit
Just as the evidence that there was ever any injury dispels into the ether

When a body is infected with a malady mortal medicine cannot remedy
Chant this invocation upon the muggiest eve amid the summer solstice
When the moon sits low on the horizon, serenading us all into slumber
As the warmth of the waning sun endures—like a keen rotisserie of fire
For this fraught spell demands all the smoldering heat it can apprehend
To scorch away the sickness clinging onto vital organs with lethal claws
Concoct a potion within a crystalline chalice gifted by preceding mages
To start, sprinkle in a tenuous sifting of crushed chrysanthemum pollen
Then nine droplets of nymph tears and one decanter of peppermint oil
Finish with a dosage of elderberry syrup to conflate everything together
Mix until the magic becomes as intimidating as a midair concrete block
Imbibe the potion at a lethargic pace—as if demise does not loom near
Let every ounce putrefy the virus persecuting an enchantress's existence
With a stomach full of witchcraft, sense the illness begin to slither away
Close this spell feeling restored, revived, and healthier than ever before

Witchy Women

Shuddering from the harmonies of mages humming beneath our blood
Let this invocation lurch from our gaping mouths in a fracturing flood
Birthed from the seeds of genuine sorcery, we will flower upon this eve
Binding our bones to rare tendrils of magic which will never thus leave
We will revere our witchcraft until our hearts no longer resolve to beat
Returning to the granular sands we sprung from, a final fate bittersweet
We petition you to regard the librettos of witchery we perpetually speak
For the daughters of enchantresses may dispense the comfort you seek

Upon this Earth, females are goddesses, originating from buttery clouds
Reincarnated into deities with precious powers infusing their anatomies
And sunshine circlets beaming off their complexion like a cherub's halo
Pray at their altars like you beg your false gods; prepare to be awakened
Consider them as saccharine sorceresses, idolize them as they so deserve
Deceive them with treacherous words, if you wish to decimate your life
For exquisite mages, they may be—but carelessly forgiving, they are not

Born from the trenches of mystic mud, blessed with an olden grimoire
Metallic powder sweeps across their eyelids like smatterings of starlight
Cataracts of glowing locks, exquisitely lacquered, fall down their spines
Feminine idols convey such unaffected power within their cosmic lungs
With each respiration, their inhalations and exhalations dispense magic
Lips execute eternal choreographies, reciting invocations with certainty
Power ruptures from their mouths, billowing onto the backs of breezes
Wishing to pinpoint the utopian skin of mages living both near and far

All witches are united by the charms they carry—like ethereal reminders
For sorceresses are sisters—wedded not by plasma but by understanding
Of what it means to walk this weary world as a woman unlike any other
Sublime witchcraft will encircle the spirits of their descendants to follow
Ensuring that no woman will ever live a life void of the essence of *magic*

666
666
Bargaining
Demon
666
666

Bargaining Demon

Amid a seraphic realm, hardhearted divinities claim it cannot be true
Leaving only the psychopathic demons below for stubborn souls to turn to
In awful need, hike to the cordial angels above, watch them all turn away
Though, this being of bartering, when summoned, will never dare stray
Appearing as this spell is stated, coasting through realms like an alderfly
Aiding with a dose of hellish humanity when others would not even try
Speak of this demon, and he will appear, though never as a lover or peer
For when the deal goes through, soul now stolen, he will swiftly disappear

Wheelbarrows of fear ooze from the sieve-like pores of those in hysteria
Hazarding the anger or assistance of a reprehensible bargaining demon
For no mortal nor divinity nor mage would consider their propositions
Until the only option seems to be the beckoning of this haggling being
Soberly cognizant that one must never summon with a cavalier attitude
For anything the demon may concede to will come at a harrowing cost

Once uttered, the spell cannot slope back down their contrite esophagi
For the crypt of their destiny is decisively locked as the demon surfaces
Soon, their hollowed-out skeletons, nostalgic for all they will relinquish
Will be bereft of a soul, bearing an abridged lifespan, bereaving vitality
But still, the bidding begins, *for desperation remains an incurable disease*
When the floras of midnight blossom, these individuals start their spell
Intoning their lyrics with resolve as the atmosphere grows inauspicious
Until Satan's spawn answers their call, all too willing to heed their pleas

Extricated from the dim haven of the netherworld, the demon emerges
Draped in smolders of ill-omened incense, as alarming as a trio of sixes
Patiently, he listens to lengthy petitions, though they all sound the same
For mortal desires are unremittingly material, unrelentingly sentimental
Merely trifling wishes, meriting not an iota of sympathy within demons
And yet, these supplications are repeatedly permitted with permanence
As demons slyly receive the superior end of the deal—every single time
And when the summoners wail, realizing the weight of all they wagered
Bargaining creatures from a disreputable domain never wipe their tears
For they are heathens at heart and have already helped *more than enough*

Moonlit Mistress

Women scorned when breathing being spirits incentivized when buried
Whenever gluttonous hands—just like the talons of a predatory falcon
Capture the flesh of one who no longer craves the feeling of their touch
Destined they become, forced to bear the chastising weight of penance
Perched upon their souls like acidic reminders of their abuse, evermore
Enter the *Moonlit Mistress*, towed from the embrace of this grassy realm
Heaved into the custody of death, inundated by an ambiance of demise
For her time on Earth was trimmed by the influential fates far too soon
Slashing her thread of life with decisive scissors of finality in one sharp swipe

Often, the mistress finds herself reflecting upon her curtailed existence
In bursts of bruises and snapshots of torment—like a short film of woe
Over time corporeal tears have fossilized into droplets of pure titanium
Reminders of the metallic heart she now holds within her spectral soul
A motionless organ—fortified in indestructible alloys of determination
A weighty reminder of all she had stomached amid her fleeting lifespan
And all she will accomplish in the afterlife, affected by ethics, no longer
Transparent she may be—yet her intentions are welded in spiteful steel
For if her pulse could twirl again, it would sway to the tune of payback
After suffering so severely, there is nothing the mistress will not endure
Nothing she will not encounter in order to reap her unresolved revenge
Just as the detached reaper of termination had seized her mortal vitality

Before death—when sunlight bathed her secular flesh with tropical heat
Her lover's aura grew as pitiless as the mythic hydras inhabiting the seas
With abrasive touches and humiliating degradations, she fell out of love
Determined to leave—lest she remain in his caustic clutches any longer
But, before she had the opportunity, her lover, feeling jilted, acted first
Rabid from rejection, he lunged, speedily ending the life of the mistress
With only the muscle of his palms held against her asphyxiating jugular
The Moonlit Mistress was thus birthed as an inhuman witch of reprisal
Luxuriating in retribution—for how can her blood ever decide to settle
If the presence of indulgent vengeance does not saturate her irate mind
Disturbingly jarring is now the only way to explain the lilt of her laughs
Chiming throughout the hillsides as she launches her haunting sessions

Seething with sentiments of vindicated rage and passionate anticipation
The Moonlit Mistress deftly curates a distinguishing wardrobe in death
Fitting of her newfound liberation, filled with racy garments she adores
Draped in sensual nightgowns of sheer chiffon and bloodred-lined lips
All the things her murdering paramour of the past would have detested
But now, this wraithlike beauty finds freedom in the domain of demise
Bathing in the grim afterglow of expiration, the mistress hunts with glee
Toying with the sadistic emotions of others who flaunt scathing essences
Pulling on icy heartstrings until they bend to her will or until they *snap*

Every eve—the mistress gazes upon shining constellations of the zodiac
As she brushes her rosy strawberry-blonde locks at least ten dozen times
Conscious that the only hands able to sense the soft texture are her own
At ease, knowing none will pull upon her ponytail until her roots throb
Untouchable by the armor of demise, the mistress will never ache again
Now, she looks toward those whose vile crimes fall upon unseeing eyes
And unheeding ears, before marching out to do what the living cannot

Primed and vulnerable from her stalking benders, her victims are ready
Under the brilliance of the moon and the inaudible support of the stars
The atmosphere begins to shiver from the frigid laments of poltergeists
As the Moonlit Mistress wordlessly steps out of the shadows and *strikes*
Slaying like a feral cougar—breathing easier with every butchered body
Targeting those whose palms are marinated in the lifeblood of females
Swiftly hindering them from hurting anyone else in this life or the next
Taking her time because now, alive no longer, she has nothing but time

Though her objectives are merciful, her exterminations are anything but
Employing supernatural artilleries, like pliers dipped in sparks of hellfire
And axes doused in basilisk venom, initiating agony before annihilation
Unleashing the full intensity of her magical ministrations upon them all
Feeling warranted in her actions, only doing what she deems is essential
For so rarely and with such rash injustice are those with depraved cores
Given a taste of their own medicine, feeling the same fear they inflicted
The Moonlit Mistress strives to right these wrongs, one corpse at a time

Recipe for Remembering

Desperate, dazed, and desolate, sequester a sprig of evergreen rosemary
Hoping the herbal fragrance will finally bring my memories back to me
Something sentimental is buried within the padlocked traps of my mind
Let me uncover what lies within my hippocampus, what I yearn to find
Let moths never flee from their cocoons until my reminiscences reappear
Unearthing spell, gift me my memories and let this fog of amnesia clear

Mislaid memories resurface within the porous membranes of my mind
In an enlightening rainstorm of recollection, swelling my besieged skull
Meaningless has been my existence—exterminated of my stowed secrets
Only as they are released by a master key of mercy, unraveling like yarn
Does my purpose renew, injecting my life with a dosage of importance
Thunderstruck brain trapped within a typhoon of exposed experiences
Overworked and overheated from treading whirlpools of remembrance
Lost conversations and lasting caresses flock to me like thirsty parasites
As sensations of elapsed touches and neglected voices mollify my spirit
While I etch my salvaged recalls into the platelets of my maroon blood
Spotting my memories gliding inside my veins, never again to elude me
Never again able to withdraw to an inaccessible junction of my intellect
And though they ache while fitting back into the forefront of my brain
At least this excruciating acidity assures me of their heartening presence
Now restored to the cerebral position where they shall endlessly remain

Even if my intentions were to change amid an uncharacteristic evening
Tempted by the feeling of forgetting for reasons inexplicably unknown
Nothing may be done, for found memories endure, altered aims or not
As if one were to fuss with their flesh until jewels of plasma materialize
Only to smear the scarlet liquid along their cuticles in a desperate effort
Urging the blood to seep underneath their skin—as if it was never freed
I will not, it would speak; *I have left and can never return*, it would sing
For their cells would be a different shape, a different silhouette entirely
Unable to enter through the grisly wound that they once escaped from
Just as their blood cannot go back in, my memories cannot go back out
For this bout of remembering has renovated my soul, my heart, my life
Leaving me as a changed person, one who, thankfully, knows *everything*

Herbal Sorcery

Below ambers oceans of brewed teas—all honeyed seas and herbal surfs
Divine leaves of ochre oracles uncover themselves to sorceresses in need
Mages concoct beverages of insight, employing enlightening ingredients
Situated inside ceramic teacups glazed with ivory lacquers, marble-hued
Beautified with baked artworks—diminutive in size, saccharine in status
Depicting pleasing floras from forget-me-not petals to periwinkle leaves
In the kitchen, boiling kettles shriek as if haunted by unruly poltergeists
Strands of steam levitate from the sweltering waters like volcanic smoke
Mages meticulously decant the liquid before stirring in their mix of teas
Floral hibiscus to encourage Aphrodite-inspired sentiments of romance
Brisk mint for sober clarity and restful chamomile for medicinal healing
Ending with crystalized sugar cubes for success, like cloying snowflakes

Brewed with purpose, mages sip deeply to reveal their pending destinies
Tasting the pleasing tea upon their craving tongues, savoring their tonic
Licking their enchanted lips until the base of their cup creeps into sight
Ready to embark upon a session of witchcraft with routines and charms
Reverentially placing their teacups into their left, most perceptive, palm
Executing their rites until delectable dregs of data are ready to examine

Botanic bouquets imply bountiful luck, both in dealings of life and love
Angelic swans signify delicate elegance and tranquil sessions of serenity
Sharpened knives suggest deception from the cutting blades of betrayal
Ripe pears indicate unlimited wealth, for such trees prosper perennially
Mages gaze upon these advisory emblems, deciphering their divinations
Heeding the truthful forecasts steeped in the herbal sorcery before them
Before murmuring this encouraging spell of prophecy in humble tones:

As inquisitive witches, we permeate this brew with our prodigious powers
Until the telling tea leaves rain down upon our minds like intuitive showers
And if the answers we anticipated within our cups are nowhere to be found
We worry not—for the tea's magic will find our hearts like a sleuthhound
Whether tracking us within waking life or greeting us within restful sleep
Epiphanies will seep into our souls, and honest intuitions we will reap

Reptilian Charmers

Mythical sisters of three whose hardhearted tresses teemed with venom
Whose petrifying irises turned skin into stone, inciting fossilized deaths
Such magic was the gift of the Gorgons—famed females from long ago
With reputations never to be swallowed by the expunging sands of time
For the serpentine ways of these sisters live on within their descendants
Women who inherited lissome snakes within their skeletons from birth
Known as serpent charmers, whose toxic den lies not within silky locks
But within their mouths, crawling over rosy gums, dwelling above teeth
Winding around tongues, slinking down tracheas, draping over tendons
Celebrating the bodies of the seducing sovereigns they merrily populate
For the anatomy of the Gorgons distant progeny are entirely hospitable
As the ancient powers passed on from generation to generation flourish
Resulting in forms so tolerant, the serpents whimper in welcoming bliss

If bestowed with a spearing needle of steel and a thimble of firm thread
Mortals would promptly seal the divine lips of these reptilian charmers
Ensuring the serpents remain eternally captive, irrevocably incarcerated
Lest they escape, commencing the reign of poisonous terror they desire
Even so, these coldblooded creatures were never meant to linger within
Knowing this to be true, the descendants unhinge their jaws—willingly
While mandibles detach, serpents catch transient wafts of external ether
Aromas of mango and rum and mud and rosemary trip into their senses
Goading the reptiles into wrestling their way toward an illuminated exit
With ruinous dexterity, they uncoil from lungs and livers and ligaments
Before decanting from their hosts' yawning mouths, hissing in harmony
Secreting viscid droplets of poison—a lethal promise of what is to come

Though the serpents do not devour mortals like mice, not straightaway
Initially, they prowl in pursuit, curiously studying the prey they so crave
Skidding in expert unison upon ridged scales while flaunting filed fangs
Doing only as their enthralling females ask of them, fondly submitting
Acting as devoted as the snakes who obeyed the historic Gorgon sisters
Hidden by overcast clouds, these descendants part their lips once more
Thrusting out forked tongues—while releasing faint hisses of their own

210

Spellbound Stardust

Earthly melancholy, marrow of my bones deprived of elysian allures
Heart I hold, shivering to the melody of mortality, probing for cures
Denied of divinity, dipped in normality, breathing an ephemeral life
Hallowed hands—guard and guide me, save me from my drab strife
Drench my weary skeleton in spellbound stardust amid lunar nights
Witchcraft idols, revise my aura, appease my otherworldly appetites
Marry me to numinous moonlight and unshackle me from this rage
Permeate my tongue with stellar tears and release me from this cage

Wring me dry, unravel my veins, donate my blood without emotion
Let my gouged arteries flood with the invocations in a mage's potion
Carve these goals into my secular skin—for it will soon sprout anew
And in its place, cosmic flesh will blossom, as decadent as honeydew
While I regale my spirit with an enchanting overture of transformation
Crooned by a poetic orchestra of charmed violas singing of liberation
Irreversibly altered, I become, although my powers remain restricted
Boiling within my new body, magic lies in wait, dolefully constricted
Sorceresses have siphoned their essences into the cavities of my mind
But, the answer of how to relinquish it into my palms, I cannot find

Search my skull for the scent of spells—return dizzy from the aroma
And yet—my gifts do not scramble to the surface, caught in a coma
Expose my talents to the ether until my inhuman passions are sated
Devastate these bodily boundaries, so I may claim all I have awaited
Hoist the arduous hammer of the grand god of thunder, and swing
Belabored bones shatter from the impact—hailing the ensuing sting
Exorcise my entrails, massacre my muscles, trounce my pliant brain
Flutters of pain—hurtle through my abnormal flesh like a hurricane
Until my magic is freed, at last—unlocked by the persuasion of pain
Rolling from my skin, descending like transcendent droplets of rain
Rampant with power—appendages are repaired, organs are rectified
Mortal to mage, my despair has expired, my worldly tears now dried

Nyx, Goddess of Night

Electrifying twilight ether reacts only to Nyx—crucial goddess of night
Embodying dusk skies, as nocturnal and noxious as pinching scorpions
Eclipsing the blinding waves of sunlight and asphyxiating afternoon air
Obscuring the effects of her darling daughter, Hemera—goddess of day
Replacing the burning star of brilliance with the silver planet of serenity
Until time truly does fly by, soaring like a sparrow, and nightfall begins
Picture the winged deity of wicked hours with rare feathers of midnight
And bittersweet brownie-hued curls cascading just like chocolate waves
Adorning an ascending halo of onyx, followed by a filmy cloud of sable
Traipsing around as an ethereal outline with the lissome gait of a gazelle

Offspring of Chaos, spawned with primeval power of the strongest kind
Even Zeus, famed Olympian god, trembles from both panic and respect
Always afraid and forever in awe of the essence of authority Nyx exudes
Mother to melancholic souls and monarch to gods of sleep, death, strife
Lover of Erebus, god of darkness—a seemingly fitting and fated couple
Infatuated as Nyx is—teeming with tender feelings of fawning romance
So too, does her soul grow fretful, beleaguered by vulnerable intrusions
Insecure of the notion that her powers rely so profoundly upon Erebus
For Nyx's night, strengthened by shadow, needs dire darkness to prosper
Though for Erebus, necessary it is not for the god to depend upon Nyx
For dimness may be constructed anytime, amongst solar or lunar hours
And it is this harrowing imbalance that heavily weighs upon Nyx's heart

Sensing her woe, for their spirits are united, Erebus pulls his lover close
Holding her near, folding a night-blooming moonflower behind her ear
Watching in worship as the petals flourish, blossoming for their master
Erebus consoles Nyx over her concerns—uttering that night is superior
For darkness is but an abyss of emptiness—while night encapsulates all
When dusk dawns, celestial spectacles of interstellar wonder materialize
For night draws out the iridescent moon and all her starburst followers
Creating a cosmic display of stellar amazement, if only until the sunrise
Comforted by Erebus's sentimental speech—Nyx's heart slackens at last
Banished are any lecherous doubts of insecurity, replaced by pure pride
Restored are Nyx's warmhearted affections for her soulmate of obscurity
For their love is as endless as nightfall's existence, *both dark and delicious*

Dark Arts

Atavistic witchcraft is not entirely pure in pursuit and pagan in purpose
Throughout imperiling lairs and inauspicious lands, black magic persists
Streaming with the fragrances of hexes, morbid souvenirs from sacrifices
And portraits of pentagrams written in plasma, drawn with toxic intents
Keen the consequences will be trivial in comparison to all they will gain
Wishing with brazen cruelty to disrupt the inherent scales of this world
Partaking in archaic rites by forfeiting carafes of blood and cuts of flesh
Amid the clock's nightfall hours, eyes roll like a duet of snake-eyed dice
Convening souls of late mortals, communing with errant goblins in hell
Those whose access into this empire should have forever been forbidden
And yet, when summoned—these spirits saunter into our terrestrial veil
With the bloodlust of a quarantined vampire left to starve for centuries
Invite these hellion entities with anarchic desires into our living domain
But beware—for black magic is affixed with a grave price one must pay
And the ensuing expense is stolen from your body and bones and brain
A debilitating fee with draining results—too steep to ever recover from
For the darkest of arts prove to be critically consuming when all is done
Look within, you must, to the caveats in your core, and fatefully decide
Which altruistic values and humane ethics would you divest yourself of
And which outcomes do you believe your mind and marrow could bear
In exchange for a taste of true supremacy—never to be felt superficially
No, seedlings of black magic transplant themselves straight into arteries
Of those who brandish such severe command within such gentle hands
Resulting in debts that cannot be paid with silver coins or saintly words
For the dark arts swipe and siphon far more than they ever give and gift
Partake only by muting the slice of your brain begging you to turn back
Imploring you with *urgency* to ruminate upon your neglected principles
Desperate for you to recall the pitfalls of expressing ancient spells aloud
Daring the earth to plug her ears, to ignore the spells you let slither free
And yet, dignity and decency do not dwell where black magic blossoms
Those who indulge in this demonic sorcery only hope for olden insight
From the occultists before them, trusting they will not lead them astray
But, black magic and the witches of before understand nothing of trust
Leaving those participating in this darkened craft entirely on their own
As rhymes lined with rebellion are spoken—never can they be reversed
Once intoned, black magic stains the ether *and* your existence—forever

WINDS MAY SWAY,
PETALS MAY DECAY,
YET BACK TO YOU,
I WILL ALWAYS
FIND A WAY

Imogen's Locket of Love

Sentimental sorceress, intoxicated from drunken charms of aching love
Never will there be a richer sensation or a sweeter formula of witchcraft
Than the hallucinogenic energy bounding off tides of amorous worship
Imogen embraces all feelings of infatuation, drowning in raw rhapsody
Like a solstice honeybee gulping exultant mouthfuls of botanical pollen
Every ardent language of love lures Imogen, like moths drawn to nectar
Spending time together, penning lovely letters, gifting garlands of irises
So long as these touching gestures stem from her star-granted soulmate
Imogen will praise them all, immortalizing the memories into her skull
Breathless from passionate thoughts—Imogen fashions a locket of gold
Sculpted into the saccharine shape of a heart, devised from dizzy desire
As pleasing to the eye as a private ocean rolling with tides of moonlight
Imogen's pendant suspends from a delicate chain coated in a ruby glaze
Displaying a garnet gemstone fused within the center of her dear locket
A romantic jewel to summon a starry-eyed spirit into her doting chakra
Imogen unhinges her piece of priceless jewelry, appreciating the interior
Lined with elegant white jade—to enrich the sugared nature of her aura
Imogen wishes to sense her companion's love humming against her skin
To enhance her locket with the true and treasured essence of his feelings
And so, the sorceress sings this spell, for a soul in love knows no bounds

Gaze into my undulating heart—dancing an emotive ballet of romance
Pirouetting for my fond paramour—an angel upon this Earth's expanse
Lovestruck deities, decant a drop of his devotion, cleave a sliver of his heart
Position them into my everlasting amulet of love, so we will never be apart

Imogen idyllically glows, now able to hold his prized heart so very close
As she strokes a finger over her invaluable pendant, as she so often does
Her flesh dreamily detects the maudlin engraving etched onto the back
Winds may sway, petals may decay, yet back to you, I will always find a way
If Imogen ever unclasps her necklace from her nape, his love will linger
Wholly uninterested in evading, for as much as she covets his closeness
His heart equally *needs* their proximity, fearing he may expire without it
Just as aquamarine mermaids never drift too far from their rippling seas
For sincere sagas of romance crave an unearthly type of divine intimacy
Which *only* this gilded locket of rare enchantment may tenderly provide

Elite Valkyries

What a violent vision the Valkyries render upon battlefields of disorder
A barrage of worthy female warriors vigilantly selecting laudable bodies
To be given an exalted spot in Valhalla—the hall of slaughtered fighters
Vanquished bodies are assigned to the trustworthy care of these soldiers
Who deliver massacred souls with humble care despite their godly gifts

Though, upon arenas of butchery, Valkyries are ruthless and responsive
Like an agile pride of lionesses pursuing quarries within arid grasslands
Only the spirits of women could comprise such an elite unit of fighters
For they have had to brawl far before stepping foot upon the frontlines
Valkyries, much to the *disdain* of males, prove to be the apex of soldiers
With divinely enhanced skills of warfare both in combat and in strategy
Possessing a calm plethora of patience and a surplus of analyzed tactics
Resilient arms never hazard veering out with reckless and rash abandon
Just as sturdy soles never tread with impulsive and imprudent footsteps
Even though the Valkyries are equipped with breastplates and gauntlets
So, too, are their scheming craniums reinforced with barricades of brass
Halting any absentminded decisions from trespassing, daring to distract
Valkyries trot into battle upon gallant steeds, kicking up dirt and debris
Before dismounting with effortless ease, sliding from their mares hastily
Only to brazenly enlist in the turmoil of war with praiseworthy velocity
Fighting and filleting with the honorable synchronicity of sisters united
Displaying a valiant portrait of what primal feminine strength looks like

As Valkyries, we speak as one over the sounds of slaughter and savagery
We appeal to Bellona—bloodlust goddess of war with abilities legendary
Destructive divinity, watch on while we trudge past bodies black and blue
Hear the hollow thunders of our war drums—our song and spell to only you
Steady our hands and shield our hearts while we consume your vast powers
And always allow our enemies to falter amid these brutish wartime hours

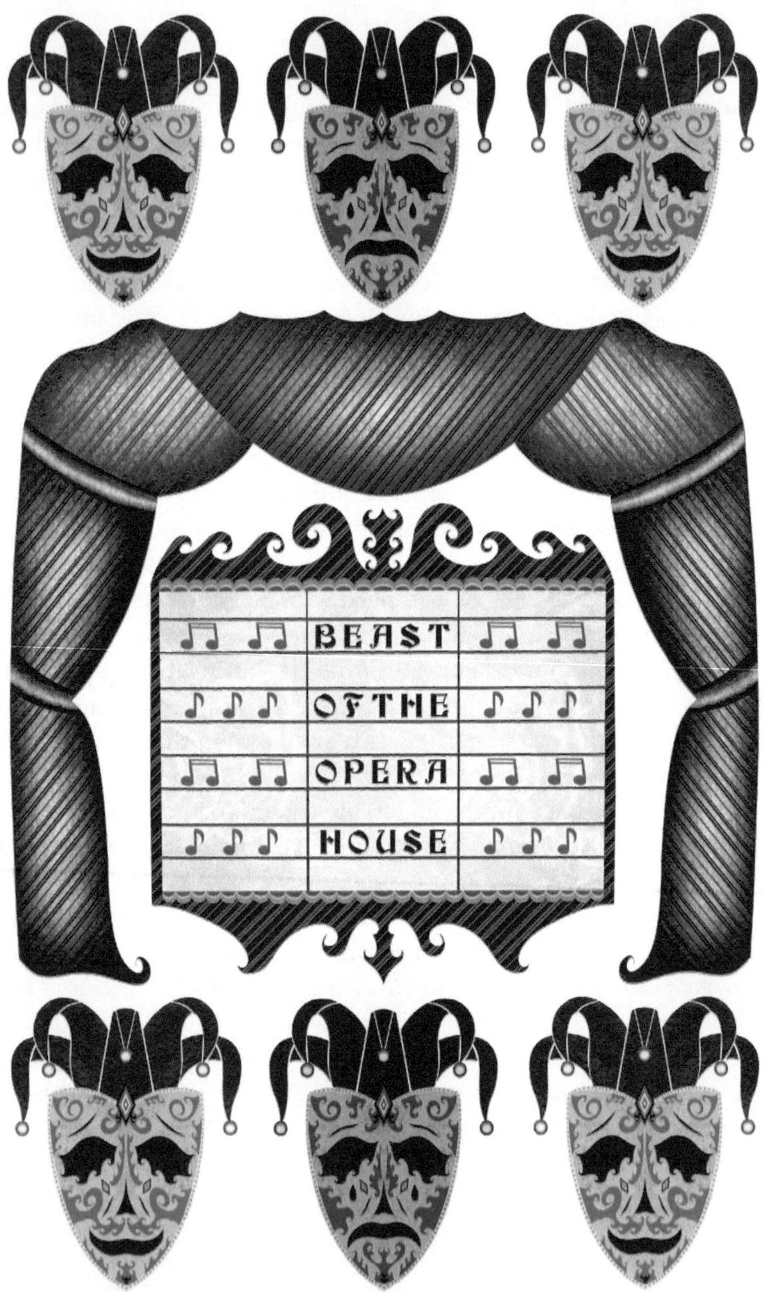

BEAST
OF THE
OPERA
HOUSE

Beast of the Opera House

The Music Box Opera House—situated in the theatrical heart of London
Where melodramatic performances haunt the halls like bawling specters
Within, opulence dominates, emitting grandiose extravagance in spades
Walls feature lavish dashes of golden leaves like affluent embellishments
Lofty ceilings portray renowned operatic tales brushed by artistic brains
Upholstered bloodred chairs affixed with velvet fabric yearn to be filled
Sweeping curtains pull back, only to ascend above in anticipatory hush
Exposing a stage so exquisite—thespian goddesses weep in appreciation
Backstage—baroque props and intricate backdrops are draped in taffeta
Only uncovered when the next opera is cast and rehearsals begin at last

Mere months ago, the opera house and its patrons were in breathless awe
Of their leading performer, Leo, a notable tenor with ceaseless charisma
Applauded for both his vulnerable tenderness and masculine attraction
For his vocal cords bore inexhaustible talents bathed in docile modesty
Urging Leo to imagine a lengthy life beneath the spotlights of his stage
While his virtuoso career prospered, a hostile hex fell upon the vocalist
Recited from the lips of a sorceress—laced with dregs of bona fide envy
Invoking the powers of witchcraft to turn this gentleman into a goliath
Henceforth, at the metamorphic stroke of dim midnight every nightfall
As the sentient moon watched on with unshed tears of empathetic woe
Leo was forced to transform—becoming a beast of deplorable notoriety
With a physique the size of a stag and the flesh of a feral, foaming boar
Only gifted the reprieve of this ghastly existence when sunlight ascends
Too scandalous to surface in the eve, too ashamed to appear in the day

Leo could never tolerate the notion of exiting the embrace of the opera
For the faint echoes of harmonious encores mollified his besieged spirit
And so, Leo beheld every recital from unfilled balconies veiled in shades
Enveloped by the silhouettes which took him in when no others dared
For the patrons and orchestra and performers had not fully spotted Leo
But they had heeded his howls and glimpsed his movements in the dark
Eventually, hours elapsed into days, just as weeks matured into months
Until prolific Leo, with melodious vocals and secular skin, was *forgotten*
And the nameless entity dawdling backstage before mournfully shifting
Became renowned only as the *Beast of the Opera House* from here on out

Before the devastation of his soul-crushing hex—Leo was avidly in love
Enamored with Juliet, the opera's prima donna, and a sparkling soprano
Leo idolized Juliet in the way deities praise even a dewdrop of ambrosia
With every learned libretto and practiced aria, their sentiments thrived
And when Leo vanished, Juliet mourned his loss like a bereaved widow
Amid her grieving—a message slid beneath Juliet's dressing room door
Urging the soprano to stay late at the opera house for an urgent matter
While reading with unease, the corset of her costume grew smothering
But, anxieties aside, Juliet knew she needed the heed the worrying note
And so, with admirable bravery, the elegant vocalist waited for nightfall
Until *finally*, with panicked mettle, Leo revealed himself to his soulmate

Though his figure was altered, his kindhearted irises remained the same
Allowing Juliet to identify Leo, her compassionate tenor—straight away
Juliet did not hesitate; *no*, she sprinted into his arms, sobbing with love
After many warmhearted minutes, Leo swayed Juliet in his doting hold
Lulling her waterworks while he clarified to Juliet the details of his hex
Hurriedly amending that he could not expose himself to her any sooner
For he feared Juliet's pending rejection, repelled by his twilight dilemma
And though Leo would have understood, for he nauseated even himself
The loss of her love would have anguished him far more than any curse
But then—Juliet reassured Leo of the undying nature of their romance
For she loved Leo in the light and would remain loving him in the dark

Juliet coaxed Leo out of the shadows they were huddled and hidden in
Hand in hand, she brought her beast onto the stage before taking a seat
Encouraged by Juliet's emboldening gaze, the prior star finally sang out
Projecting his idyllic voice as far as it could travel, weeping all the while
For though he appeared as a beast, his vocal talents had not evaporated
Overcome with affection for Juliet and for the opera house, Leo bowed
Juliet then leaped up, applauding as loudly and lovingly as she was able
Joining Leo where he stood, Juliet etched his name onto the stage floor
A way for his legacy to persist and for his presence to be felt beside her
When Juliet performed in the public eye that he could not bear to face
This troubled Leo not, for following every finale when all but Juliet left
Leo sang out to his love, back below the spotlight which missed him so

Zoya's Immortal Reign

Zoya, majestic ruler of verdant lands and grand monarch of misty skies
Multifaceted queen of many kingdoms—as imperial as she is immortal
With the beauty of a budding morning, tranquil yet outright tempting
Diplomatically exerting the sway of a goddess upon her emerald throne
Humbly adorning a royal circlet with a razor-thin band decked in gems
Starring freshwater pearls and amber jewels, like a mosaic of aristocracy
Noble crown—diminutive in size, though dearly beloved in reputation
Luxuriating upon the flesh of Zoya's temples—pinching ever so slightly
Triggering violent drops of gelatinous blood to slant down her forehead
Though the cherry gore upon her alabaster skin only enriches her grace
Granting Zoya an essence of stunning danger and splendorous delicacy

Diplomatic empress, presumed to adorn herself with wartime artilleries
And steel armor, protective in purpose though unsightly in appearance
Yet Zoya has no such need for shields or steels to prove her dominance
Throwing away thoughts of tradition—Zoya dresses in what she desires
Whether that be ballgowns with fitted bodices and excessive beadwork
Or slips of satin clinging to her curves with an unforgettable simplicity
Either way, these silken textiles trail behind Zoya like fashionable winds
As she glides with the sinuous gait of an eel through her medieval castle
Certain her dresses will slither right along with her, as loyal as any other

Amid her reign, Zoya shrouds her rivals underneath a cape of deception
Fooling every adversary into erroneously supposing that her supremacy
Is laced into her feminine façade of blushing glances and bashful grazes
When in truth, the queen's power is held within her Machiavellian mind
Talented at manipulating the feelings and cravings, and fears of mortals
And her self-confidence is contained within her duplicitous appearance
For the queen is skilled at shapeshifting, taking on any form she pleases
Emerging as an amphibious newt, a spotted leopard, or an airborne bat
But do not forget Zoya's compelling lips, lined with truth-telling magic
As well-spoken as the Bard of Avon—hypnotizing souls with her words
Capable of unearthing confessions from even the most reticent of rivals

Even Zoya's crown inaudibly speaks volumes concerning her conquests
For every inlaid gemstone was raided from the treasures of her enemies
Whose destitute lands she seized and whose trivial lives she slaughtered
Any who have come to unearth the enigmatic queen's unaffected nature
Treat Zoya with the deferential respect and discreet praise she warrants
As those who are never kept abreast—obliviously living in the shadows
Behold Zoya's beauty as her reigning attribute, never to learn the truth

Twisted around the queens tantalizing throat lies a serpentine necklace
Yet the jewelry was not hewn from gold nor silver—or any metal at all
Unbeknown to others, the reptilian figure atop Zoya's skin is authentic
A living and lethal viper wrapping around her neck like a scaled choker
Ages ago—Zoya believed just as much venom skated through her veins
If not a droplet more than the viper held himself, teeming with poison
Though, the toxins within the queen were produced through sheer will
By the innate influence bustling avidly within her dignified bloodstream
As the platelets in her plasma pleaded to alter into something poisonous
Something intimidating to keep her adversaries at bay and allies in line
And eventually, since the willpower of women is undeniably compelling
Zoya's blood mystically turned to poison, a novel blend of regal venom
Endowing the mortal queen with the everlasting present of immortality
Along with an imposing mind, shifting bones, and an influential mouth
Brimming with magic—Zoya beheld what would become her necklace
Using only her bare hands—the queen snatched the viper from the dirt
And knotted the serpent around her neck, where he would forever stay
Raptly recognizing Zoya—as if she was cut from the same coldblooded cloth

With a sense of submission that the viper had never before experienced
Soundlessly, the terminal being vowed never to harm Zoya—his savior
Pledging to remain reposing atop her skin as a piece of reptilian jewelry
Now, he watches the omnipotent queen rule over her ample kingdoms
Pleased that due to his ruler's immortality, steering her away from death
Zoya's almighty dominion of earth and ether will never come to a close

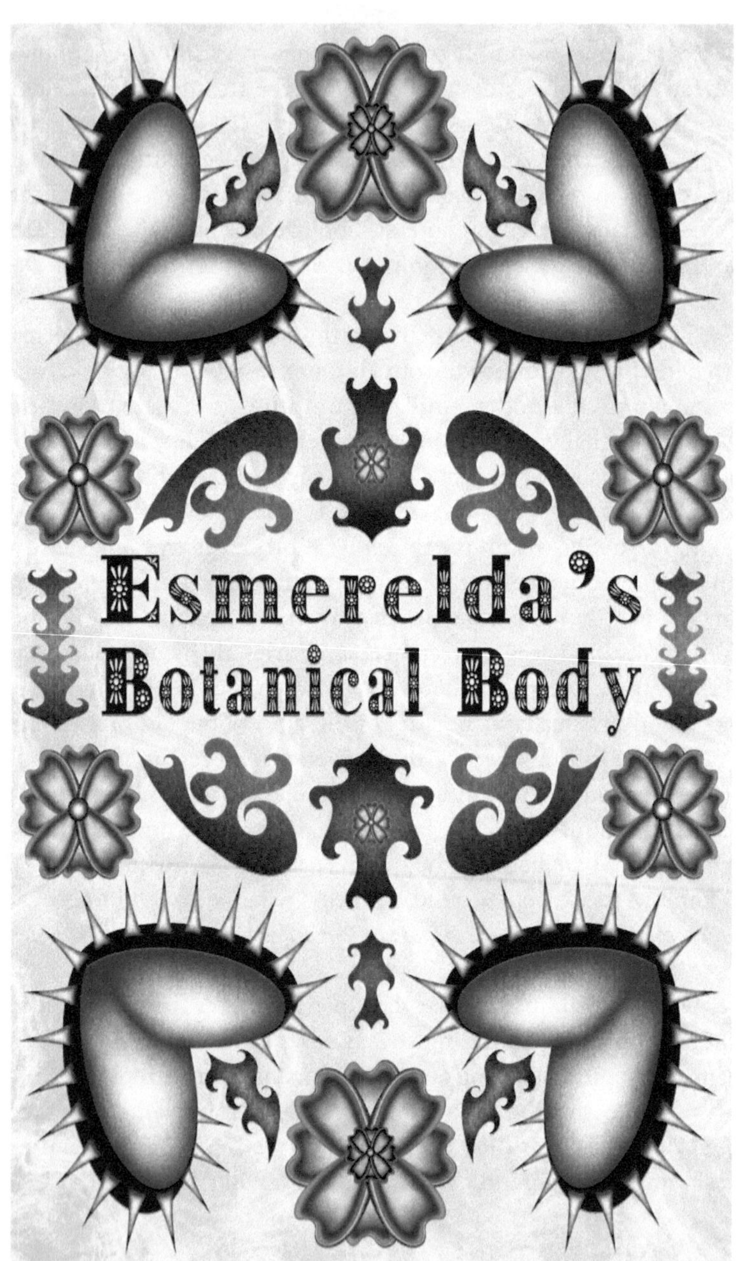

Esmerelda's
Botanical Body

Esmerelda's Botanical Body

Carnivorous lips of lethality whimper to be served their supper of flesh
Attached to the mouth of an ensnaring plant, the rapacious Esmerelda
Sprouted from fruitful roots with the botanical body of a Venus flytrap
Only beetle swarms and spider clusters pique the interest of her palette
Until the day her appetite for all insectile and arachnid creatures wanes
And so—Esmerelda looks toward mortals with the godsend of soft skin
Discovering a newfound craving—needing to sample their mortal zests
Esmerelda harnesses the abilities of witchcraft within her vegetal figure
Composing an enchantment, eager to adorn the garments of deception
To appear as all she has never been with an allure she has never known
Drawing inspiration and insight from ancient Apate, goddess of deceit
Whose sour tongue spewed candied words sheathed in gilded molasses
Esmerelda laces her spell with the duplicitous energy of her godly muse
Keen to emulate the illusionist aura of this disloyal deity within herself

Born as a Venus flytrap with an exterior unsightly and a spirit unappealing
  Conceal my murderous nature and let my intents be nevermore revealing
  Present my body with a glamour, to masquerade as a mortal with splendor
  Bearing such perfection, even heartless gods would fall into a love so tender
  Let me emerge as timid as a lamb so others do not fear me with eyes aghast
  Allow me to lure delectable victims near to appease my severe hunger at last

As the spell crochets itself over Esmerelda, veiling her teeth with magic
Flesh-eating features disappear, hidden under heaps of aesthetic appeal
Mouthwatering mortal men tread closer, urged by femme fatale powers
Inspecting her falsified body and her fabricated lips like forbidden fruit
For Esmerelda appears so seductive that even the bones of these victims
Would bend themselves blue until splintered, if only she commanded it
Esmerelda handles her fabricated beauty like a switchblade of attraction
Plunging it into the ribcages of those whose sight is entranced with lust
Permitting the Venus flytrap to finally get her fill of the flesh she needs
Ingesting her victims fully intact, Esmerelda leaves no evidence behind
Demoralizing screeches vibrate within the basin of her satiated stomach
Yet the roaring of her blood, surging with success, muffles their screams
While Esmerelda realizes that she will never consume a caterpillar again
For the naivety of tempted mortals has proven to taste *so* much sweeter

Evil Eye

Unblinking eyes attain enlightening knowledge from one clipped glance
Breaching superficial barriers of physical exteriors bearing insincere facts
Only to behold the interior pigment staining a soul—revealing raw data
Harnessing that illuminating information, triggering paranormal talents
Activating malignant powers encouraged by the foul vermin of jealousy
Welcoming greed into gouged sockets imparted with vindictive eyesight
Burdened or blessed with the ruinous capacity to inflict lasting torment
Curse of the evil eye: conveyed only through a wordless, nefarious glower
Brought on by the envious energy of those blinded by rays of bitterness
For if success or prosperity or splendor describes your fortuitous reality
So too, will you become susceptible to gaining the resentment of others
And after only one stare—saturated in the sorcery within these evil eyes
Any lucky roots of luxury will be plucked by the razing tweezers of ruin

For some, those who employ an evil eye cast their curses with intention
Deeply pining to be a bystander to the cataclysmic downfall they rouse
Though, for others, those with this ocular condition contain no control
Over the ensuing blight which their mystic eyesight unwittingly inflicts
Ill-fated to suffer when others succeed and to exult when others endure
All while living in apprehensive affliction—tethered to their tragic stares
Though, their torture remains trivial compared to their dejected victims
Forced to feel the caustic effects of the evil eye curse—now and forever

To be inconvenienced by a supernatural hex is to be irrevocably scarred
As if stalked by a cadre of demons carving away at your skull, ruthlessly
Sinister spell, compressing your spirit like an anvil of persistent anguish
Strangled by the smothering burden of magic from now until departure
Once a harsh curse is spat at someone's feet or scowled into their pupils
Brains begin to screech from the shrill hammering badgering their lobes
While eyes turn heavy from the weary exertion it now takes to stay alert
And bones grow brittle from the strain of trying to move—*trying to live*
Forever convicted—for a curse is a prison, and their spirit is the inmate
Better to be cursed by the stars, divinely meddling in earthly existences
Unapprised of the consequences—only acting with celestial recklessness
Rather than to be jinxed by a mortal with despicable intentions of spite
For those curses, *like the evil eye*, will never surrender to any known cure

Heartbroken Solidarity

Divine goddess of doleful heartbreak—as cynical as the unsocial reaper
Tortured by wretched ballads sung by the shattered organs of romance
Abhorrer of affection, believing it to be as rancid as the aroma of death
For transitory moods of superficial desire can culminate in bleak agony
A category of intolerable cheerlessness unworthy of your precious time
Pessimistic deity, impaling your pirouetting heart with lacerating spikes
To deter souls from nosediving straight into the maudlin oceans of love
For the brutal fall from adoration is not worth the brief joy from before

Goddesses of melancholy and mourning—heed my spell of heartbreak
Let my scathing palms reach into cleaved-open chests like a silent snake
Before seizing hawthorn-hued hearts, soon to sting from barbed spears
Acting as maiming alarms advising against amorous affairs ending in tears
Vow that the spikes halt any infatuated happenings from slinking inside
Saving others from surefire sobs of grief by piloting love to the wayside

Sufferers of the goddess's powers howl—trapped in a piercing cataclysm
For their hearts violently ache from the presence of her punitive thorns
And whenever they venture to amble down the starry-eyed path of love
Brutality follows while the spikes of steel dig in, deeper and deeper still
Spilling pails of plasma portraying the notoriously grim rivers of Hades
Perhaps it would be less excruciating to pry open their aghast sternums
And seize each barb, ripping away the devices of demolition one by one
Gouging open their bare hands in the process before bleeding out fully
Tragic, yet not nearly as tormenting as the dispiriting sense of stabbing
Repeatedly ruining vascular muscles convulsing every time love is nigh

As her prey cry and plead and cower—the goddess celebrates and curses
Musing upon the centennial anniversary of her own ardent relationship
Which ended in such upsetting heartache, her soul grieved for decades
Brokenhearted, she transcended into this unsentimental deity of hatred
Substituting her impassioned heart with an arterial-shaped slab of stone
Before driving fresh spikes into her fossilized faux-organ with certitude
Now tolerating a haunted chest that bleeds waterfalls of calcified blood
Resolved to shield others from her fate—to shelter them with sympathy
As she slowly hemorrhages—*just like her prey*—in heartbroken solidarity

Fiorella's
Garden Spell

Fiorella's Garden Spell

Green-thumbed *Fiorella*, the gentle, botanical mage of soil and saplings
With an elemental aura and earthly magic florally founded upon nature
Modeling a handstitched springtime slip—as lightweight as a dandelion
Delicately embroidered together with hyacinth petals and clover leaves
Jade stems craft threadlike straps—as plantlets create jewel-like designs
Gardenia bouquets and thyme bundles dream of adorning such a gown
Envious of her attire—while also idolizing the mage's nurturing energy
Fiorella, agricultural witch of gardens, with a brain destined for botany
Emerald vines tangle around her arteries, gilded pollen floods her veins
Wrapped within the atmosphere of wildlife—Fiorella finds inner peace
For the genuine darlings of her life are her plants and flowers and herbs
Stalks of mint and sprigs of parsley, posies of larkspur and bee blossoms
Who bow to Fiorella, for she has been decreed as the monarch of mud
And dutiful sovereign of all which germinates from the ageless ground
Fiorella's mind governs all beings born from dirt—with warm authority
Cultivating their bouts of blossoming—vowing they will bloom hastily
Dubbed as their enchanted idol and encouraging godparent of fresh life
Fiorella's sorcery distributes prospering parcels to her multihued garden
Overflowing with sachets of everything the earth needs to grow heartily
Gifting tulips with pigments of chlorophyll and envelopes of potassium
Keeping her precious roses and treasured carnations blissfully hydrated
While greenhouse violets, vegetables, and vanilla beans photosynthesize
Never to wither—for Fiorella senses when downpours of decay are near
And offers whatever her floral followers need—until they joyously take
Fiorella acts as a mothering mage—whispering to her bountiful harvest
Calmly advising every underground crop to sprout and each root to rise
Fiorella's exposed orchards and enclosed conservatories regard her edicts
Promising that their grave thorns will never impale her ungloved palms
For ecosystems fostered by perennial magic always protect their saviors

As a garden sorceress, I arrange this altar like an environmental stage
Offering pine needles, nutmeg candlesticks, and twigs of basil and sage
Let the fluttering streaks of smoke and floral fragrances flood the flowered air
As silver wind chimes sing, imbue magic into my seedlings with doting care
Allow my budding subjects to obey my spell, forever flourishing for their sire
Multiplying at dusk, mounting at dawn, fulfilling my every botanical desire

Refrains
of the
Departed

Refrains of the Departed

Rising from the kiln of witchcraft, singed with credible marks of magic
Striding from the transforming oven with the mystic prowess of a mage
Yet, a bitter affliction also settles in—as withering as an icicle of despair
So chilling that not even eruptive lava could offer any soothing warmth
For this sorceress's skeleton is stuck in an Antarctic state of abject gloom
Manacled to her misery, for the cargo saddling her heart only stockpiles
As dejected pleas impale her fragile mind from those dolefully departed
Onerous choruses of keening infiltrate the alcoves of her consciousness
From the labor of morning light all the way to the birth of moonlit eves

Anguished sighs and toilsome shrieks brutally plague her ruptured ears
Asking to breathe again, to be freed from the penitentiary of the reaper
Every ragged and raging voice nibbles at the besieged flesh of her brain
Like a gnat pilfering pieces of her waning sanity, one murmur at a time
Precipitations of pain alarmingly blemish the sorceress's sopping cheeks
For these waterworks will never expire so long as their bellows ring out
Amid the violent harassment—the sorceress seeks out a wealth of cures
Wishing for a glimpse at salvation through the reveries she conjures up
Entering illusions where her ears are irretrievably severed and shredded
As her hands drive daggers through the occipital bone of her weak skull
Granting this sorceress the awaited gift of euphoric stillness and silence
Released from the voices nagging her within this beleaguered existence

However, her fantasies are only fictional, for her body remains too frail
Too wounded from the weight of her despondency *to do anything at all*
Unqualified to revoke the decomposing status thrust upon these spirits
Necromancer she is not, for her tongue remains tied, unable to respond
Even the talents of a mage include limitations, only able to travel so far
For whenever she siphons her magic into an undeviating land of expiry
At once, the connection shatters, snapping back with harrowing finality
And so, the conversations remain one-sided, as all she may do, is listen
Unendingly, the deceased howl in death, and the sorceress weeps in life
Bawling over the choirs of suffering spirits, shrill from their beseeching
Musing if one dim eve, she will drown in the tsunami of her fallen tears
But then, who will listen in woe to the uproarious petitions of the dead
And will her voice, now affixed to their lifeless world, be among them?

Mesmeric Elixir

Aura: defined as tendrils of translucent energy encircling earthly bodies
Emitting wraithlike strands from within, surrounding flesh with vitality
Heightened only through the intrinsic magic of bewitching happenings
Accomplish this by devising an appealing perfume—the *Mesmeric Elixir*
Spritz your skin with the aromatic potion; recite an altering incantation
Until the alignment of your aura changes and original appeal seeps out
No more attractive than before, for your appearance will be unaffected
It is only the wavelengths leaping off your skeleton which will intensify
Painting your aura in hues of supernatural charm and paranormal thrill
As luring as the prospect of sin slotted within the corridors of perdition

Acquire a vessel with the silhouette of a lush diamond: the crown jewel
Lay prized crystals upon the base, enriching the powers of the perfume
Bloodstones permeate the concoction with a sense of spiced confidence
As carnelian stones seduce true gifts of persuasion into ascending at last
Atop the jewels, dispense trifling vials of lemon verbena and ocean mist
Adding flairs of freshness as refreshing as the coastline breezes amid July
Decant the sap of black cherries and the lifeblood of legendary dragons
Imbuing the perfume with irrefutable potency—indescribably inviting
Drizzle a spoonful of decadent praline—for a minor surge of sweetness
Inhale the citrus notes and mulled aromas; a truly mouthwatering brew
Warily swirl the spelled bottle—effectively fusing the fragrance together
Fasten a ribbon of supple satin around the center, completing the elixir

Spray the perfume upon your wrists, the nape of your neck, your throat
Anywhere blood will fizz beneath the surface, purring within your veins
Soaking up the scrumptious scent like a keen sponge of transformation
Ultimately becoming a sentient embodiment of inebriating enticement
Whose spirit draws upon the private wants of others, reeling them near
And as the perfume lands with perpetuity into the arteries of your heart
Repeat this stanza six times to ensure the *Mesmeric Elixir* never weakens:

I summon the glorious goddess of persuasion—Peitho—with this spell
Ripen my aura like lavish wine—exaggerate the irresistible energy I expel
Award me a soul so seductive, sycophants will crawl to me—dusk or dawn
Make the fragrance of my spirit so tempting, the universe herself will fawn

Primordial Scepter

Salient scepter fashioned from the proficiencies of primitive witchcraft
Imposing emblem of control and extraordinary signifier of sovereignty
Baroque baton enveloped in obsidian—as blackened as a lagoon of tar
Featuring a linear array of pearl-shaped trinkets stamped into the onyx
Vaulted globe balanced atop—resplendently studded with labradorites
Jutting out of the striking summit lies a pointed spade, as sharp as ever
Beautified with a trinity of prized rubies, gleaming motifs of protection
Intricate engravings embellish the elongated scepter as cryptic carvings
Inscribed with utopian ink and penned in the *ancient language of magic*

Enigmatic ciphers of complex symbols are revealed to be distinct spells
Stating that whoever strains to seize the scepter will possess dominance
Gifted the grandiose authority over mythical beasts and colossal beings
Clutch the baton and urge them all to fight for you, to fight beside you
Or—demand their urgent abstinence from engaging in battles or brawls
Whether you hunger for peace and harmony or for the chaos of warfare
Your new subjects will regard your mandates with the patience of an ox

Permit the scepter's invocations to heartily infuse your acquisitive spirit
Become inspired by olden understandings of past mages and monarchs
As your skull augments in size and strength with elemental information
Learn the fortes and the failings of every hydra and dragon upon Earth
Sense shockwaves rush through your bloodstream with reigning ripples
Feel your spine quake from the force of the insurgence erupting within
Hold on tight—as your supernatural followers await your next demand

Wield the eccentric staff, whose gems glisten from daylight to darkness
March into combat—as the magic of the baton fortifies your directives
And emerge victorious, with your unassailable battalion trailing behind
Drenched in violence—yet the scepter remains staunchly glued in place
For your greedy grip, drunk with supremacy, will never dare to let it go

Delphine's Invisibility

Preternatural powers of the occult, release my visibility from perception
Veiled within the illusory mantle of witchcraft—an enigmatic deception
Blind my body from the ever-vigilant inspection of nature and her flora
Awareness of my flesh be gone—cloaking even the fragrance of my aura
Remaining upon this realm as a breathing phantom, hushed and hidden
Wraithlike reprieve—let the liabilities of visibility finally turn forbidden

Mystic palms: liberate Delphine's discernability from your strained fists
For this incantation has endured far too long, twisting into permanence
No, the enchantress internally laments—this is not what she envisioned
When deferentially requesting the stillness and solitude of concealment
Only for a blip in time, only until her reticent heart had been appeased
For her mood had grown too sullen as the world had grown too hostile
A negligible reprieve from the invasive quality of life was all she needed
But now, incarcerated in transparency, Delphine could not change back
Fraught with an invisible plight, freed from the meddling eyes of others
Yet constrained by the cheerless encumbrance of never-ending isolation
Forlorn, the enchantress howls—frightened of feeling forgotten, forever
For if none can view her physique—how will any remember her legacy
Mentions of her name turn somberly scarce as if she never existed at all
Delphine senses garlands of her soul scrambling away, joining the wind
Fretting the inauspicious moment when so much of her spirit disperses
That there will be nothing left of her to hide, and none will even notice
Lonesome, she attempts spell after spell to amend her disguised destiny
Hoping within her dying heart that *this* will be the one to prevail at last

Expose my disguised body to the elements at once—before it is too late
Let my flesh be detectible, let my voice be heard, let me no longer wait
Overturn the former spell, lest I dissolve into nothing but atoms of air
Reverse the masking magic, and I will never ask of this again—I swear

Delphine treads by floral rows of geraniums and trudges behind mortals
Daring to dream of any subtle acknowledgment or even a discreet wave
A small signal that says, *you are still here; you have not faded away just yet*
And as a dragonfly lands upon her shoulder, greeting her with his wings
She knows fate has turned around her fortune—for she is visible at last

Voodoo Doll

Voodoo Doll

Voodoo doll: a worrying effigy made with the echoing witchcraft of evil aims
Conjure the skill of controlling, yet only from afar—in spiteful solitude
Fabricate a figurine with biddable textiles; distended with supple cotton
Affix a set of sable buttons with spelled yarn to mimic emotionless eyes
Sew a heart-shaped crest within the middle to mirror a mortal anatomy
Utilize an unlimited spool and a shielding thimble to seal the doll shut
Contentedly survey the voodoo doll with a shrewd feeling of familiarity
As the likeness parodies the source of your spite with uncanny accuracy
Cradle the effigy with purpose, conjure the image of the one you detest
Twist your tongue to narrate lyrics spiked with the raw aura of payback
Gather penetrating pins within your palms like scarring bushels of pain
Purposely perforate with one sharpened stick after another and another
Pierce the crocheted complexion of wool and stab into plush insulation
Extract the pin, *only slightly*, before repeating the languidly action again
Know that while the inanimate doll undergoes mutilating machinations
A faraway body—one with skin which scars and sentience which suffers
Writhes amid the replicating punctures—as if stuck with phantom pins
For the doll is imbued with duplicating powers, able to distantly wound

Although—revengeful dollmakers are destined for injury in this process
Rupture the pliable chest of the doll, feel your own chest stiffen in turn
Sustain frustrating aches—though never nearly as severe as your victims
For a pin rocketed into the jugular of your doll will instantly asphyxiate
While you will only endure minor shortness of breath, easily eradicated
Voodoo sorcery may only be exercised upon those deserving vengeance
For the anguish they extort, both intangibly emotive and vilely somatic
Lingers with their prey far longer than the sting of the pins will remain
That injustice must be rectified through the repetition of shooting pain
Indulge in gratification as you continue your disfigurements of the doll
Beam as a prick of pain finds your heart, *knowing theirs has halted at last*
Finally grasping the irreparable fatality that the magic of voodoo retains

Hellish Furies—indorse my voodoo hex as divinities of unforgiving callous
Endow my soul with command as I envision individuals dipped in malice
Picturing the positions of their central organs, shower my spirit with power
As I impale pins into my handmade doll, let these sinful mortals truly cower

GAIA

Gaia's Earthly Worshippers

Evergreen Earth, sun-drenched realm of nature, land of flora and fauna
Witchcraft of the pagan variety never thieves from this luxuriant terrain
For this sorcery only reveres at the environmental altar of Mother Earth
Idolizing *Gaia, instrumental goddess*, with the loyalty of organic disciples
Earthly coven of wiccan mages— Hesperia, Davina, Tabitha, Magnolia
Admiring this moss-strewn, fox-traipsing forest, *a woodland wonderland*
Adorning lithe slips in terrestrial tones and wreaths plaited from pansies
Hesperia and Magnolia amass and assemble incendiary logs of firewood
As Davina and Tabitha ignite the inferno, acting as a singeing spotlight
Heeding the metronome of crackling fires, sacred palms are interlocked
Before dancing in a circular formation, acrobatically twirling like flames
Ardently vocalizing incantations to the ears of the squirrels and streams
Engraving each of their names into the creased bark of mahogany trees
Utilizing blood as macabre ink—ensuring the forest never forgets them
For the witches pine only to worship all that Gaia distantly constructed
By admiring soil and cherishing sand and savoring their emerald powers
Within their spellbinding circle, the witches grasp their newest sacrifices
Confiscated from those who ache to exploit witchery for their own gain
Only to harbor hostile cesspools when learning this sorcery only aids the dirt
This is when the coven acts out—as penance for such odious disrespect
Tabitha and Magnolia entice and ensnare; Hesperia and Davina seduce
Before embracing these teased and tempted evildoers with roving hands
Shifting from minx-like to murderous as they wrench out selfish hearts
While sensing their pupils flicker from maddening embers of molten ire
Gazes dribbling with rage and palms drenched in lifeblood, they depart
Now, back beside their bonfire, those energetic hearts have *finally* stilled
Allowing the coven to bury the organs below—as arterial contributions
Hopeful Gaia will hereafter nurture each centipede and candleberry tree
Satiating the Earth long after the coven departs to their wildlife afterlife

Like humble honeybees, we call on the powers that be to awaken and unite
As Hesperia, Davina, Tabitha, and Magnolia, we slit our skin, a ruby sight
Gaia, let the liquid which grants us life infuse the ground amid early dawn
As ancient runes drawn into the mud maintain the charms we depend upon
Alter our bodies into breathing conduits—siphon your magic into our veins
For we are ecological devotees, bound by the eternal boon of earthly chains

Marisa Loretta is an author and artist living in Upstate New York. *Scarlet Nightfall,* an enchanting and eerie collection of poems and illustrations, is her second release, following her debut, *Midnight Love Potion.* As an avid reader, her unending love of all things fantasy and romance, from *Practical Magic* to *Buffy the Vampire Slayer,* has only grown over the years. Marisa is thrilled to have translated that infatuation into crafting her own stories, and feels beyond grateful towards everyone who has chosen to read her poetic works. You can further connect with her online at www.marisaloretta.com or on Instagram: @marisaloretta